# KING'S
# PASSION

# KING'S PASSION

**ESSENCE BESTSELLING AUTHOR**
## ADRIANNE
# BYRD

ARABESQUE®

Recycling programs
for this product may
not exist in your area.

KING'S PASSION

ISBN-13: 978-0-373-53445-6

www.kimanipress.com

**Printed in U.S.A.**

To Alice: Forever my inspiration

## ACKNOWLEDGMENT

To my family and friends, thanks for all the support and love that you've given me. To my editor, Evette Porter, for helping me through one crazy year. To my wonderful fans and readers, thank you for allowing me to do what I do. It's always a pleasure to entertain you. I wish you all the best of love.

## The House of Kings series

Many of you have followed the Unforgettable series, which morphed into the Hinton Brothers series. Now I'm introducing you to the Hintons' playboy bachelor cousins—the Kings.

Eamon, Xavier and Jeremy along with their infamous cousin Quentin Hinton are business partners in a gentlemen's club franchise called The Doll House. One of their most popular and lucrative specialties is their bachelor party services. And with clubs in Atlanta, Las Vegas and Los Angeles, the brothers are determined to make sure their clients' last night of bachelorhood is one that they'll never forget.

In *King's Passion,* Eamon, the eldest brother, books a high-end client, Marcus Henderson, for an over-the-top, bachelor-party extravaganza. According to the best man, there's to be no expense spared for this wild night. Even Eamon gets caught up in the excitement. But things take a detour when the groom-to-be gets so plastered that he ends up marrying one of the hired strippers. When the dust clears and the alcohol wears off, Eamon has another headache to contend with—the angry ex-bride-to-be, Victoria Gregory.

Next month, look for the second title in the House of Kings series, *King's Promise,* featuring Eamon's brother Xavier King. And in August, read the final book in the trilogy, *King's Pleasure,* featuring Jeremy King.

Remember, in love, never bet against a King....

Adrianne

# *Prologue*

Quentin Dewayne Hinton was at a crossroads. Actually, he'd been there for quite some time. The hard part had been admitting it. Once upon a time, his father had told him that "pride was the bane of all men." If anyone knew that, it would be his father. Roger Hinton was a proud man who ran his family like a corporation. His God was the Dow Jones, and his heart and soul belonged to the numbers in his bank account.

Chuckling at his analogy, Q climbed out of his black Mercedes and gave the parking deck a casual glance from behind his Oliver Peoples sunglasses. He slid his hand into the pants pocket of his gray, tailored Italian suit while he opened the glass door to the high-rise building with his other hand. Though he was nervous about this meeting, one would never know it by his confident stride through the Peachtree Tower. Inside the massive, ornate lobby, Quentin kept his focus straight ahead toward the brass elevator doors.

As luck would have it, a very tall and very beautiful woman stepped into the compartment behind him as he pushed the button for the thirty-third floor. As usual, he started his inspection from the feet up. Pretty toes, nice ankles, firm calves. So far, everything had his imaginary dog tail wagging. Amazing legs, slim waist—by the time he made it to the woman's long neck, he was turning toward her ready to spit his best pick-up line.

But then the image of Alyssa Hinton's face smiled.

Quentin jumped back.

"You know it never would have worked between us," she said.

"What?" He blinked and then snatched off his shades.

"Are you okay?" the beautiful woman who was *not* Alyssa asked, frowning at him.

Quentin quickly glanced around the small compartment and saw that they were the only two people in the elevator.

"Sir?" The woman's brows dipped in concern and suspicion. "You look like you just saw a ghost."

"I…uh." He straightened his shoulders and cleared his throat. "I guess I was awed by your beauty."

The woman's expression clearly reflected that she wasn't buying his answer and she inched closer to the corner of the elevator car.

Q didn't blame her. He rubbed his eyes and slid his sunglasses back on just as the elevator arrived on his floor. He tossed the woman another quick smile but then rushed out of the small compartment.

*Pull yourself together, man.*

He squared his shoulders again and marched toward

suite thirty-three hundred. Once in the quiet office, he felt another wave of relief to see the lobby was empty.

"May I help you?" the receptionist asked from behind the counter.

Q approached the girl-next-door ebony cutie with a smile. "Yes. I'm here to see Dr. Turner."

"Name?"

"Quentin Hinton."

The woman looked down and ran her finger over a column of names in her appointment book. "Ah. Here you are. If you can just sign in for me here." She handed over a clipboard.

Quentin took it and the pen and scrawled his name. When he looked up to hand the clipboard back to the receptionist, Alyssa smiled.

"The doctor will be with you in a second."

Q blinked and then snatched his shades off again.

The receptionist frowned. "Are you all right?"

*You mean other than my seeing things?* "Yes. I'm fine. Thanks." He quickly turned toward the waiting area and commanded himself to pull it together. He sat down and slipped his sunglasses in the inside breast pocket of his coat jacket. A second later an office door to his right opened.

A tall, older dark-skinned brother in an Armani suit crossed the threshold while still shaking hands with an attractive, red-bone sister who was needlessly hiding her curves in a black, shapeless skirt-suit.

"Thank you, doctor," Mr. Armani said, cheesing at her as he released her hand.

"I'll see you next week," Dr. Turner replied, smiling before turning her soft brown eyes toward Quentin.

"Mr. Hinton?"

"Yes." He stood up, feeling his nerves twist.

"Hello. I'm Dr. Julianne Turner. Won't you come in and have a seat?"

Q forced a smile and strolled into the office. He hesitated for a second before he took his seat in the chair in the psychiatrist's office. He shifted a bit, trying to make himself comfortable, but that wasn't possible on the first visit.

"You look uneasy," the doctor said, removing her golden pen from her breast-pocket.

"Nah. Nah," Quentin said, shifting some more. "I'm good."

"Uh-huh." Dr. Turner clicked the back of the pen and started writing.

Q frowned. What the hell had he done to warrant her writing something down already? He leaned forward to read her handwriting on the yellow tablet, but before he could make out the words, the doctor looked up with a knowing smile.

"So what brings you here today…do you mind if I call you Quentin?" she asked.

"No. Please do." This should've been the one question that Quentin was prepared for. But instead his brain zoned out, leaving him staring at the doctor as if he was waiting for an answer.

"Please don't tell her that you think you're still in love with me," Alyssa said from across the room. She was wearing those wonderful tight blue jeans and the white top that she'd worn the day they had gone horseback riding together and the first time he'd kissed her under an oak tree.

"Mr. Hinton?" Dr. Turner interrupted.

He paused for a couple more seconds and then said, "Love."

Dr. Turner's brows arched upward at the answer.

Across the room, Alyssa groaned.

"Are you in love, Quentin?"

Q's head turned toward Alyssa, but she was gone. "I thought I was."

"But you're not sure?"

Silence.

"Quentin?" she pressed.

He faced her again. "Let's just say that I don't understand love. How it magically appears, puts you in a spell and then *poof!* After that, you question whether it was ever there at all." Sensing that he wasn't making any sense, Q cleared his throat. "Maybe I should lie down."

"If you like," Dr. Turner said as she scribbled away on her notepad.

Q assumed the position on the doctor's leather chaise and leaned back on the arm. "You know, my brothers have been telling me for years that I needed to see a shrink."

"Are you here at their urging?"

"No."

"So you wanted to come?"

Pause. "More like I needed to come."

Scribbling. "And why is that?"

Quentin lowered his gaze from the ceiling to stare at the floor-to-ceiling glass window to see an image of Alyssa in her white wedding gown, checking out her reflection. "I'm afraid that I missed my one chance."

"At love?" Dr. Turner asked.

Alyssa spun around and shook her head at Quentin. "You don't love me."

"Quentin?"

"Yes," he said simply. "The woman I thought was for me married my brother two years ago. I went to the wedding, stood in line with the other groomsmen and watched

Sterling marry the woman of my dreams—then I left and haven't seen them since."

"So you're estranged from your brother?"

"With Sterling—yes." Q shrugged. "I still talk to my other brother Jonas from time to time. But it's not the same. He's happily married with children and…everything has changed. Everyone has changed. Everyone is falling in love," Q chuckled. "Who knows, maybe something *is* wrong with me."

"You don't really believe that, do you?" she asked.

Alyssa shook her head at him.

"I don't know what I believe. Once I lost Alyssa, I swore off love and renewed my vow to be a bachelor for life. And why not? There are more than enough women out there who'd love the pleasure of my company. You know what I mean?" He turned his head and caught a glimpse of the doctor's long legs. *Nice.*

Dr. Turner cleared her throat.

"Sorry." Quentin smiled and turned back around.

Alyssa rolled her eyes.

"Anyway," Q said, "like I was saying, bachelorhood is for me. So I figured that birds of feather flock together, right?"

Scribbling. "You tell me."

*This is like talking to myself.*

"It beats talking to a woman that's not really here," Alyssa said, twirling around in her dress.

Quentin rolled his eyes but had to concede her point. "Well, I considered my business partners and cousins Xavier, Jeremy and Eamon a part of my flock. Well, maybe not Eamon so much—but definitely Xavier and Jeremy. They all loved women as much as I did. None of them wanted to settle down with just one, which actually made them the perfect partners in The Dollhouse."

"What's The Dollhouse?"

"Only the hottest gentlemen's clubs in the country, of course I'm a little biased." A smile eased across Quentin's face as his chest expanded with pride. "We're in Atlanta, Las Vegas and Los Angeles. But the *big* moneymaker is our side business called Bachelor Adventures—where we host the wildest bachelor parties ever. The women have their day, the men have their night. You know what I mean?"

*Scribbling.* "So you and your cousins provide a service for men to enjoy their last night of bachelorhood?"

"That was the plan."

"Until?"

Q drew a deep breath. "Until love showed up. What else? Then they started to fall one by one. Take Eamon for example…"

*The Reluctant King*

# Chapter 1

"Welcome to The Dollhouse, Las Vegas," Eamon King shouted above the crowd, raising his glass to toast the raucous bachelor party as fifty or so guys entered the V.I.P. section of his exclusive Vegas nightclub. Most of them whooped and hollered, and fist-pumped over the loud, pulsing music—a clear sign that they were married men who'd planned to go buck wild on this rare night away from their wives. A few of their eyes were already bulging at the sexy-looking women who worked at The Dollhouse.

"Now, which one of you is Marcus Henderson?" Eamon asked, his gaze combing the crowd.

"Right here," they shouted and then pushed a six-foot, pencil-thin nerdy-looking brother in black-rimmed glasses.

Eamon ignored his private thoughts about the guy looking like a stereotypical paper pusher and hooked one of his muscled arms around the man's neck. "All right,

Mr. Henderson," he boasted. "As one of the owners of this establishment, I want to personally guarantee you that tonight will definitely be a night that you will *never* forget!"

"Whooo-hoooo!" Henderson's party shouted.

"Last night of freedom," Marcus joked shyly.

"Plenty of time for you to change your mind," someone shouted from the crowd.

Although there was a smile on Marcus's face, Eamon detected a note of uncertainty in his voice. He gave Henderson another casual glance and thought to himself that if this man had found a woman—*any woman*—to say yes, then maybe he'd better get on his knees, say his prayers and seal the deal as fast as he could.

"Ladies! Please come on up here," Eamon shouted.

On cue, Shawn, Brittani and Cassie strolled into the V.I.P. room smiling from ear-to-ear in their metallic gold Daisy Dukes and matching bikini tops. In their hands each one carried a golden ice bucket with a bottle of Cristal.

All the men's eyes grew even wider and their mouths sagged to the floor.

"Good evening, gentlemen," the beauties greeted in sync.

"Oh sweet baby Jesus," Marc mumbled.

Eamon reached over and nudged Marc's chin so that he'd close his mouth before he started to drool. "Now gentlemen, these three ladies will be your hostesses for the evening. If there is *anything* that you need, your hostess will take care of you. But first…" Eamon walked to the back of the V.I.P. room and stepped onto the stage and grabbed the microphone lying on the lone chair next to a stripper pole. "I need the man of the evening to come on up here."

The men clapped and shoved Marc forward.

It was clear that he wasn't used to the spotlight as he seemed to tuck his head down and had trouble making eye contact as he made his way up to the stage.

Amused, Eamon shook his head and then swung his arm around Marc's shoulder and directed him to face forward. "Now. We at The Dollhouse have something special for you, my man."

One side of Marc's lips curled upward as he asked in a quivering voice, "Really?"

"Ooooh yes. I have a special girl in mind for you. " He tossed him a wink and then signaled to the DJ. The music quickly transitioned into Li'l Wayne's "Lollipop." To the crowd Eamon said, "Gentlemen, won't you welcome to the stage DELICIOUS!"

A gold-and-silver disco ball descended from the ceiling. The men gave enthusiastic barks and shouts as The Dollhouse's number-one moneymaker, Delicious, stepped onto the stage, working her hips like a figure eight and rolling her chest so that the small tassels on the ends of her gold pasties spun like mini-helicopters.

The crowd went wild while Marc stood like a deer in headlights and Eamon exited the stage and handed off the mic to one of the hostesses. Delicious knew how to work a crowd and within seconds, she had them all eating out of the palm of her hand.

As Eamon worked his way to the back of the V.I.P. room, he spotted his brothers, Xavier and Jeremy, with their arms folded and leaning against the back wall. The three of them were similar in build and coloring: tall, milk-chocolate brown with solid, sculpted muscles. Of the three, Eamon sported a pencil-thin goatee, a slightly squarer jaw, with eyes that were slanted like Tyson Beckford's. While Eamon and Xavier stood at an even six-four, Jeremy, the pip-squeak, came in at six-three and three quarters. It was hardly noticed by others, but it made for endless teasing by his older brothers.

They were all pretty laid-back. They were very close having grown up in a family that didn't have a lot of money, but plenty of love. Their parents had taught them the value of hard work and didn't accept any excuses. The three put themselves through college and then went into business together. They weren't as rich as their cousins, the Hintons, but they each had a couple of million in the bank.

"What are you guys doing here?" Eamon asked, suspiciously.

"Damn. What? No hug or 'how in the hell are you'?" Xavier shouted above the music, smiling.

Eamon lifted a brow. His brother was showing a little too much teeth with that smile. "I'll hook you up at the next family reunion." His gaze then shifted to Jeremy who was acting like he'd never seen Delicious perform before. Playing along, Eamon folded his arms and turned back toward the stage.

Marcus Henderson sat in the chair center stage, looking like he'd died and gone to heaven. His ebony goddess backed up her beautiful, oiled, brown booty with a disappearing gold string down the middle up on him and then started bouncing her round cheeks until he was damn-near hypnotized.

"WHOOOOOAAAA!" His friends whooped and hollered as they crowded around the stage and tossed bills of every denomination onto the stage.

Marc's mind spun like a pinwheel while money rained down on him and this goddess of the stripper pole like they were in their own little money globe.

Delicious bent over at the waist, giving him a better view of just where her mysterious gold string disappeared to before effortlessly making both cheeks clap.

The erotic applause made Marc tug at his collar. Even though the sucker was already open, it still felt as if it was choking him. Completely wiped clean from his mind were any thoughts of the woman he was going to marry tomorrow. In that moment, all that mattered was Delicious. She gave Marc an erection so hard that he swore he could feel his inseams popping.

Marc turned his head, while his jaw elongated and his hands trembled with want.

"Your boy is looking like Gollum up there," Xavier chuckled.

Jeremy turned with his fingers creeping toward Eamon's face. "Precious. I must have the precious booty."

Eamon swatted Jeremy's hands away from his face and then rolled his eyes. "Grow up."

That just succeeded in making Jeremy laugh. "Testy. Maybe we should arrange a private lap dance for you, as well. You need to relax." He put his hands on Eamon's shoulders and started rubbing. Since he didn't know what he was doing, the shoulder rub hurt like hell.

"Will you two just spit it out. What the hell do you want before this fool lands me on a chiropractor's table?" He shrugged Jeremy's hand off his shoulder, but then turned in time to catch his younger brothers sharing a look. "What?"

Xavier sucked in a deep breath. "Maybe we should talk about this in the office?"

Eamon frowned as a ball of anxiety picked up speed in his chest. "It's that bad?"

His brothers stood mute blinking at him.

Cursing under his breath, Eamon cast a quick glance back at the stage. Delicious had Marc's face planted in between her chests while she slapped both cheeks with her fresh-out-the-box silicon-filled breasts. When she finally pulled his head back again so that he could breathe, Marc looked like he was in love.

"Another satisfied customer," Eamon chuckled. But when he looked back up at his brothers that ball started rolling again. "C'mon. Let's go to the office."

The three Kings exited the V.I.P room and entered the main floor of the club where it looked as if they had a full house. Prince's old-school jam "Get Off" pumped through the mounted speakers while seven of his hottest women on seven different stages worked golden stripper poles while their customers rained money on them.

As the Kings traveled down the glass staircase, a harem of belly-dancing strippers were coming up for the bachelor party's next set. Eamon plastered on a smile as he glanced down at his watch. "Running late, ladies."

The women gave him meek apologetic smiles as they continued running up the stairs. At the bottom, Azizi, an African beauty with gorgeous coal-black skin, waited with a sly grin…and a goat.

"Now that's something you don't see every day," Xavier said with mild amusement.

The brothers stood on the side of the staircase so that Azizi and the goat could climb up. Right behind her were a dozen dwarfish women, no more than three and a half feet tall, dressed in two-piece black cat costumes with furry ears.

The look on Jeremy's face was priceless. "What kind of freaks are you hosting tonight?"

"The kind whose credit card is approved when I swipe it," Eamon laughed while he threaded his way through the thick Saturday-night crowd. He could literally hear the *ca-ching* of the cash registers as he watched the army of bartenders, waitresses and dancers scurry about.

The success of The Dollhouse defied the odds and

baffled all their competitors—not only in Atlanta, but also in Las Vegas and Los Angeles. But the Kings believed, as their father had always taught them, that the fundamentals were what made success: vision, integrity, talent and communication. After that was location, location, location—marketing, marketing, marketing—and cash, cash, cash.

That last part—the money—was particularly hard. When Xavier and Jeremy first approached Eamon about *expanding* their small adult nightclub and laid out an impressive business plan, he was skeptical. The normal movers and shakers who did what his brothers were suggesting usually came from old money. They argued about it for so long that he finally tossed up his hands and told his brothers that if they could find the money to finance their grand fantasy, then he would go along.

He should have never underestimated Xavier and Jeremy. They could sell condoms to a nun if they set their minds to it. In this scenario, Eamon was the nun.

Unfortunately, their new financier came straight from another branch of the family tree, the branch that Eamon didn't particularly care for—the Hintons.

Correction. He actually didn't mind Jonas and Sterling so much. They were solid, hardworking men who didn't put on airs or walk around like they were better than everyone else. However, his Uncle Roger and his cousin Quentin were his least favorite and for different reasons.

Uncle Roger, billionaire extraordinaire, tended to walk around, thinking that everyone had a price tag on them. There was no deal too dirty and no trickery or underhanded tactic that was beneath him. In fact, the only time that Eamon had ever felt a little sorry for his cousin Quentin was when his uncle bribed him into marrying some business associate's daughter so he could better position himself on the company's board. It was no shock that Quentin took the money. After all he'd been cut off financially by his father in a feeble attempt to force him to grow up and support himself. But Q was accustomed to a certain lifestyle, and he was immune to the whole notion of actually working. So after about a year of roaming from one sugar momma to the next, he jumped at his father's offer.

It came as no surprise that the marriage didn't last, but Q reclaimed his inheritance. So when Xavier approached him with his business proposal, a deal was struck. The Kings and one Hinton became business partners provided that Quentin Hinton remained a silent partner.

"Hello, Eamon," a feminine voice floated in between the music.

He stopped and looked down just as a woman's slim hand slid up his broad chest. When he shifted his gaze to the hand's owner, he was pleasantly surprised to see Charelle. His lips stretched wider at the short, red number she had on. It showed off her long, lean and toned physique to perfection. "Hello, Charelle."

"Ah. So you *do* remember me?" She moved closer and pressed her small curves against him. "You know, six months is a long time not to hear from someone."

He laughed while his gaze dragged down her body. "If I remember correctly, you were the one who left town."

Charelle's cherry-red lips curled higher. "Silly man, you were supposed to chase after me." Her hands and arms looped around his neck. "Don't you know when a woman is playing hard to get?"

Behind him, Xavier and Jeremy chuckled. "Actually, I do," Eamon said, reaching behind his neck and, gently but firmly, pulling her arms down. "And like I told you before, I don't like playing games."

Charelle moaned and pushed out her bottom lip. "Then don't think of it as a game. Think of it like a dance."

"Oh. A dance, huh?" He playfully rolled his eyes.

"What?" She pushed on one of his bulging biceps and flashed her pearly whites up at him. "You're a man who owns a strip club. Don't tell me that you don't like dancing."

Xavier cut in. "Actually, it's a gentlemen's club."

Charelle's gaze shifted to the brothers. "Sorry. I didn't know that I was interrupting a family reunion. Hello, boys."

They quickly said their hellos.

"Then you won't mind excusing us." He started to move away.

"So we'll finish this dance later?" she asked, rocking her hips to entice him with what could be waiting for him when he was through.

It wasn't enough. "No. I'm sorry," he said, shaking his head and stepping away. "When I dance, I like to *lead*."

Charelle's face fell while Xavier and Jeremy sucked in a quick breath as if Eamon had delivered a body blow. He should have known better than to do this in front of them. They had a tendency to be juvenile.

"You're welcome to stay. Just tell the bartender I said that the drinks are on the house tonight." He stepped around her and then threaded through the crowd when she grabbed him by his trim waist.

"Is that it?"

"Did you need anything else?" he asked benignly.

"Hey, Eamon." A woman walked behind him and gave his firm butt a good squeeze.

He turned his head in time to see Hayley, one of his waitresses, sashay away. "Hey, I require dinner and a few

drinks before I allow a woman to have her way with me."
He laughed.

"I'll keep that in mind," Hayley teased and continued
to navigate her way through the crowd with her tray of
drinks.

Laughing, Eamon turned back toward Charelle whose
face was twisted in annoyance.

"Well, no wonder you've been M.I.A., you've already
moved on to the next trick."

Unfazed and, quite frankly, bored by Charelle's penchant
for drama, Eamon folded his arms. "You do realize that
you just called yourself a trick, right?"

"No. I'm calling you a flea-infested, roaming dog."

"Then you were smart to leave me when you did,"
he agreed. No matter what she said, he was not going
to indulge her by fighting. What was the point? Hayley
meant nothing to him. It was harmless flirtation between
good friends and not out of the ordinary for colleagues
who worked in their type of establishment. "It was good
seeing you again, Charelle."

Making a clean break this time, Eamon finally
maneuvered the rest of the way through the club to his
private sanctuary: the office. "Shut the door behind you,"
he instructed and then opted for the leather couch instead
of the executive chair behind his desk.

"Yes, boss. Right away, boss," Jeremy joked before
closing the door behind him. In doing so, he lowered the
volume at least fifty percent from the loud music bumping
in the club.

"All right," Eamon said, stretching back on the couch
and kicking up his feet. "Lay it on me. What's so important
that it takes both of you to fly in to talk to me?"

His younger brothers looked at each other again as if

waging a silent battle as to which one of them should drop the bomb.

"You guys are really trying my patience," he warned. "Spill it."

Xavier sucked in a deep breath. "It's Quentin."

Dropping his head back, Eamon groaned. "I should've known. What has he done now—tear up the Atlanta club again?" he asked, referring to a drunken brawl Q had gotten into about six months back.

"No. It's nothing like that," Xavier rushed.

*"But?"* Eamon asked. "Why do I hear a 'but' coming?"

*"But*...he's driving me—"

"Us," Jeremy corrected and then nodded for Xavier to finish.

"Yes. He's driving *us* crazy. We thought—"

"Actually it was Xavier's idea," Jeremy cut in again and then rolled his hand at Xavier. "Go ahead. Tell him *your* idea."

Xavier looked like he was two seconds from going for Jeremy's jugular.

"Anyway," Xavier said, cutting his eyes back to Eamon. "We were thinking that he could come out here and work with you for a little while. This is our biggest club. Surely there's plenty for him to do around here."

Eamon was already springing back up from the couch before Xavier could finish his sentence. "No. No. And, oh hell no!"

Jeremy slapped his hand against his forehead. "C'mon, Eamon. It's your turn. He's already spent time at our clubs, drinking and chasing women. It's like having a kid around that we have to babysit twenty-four hours a day."

"So when you say put him to work you meant that in the loosest terms possible, right?"

Xavier sighed. He and Quentin were actually best friends though Eamon never understood why. They couldn't be more opposite than the North and South Poles.

"I don't understand," Eamon said. "Why do we have to do anything? Quentin is a silent partner. Kick him to the curb and tell him to take a trip or something?"

Xavier raked his fingers across his finely shaved head. "Well…let's just say that he's going through a little emotional crisis at the moment."

Eamon frowned. "What do you mean?"

"He has a broken heart," Jeremy answered. "And it's bad."

"Real bad," Xavier agreed, nodding. "Sterling married the woman Q thinks he was in love with."

"Quentin is always in love," Eamon dismissed. "Give him a couple of weeks and he'll be fine."

"It's been six months," Xavier said.

"It's getting worse not better," Jeremy added.

"And what am I supposed to do? Babysit? Does it looks like I have time to babysit a cousin I don't even like?"

"You mean the same cousin that has made us all rich?" Xavier asked.

*Here comes the guilt.* "No."

"Just for a little while," Xavier continued. "He's ex-communicated himself from his family."

"No."

"He's a broken man. We're all he has," Jeremy added. "Just keep him for a couple of months and then you can send him back to…Xavier in Atlanta."

"Me?" Xavier turned. "What about you? You're his cousin, too."

"I just had him."

Eamon and Xavier stared at Jeremy.

"Fine." He tossed his hands. "He stays out here with

Eamon first, then Xavier and then me. We'll just keep him in rotation until he gets back onto his feet again." Jeremy glanced around. "Deal?"

Xavier smiled. "Deal."

They looked toward Eamon.

"I don't believe this." He rubbed a hand across his forehead, trying to get ahead of the stress headache that was coming his way.

"Is that a yes?" Xavier asked.

"All right. All right. I'll do it."

Xavier clapped his hands. "Great! He's staying at the Bellagio."

"What?"

"C'mon, Jeremy. Let's hit the road before we miss our flights."

Before Eamon could get another word out, his brothers damn near disappeared like a couple of ghosts. One thing was clear. He'd been set up…again.

## Chapter 2

In the penthouse suite in the Waldorf Astoria hotel, Victoria Gregory stood looking as regal as a queen in her Versace French-vanilla-and-gold empire wedding gown. The sweetheart neckline, gold Cinderella tiara and Harry Winston diamonds dripping from her ears, neck and wrist were the result of hours of deliberation by a committee of family and friends. The wedding planner, location, caterer, florist, musicians and guest list had all been handled with Victoria's usual meticulous eye for detail. Outside the floor-to-ceiling window, the sky was a crisp blue without a single cloud in sight.

"A perfect day for a wedding," she finally said wistfully, taking in the scenery one last time. After that, she drew in a deep breath, squared her shoulders and then whipped around toward her five bridesmaids. "Are you absolutely positive that they missed their flights? Maybe the limousine driver was late and missed them? They probably took a cab or something."

Her twin cousins, Grace and Iris, cut a strange look toward each other that instantly piqued Victoria's hackles a few more inches.

"What is it?" she asked, her voice lowering to a lethal level. If Victoria was known for anything, it most certainly was for her quick temper. It was something that she had inherited from her father and she made no apologies for it. "Tell me," she snapped with a stomp of her foot.

Lolita, another cousin of hers on her mother's side of the family, cleared her throat since it was obvious that the twins were too afraid to speak. "We called Cole's cell phone a few minutes ago."

Victoria didn't like the smirk that crept across Lolita's face. "And?"

"And…after threatening him within an inch of his life, he gave us some slurred statement about how he didn't think that Marcus was going to make it." Lolita's smirk continued curling up until it reached the corners of her mouth. "Sorry."

Victoria's hands balled at her sides while the room around her started turning a vibrant shade of red. "What do you mean he's not going to make it?" she hissed. "I have over three hundred guests waiting downstairs."

In sync, Grace and Iris stepped back while Lolita's eyes sparkled with mischief.

This wasn't the first time Victoria regretted asking her cousin-slash-arch nemesis to be a bridesmaid in her wedding, but after her mother pleaded and begged, she gave in. Since then, the heifer had been like a steel thorn in her butt. She bitched and complained and seriously thought that she had a vote on every aspect of the wedding. Every time Victoria came close to catching a case, her mother would step in and reel her back down to earth.

Still smiling, Lolita shrugged her shoulders. "I could go down there and tell everyone that Marcus has just dumped you."

The twins gasped.

"I'm sure that they'll understand," Lolita added. "Lord knows I do."

Before the bitch could bat her faux mink eyelashes, Victoria launched and snatched the girl's lace-front wig clean off her head, exposing her thin edges and mini afro-puff of hair underneath.

The twins jumped back.

Lolita screamed and then clutched at her unkempt natural hair.

Satisfied, mainly because it was a hideous wig in the first place, Victoria threw it down and proceeded to stomp on it.

Lolita finally stopped her long wail and spat, "You bitch," before launching toward the bride herself.

Two seconds before, the twins recognized the look in Lolita's eyes and finally found the courage to jump into the mix before it got too ugly. The result was them landing right where they didn't want to be: in the middle. Lolita's arms spun like a windmill trying to get to the bride while Victoria's hard fist was landing some pretty good blows on contact. A second later, all four of them fell into a heap on the floor.

The door to the suite flew open and, after a momentary gasp to take in the situation, a stream of women rushed into the room and struggled to pull them apart.

"Enough! Enough! Enough!"

Celya Gregory's strength never ceased to surprise Victoria. Before she knew it, she was peeled away from the girls, but she was still pissed at her cousin's determination to ruin her wedding day. Who does that?

The team of family and friends helped them all to their feet, but Victoria and Lolita continued to stare each other down.

"Oh, some of the beads fell off your dress," Ceyla fretted while she checked her daughter over.

Aunt Brenda settled her hands on her hips. "What on earth is going on? Have you two lost your minds?" Her head swung from Victoria to Lolita, but then her face twisted into a frown. "Child, what on earth happened to your head?"

Lolita thrust an acrylic-tipped finger toward Victoria and started shaking it. "She did it! Crazy bitch! No wonder Marcus doesn't want to marry you. If I was him, I'd run like hell, too."

Victoria's temper shot back up and she was once again in the launching mode. "Let me at her!"

This time the army of women caught her and pulled her back.

Her deranged cousin laughed as she swooped over and snatched her wig from off the floor. "I guess things don't always turn out the way we plan, do they, cuz?"

Lolita's mother, Fiona, snickered as well, but then grabbed her daughter's arm and pulled her toward the door. "C'mon. Let's go." Before they reached the door, she also added, "I guess it's a good thing that we didn't waste any money, buying a gift."

They laughed like a pair of hyenas and then slipped out of the room.

Clenching her teeth together, Victoria's gaze shifted to her mother. "Gee. I'm so glad you talked me into inviting those two."

Celya's cafe-latte complexion pinkened as she exhaled a long breath. "I'm sorry, baby. I'd hoped…"

Victoria shook her head and then turned away from her mother. She wasn't in the mood to rehash the strained relationship of her mother's older and crazy sister who couldn't deal with her own petty jealousy. Everyone could see the truth, but her mother generally saw or wanted to see the best in everyone.

It was an annoying habit that Victoria was happy that she didn't inherit. "Someone get me a phone."

"Sweetheart, what did Lolita mean about Marcus not wanting to marry you? Where is he?"

All eyes turned toward her. "I don't know, Mother. She probably made it up. Lord knows she's evil enough. All I do know is that he's *not* here."

Everyone's eyes shifted away.

Victoria resisted the urge to scream and instead turned around and stormed from the living room suite and to the elegant master bedroom with her torn chapel train sweeping the floor behind her.

"Oh wait, sweetheart. Your train." Her mother fretted behind her.

Victoria continued her steady march away from everyone's gazes. They probably couldn't wait until she was out of sight anyway so they could start calling and texting everyone that she had just been dumped at the altar. "Dumped! *Me?* I don't believe this."

"Well have you tried to call him?"

She sucked in a breath and rolled her eyes. "That's why I'm looking for a phone, Mother." Victoria grabbed her cell phone from the nightstand and speed-dialed Marcus. On the first ring, she impatiently tapped her foot. On the second, she was pacing the room. By the third, she was mentally threatening to kill her tenuous fiancé if he *didn't* answer his damn phone.

"This is Marcus. I'm sorry but I can't come to the phone right now. But if you leave a message, I'll get back to you as soon as possible." *BEEP!*

"Marcus Lawrence Henderson, I don't know where you are, but I know that you *better* be on your way to our wedding." She turned her back toward her mother and then added in a low hiss, "I swear. If you embarrass me today, there's not a rock on God's green earth that you'll be able to hide under. Get your butt here. Now!" She disconnected the call but still felt the need to stomp, scream or hit something.

"All right now, sweetheart," her mother said, coming up behind her and wrapping her arm around her waist. "Calm down. I'm sure that everything will be all right. He and the boys probably just hung out a little too late at their silly bachelor party."

Victoria's eyes rolled back so far that she could almost see behind her. "I know Kent is behind this."

Her mother sighed but didn't refute the comment. That was enough to make Victoria feel like she was on the right track. Kent Bryce had been doggedly pursuing her hand since college. Not because he loved her, but because he wanted to position himself with her billionaire father and his successful investment company. She wasn't a fool. She saw straight through Kent and all his lame attempts to woo her. So when she pivoted and selected Marcus Henderson, a simple paper pusher out of account receivables, as an attempt to spur his calculated affection, Kent proved to be quite adept and positioned himself to become Marcus's new best friend.

Marcus, being a shy man, didn't know what to make of his rise in social standing and popularity and was snookered into Kent and Victoria's chess game before he ever knew what had happened. Relentless, Kent beat out Marc's own brother for the position of best man and was primarily responsible for this harebrained idea of having the bachelor party out in Las Vegas.

Victoria protested the idea, but she was seen as feebly trying to prevent the groom from his one rite of passage. Her father even poo-pooed her concerns and said that she was just being paranoid. So here she was, waiting for the groom along with all of New York's elite society.

Victoria took another deep breath while the fear of becoming a laughingstock rose like a tidal wave. Marcus wasn't much of a party man. He didn't drink or indulge in anything crazy. All of that played a part in her selecting him as her husband in the first place. Sure. She would've liked to have done this the old-fashioned way. You met someone, there's a connection, you fall in love and then you walk down the aisle. In Victoria's world that was just a fantasy sponsored by the fairy-tale spinners out of Hollywood. In her short thirty-two years, she had found one constant in life: people only liked her for her family's money and prestige.

She was irrelevant.

Her father, Mondell Gregory, made his fortune in hedge funds and this year cracked the top twenty on Forbes's list of richest Americans. A worthy accomplishment to be sure, but it resulted in her having a rather difficult upbringing. When you can't trust those around you because you suspect their intentions had nothing to do with you, but everything to do with them trying to boost their social standing, it leads to a rather lonely existence. So she built a wall around her heart and protected herself the best way she could. As a result, she had little patience for fools and it could be argued that she was a little anal and controlling.

It was the best way to avoid getting hurt.

When Victoria attended prep school, she was dubbed the poor little rich girl because she isolated herself from the crowd. By the time she was in college, she was the ice queen—and the loneliest person in the world. The years that followed didn't improve much. She'd become an investor herself and was rich in her own right. She had plenty of acquaintances, but no real friends. She just learned how to play the game. Smile and pretend she was happy during long, tedious society events. Men did find her attractive. After all, she did have her mother's long legs and coke-bottle curves. But after a while, those same men would show their true hand and start talking more about her father than about her.

Again, she was irrelevant.

Now, despite all her careful planning and maneuvering, she was about to be left standing at the proverbial altar. Turning, Victoria walked over to the bed and plopped down. All she could do was just sit, wait…and pray for a miracle.

Forever an optimist, Celya stayed next to her side and insisted. "Everything is going to be all right. You'll see." She smiled and squeezed her daughter's shoulders.

Despite her struggle not to succumb, a tear skipped down Victoria's face.

So much for that damn brick wall.

## Chapter 3

Eamon woke feeling like he was riding an out-of-control carousel. So much so that it was difficult for him to even lift his head. He lay still, trying to recall his last moments of consciousness—without much success. He certainly remembered making a ridiculous agreement with his brothers to babysit their spoiled cousin, Quentin. And there were vague memories of him rejoining the Hendersons' bachelor party. Looks were deceiving when it came to those New York Wall Street types. Those men really knew how to party. That was saying something from a man who specialized in running bachelor parties.

Bachelor Adventures was his brainchild and operated as a side business for The Dollhouse. There was definitely a market for this type of service and it struck Eamon as a no-brainer when he'd read how much the wedding business actually made. But with everything primarily geared toward the brides, it seemed only logical to give the grooms' last night of singlehood the sort of send-off it deserved. It took some time, but soon word-of-mouth spread among soon-to-be-married guys like a modern underground railroad. They came from near and far, filling The Dollhouse's calendar in all three club locations resulting in an extensive waiting list.

So what in the hell happened last night that resulted in him sleeping on a floor? *The floor?*

At last, Eamon's eyes fluttered open and verified that he was indeed curled up on a carpeted floor. Despite the spinning and the pounding going on in his head, he forced himself to glance around. He found little comfort in the fact that there were at least twenty other people sleeping among throw pillows, colorful fabric that he thought he recalled one of the belly dancers wearing, food, shoes— hell, the list went on and on. The bottom line was the place was wrecked.

*"Neah. Neah."*

Eamon slowly turned his head and came face-to-face with a billy goat. "Morning."

*"Neah. Neah."* The goat responded and then with his thick tongue he proceeded to lick Eamon's face.

"Eeeww." Eamon jumped back and tried to wipe the foul-smelling saliva from his face. It was nowhere near enough to make him feel clean so he hopped up, spinning room and pounding temples be damned, and went in search of the bathroom. It required him jumping over quite a few sleeping bodies. The hotel suite's wreckage continued as he made his way to the bathroom and still he had no recollection of all that went on last night. Had he hit his head or something?

Amazingly the bathroom had survived whatever shenanigans they had indulged in last night and it was thankfully empty. He went straight for the sink and started splashing cold water on his face. It was an instant relief to soothe his headache and to wash away his unusual morning kiss. After he shut off the water and grabbed a towel, he finally took a look at his reflection in the mirror.

"What in the hell?" He leaned in close because he didn't quite trust his eyes. But he wasn't seeing things. Someone had written in permanent marker across his face: BOY TOY. Eamon took the towel and roughly rubbed at his forehead. The words remained. "No. No. No."

But it didn't matter how many times he pleaded or rubbed his forehead raw, the bold letters stayed stubbornly in place.

*Knock! Knock! Knock!*

Eamon jumped and then turned toward the door. "Who is it?"

"How long are you going to be in there, man? I gotta pee," a woman whined.

Eamon gave himself one last look in the mirror and then tossed the towel down. "Here I come." He opened the door and the unidentified woman raced in and hopped on the toilet before he had a chance to clear the threshold. Shaking his head, he closed the door behind him and went on to try and inspect the damage.

A few more people were starting to stir, a couple of them had more to do with the goat licking their faces and the others just look like extras in a zombie film.

"Damn. What the hell happened?" one of the men he recognized from the bachelor party asked.

"Your guess is as good as mine," Eamon told him. Though everything was a mess, he didn't see anything broken. That definitely came in handy in case the hotel came after him and The Dollhouse.

"What time is it?" the guy asked, looking at his wrist

and seeming disappointed to discover that he didn't have on a watch.

Eamon thought he'd help by looking at his own watch, but his was gone, too. "It's a hair past a freckle, apparently." He glanced around on the floor.

"Ohmigod! The wedding! Where's Marcus?"

"That's a good question." Eamon started looking around at the faces on the floor, but didn't see the groom anywhere. "I guess he has to be around here somewhere."

They worked their way around the living room and then finally headed back to the master bedroom. However, the moment he opened the door, something came whizzing toward Eamon's head. He ducked but the object hit the man behind.

"Ooof!"

Eamon shut the door and turned around. "Are you okay, man?"

The dude placed a hand over his left eye for a moment and then declared, "I'm okay. What the hell was that?"

They looked down to see that it was only a plastic bowl full of colored popcorn. Then something else hit the closed door, drawing their attention.

"What the hell is in there?" Eamon asked, almost afraid to try to open the door again.

"I think I saw a monkey," the brother behind him offered.

"A monkey?" he asked for clarification. *I don't remember a monkey being ordered.*

"Robert!" Another brother from the bachelor party called out and then raced down the hallway to join them. "Man, we're missing the wedding."

Robert, the monkey-bowl victim, shook his head. "I don't think there's a wedding without the groom."

"Is he in there?" the guy asked.

"We're just about to check, but he might have been killed by a raging monkey."

That explanation succeeded in making the new guy look just as confused as they were.

"Okay," Eamon said, starting to crouch before he opened the door again. "Everyone, be prepared to duck."

"That warning would've come in handy the last time," Robert snipped.

"Sorry." Eamon turned the knob and slowly pushed the door open.

*Oooooh ooohhh aaaah aahhh!*

Sure enough there was a white-face capuchin monkey, clearly losing his mind while he jumped up and down in the center of the bed. Eamon found himself echoing his brother from last night.

"Now, there's something that you don't see every day."

"With good reason," Robert whispered. "Do you see Marcus anywhere?"

While the monkey was busy having a fit, Eamon glanced around the bedroom and came up empty. "No. He's not in here."

At the sound of his voice, the monkey whipped his head around and with lightning speed, grabbed one of the bed's pillows and hurled it at him. Though Eamon wasn't normally afraid of pillows, he quickly jerked back and slammed the door again before the fluffy bomb smacked him in the face.

Exhaling as if he'd just saved their lives, he turned toward the men and asked, "Is there any chance Mr. Henderson left without you guys?"

"Highly unlikely," Robert said.

They turned and headed back toward the front of the

villa, checked the dry and the steam sauna, then the courtyard and then lastly the private pool. No Marcus.

"I don't know what to tell you guys," Eamon said. "He's not here. Maybe he went and got breakfast." He reached into his pocket and pulled out his cell phone. After a couple of rings, he reached Johnson's Cleaning Crew on the line. "Hey, it's Eamon. Can you go ahead and send your guys on over to the Henderson suite? Yeah." He glanced around again and spotted the goat still roaming around. "Wait. Actually, wait an extra hour. I need to call animal control first."

The moment he disconnected the call, the villa's front door opened and in walked Marcus Henderson, smiling and gushing at…Delicious. "Good morning, everybody," he said with a goofy smile.

The rest of his friends started peeling themselves off the floor while most of the women were making a beeline to the bathroom.

"Where have you been?" Robert asked.

Another guy in the villa, smiled just as broadly. "Everyone, gather around. Marcus has an announcement to make," he broadcasted like he was the King of England or something.

Intrigued, Eamon folded his arms and wondered why Delicious—a.k.a Michelle—was bouncing around and holding Marcus's hand, but he had a suspicion that he wasn't going to like it.

It took a few seconds, but everyone gathered around and waited.

"All right, Marcus," the man said. "The floor is all yours."

"Thank you, Kent." Marcus smiled at Michelle, squeezed her hand and said, "First, I want to thank you all for giving me a wonderful bachelor party. I've never had anything like it."

The small crowd clapped and Eamon was pleased that he had indeed pulled off another successful party.

"However," Marcus continued and then started gushing as much as the woman beside him. "There's been a change in plans…or rather…a change in brides."

"Please no," Eamon moaned, filling in the blanks a second before Marcus held up Michelle's hand and announced, "Delicious and I just got married!"

Eamon groaned. "Oh God."

"Ladies and gentlemen, may I please have your attention?" Mondell Gregory announced in the center of the Waldorf's Park Avenue lobby. Three hundred sets of eyes zoomed to the larger-than-life man with rapt attention. He took a deep breath and with his head held high he continued. "First of all, I want to thank you all for coming today, but I regret to inform you that the wedding has been called off."

As expected there was a collectivé gasp followed by a low, steady murmur as most of the invited guests turned to one another to express their surprise.

"However, since we are all here and since we have a mountain of food and good music arranged for you, I don't see why we can't just turn this into an old-fashioned brunch party and take pleasure in one another's company." He held up his glass of champagne, though he wished that it was something stronger. "Enjoy!" Mondell nodded his head and then downed his drink in one gulp.

Plastering on a smile, he strolled briskly back out of the grand ballroom, ignoring a few questions being thrown at him as he passed. "How did I do?" he asked his wife, Celya, once he exited the room.

"Great. Given the circumstance," she answered as she began the difficult task of trying to keep up with his long strides. "What do you think has happened?"

He took an impatient breath and then shook his head. "He better be lying in someone's hospital bed. That's all I know. If not, he's going to be once I get my hands on him."

Celya didn't like the sound of that. Instead of enjoying her daughter starting a new chapter in her life today, it looked like she was going to have her hands full trying to calm and soothe two people. That meant a full plate when dealing with her husband and daughter. They were too much alike when it came to temperament. If Marcus was smart, he'd forget that the whole state of New York even existed, because if he ever came back, it would be to attend his own funeral.

When they returned to Victoria's suite, they found her exactly where they left her. Sitting on the edge of the bed and staring at her cell phone as if willing it to ring. Grace hovered around closely, though it was clear they were also at a loss as to what to say. No one saw this coming. Marcus Henderson seemed as dependable as they came.

Mondell swore under his breath. He didn't like seeing his daughter looking so distraught and it was clear that it was eating him up inside.

"Is it done?" she asked without looking back at them.

Celya instantly went to her side. "Yes, sweetheart. Your father took care of everything." She squeezed her daughter's shoulders.

Exhaling a long sigh, Victoria leaned over and rested her head on Celya's shoulders. "Did they laugh?"

"Of course they didn't laugh!" Mondell thundered. "They wouldn't dare."

Victoria closed her eyes. No doubt her father truly

believed that, but she knew better. Right now, it was just three hundred people. By tomorrow, it will be all of New York when the news hit Page Six. Then again, maybe the whole world was already twittering and Facebooking about the whole debacle.

"It looks like I really know how to pick them," she moaned.

"Oh, sweetheart." Her mother delivered another squeeze. "Please don't beat yourself up over this."

Well who else was there? Marcus? Hell. She didn't even know where he was.

Her cell phone rang and vibrated on the nightstand.

Victoria's head popped up off her mother's shoulder and she stared blankly at the phone.

"I'll answer it," her father said, moving in to swipe up the phone.

But the idea of him tearing a chunk out of Marcus's hide before she had a chance didn't set well. "No! I'll handle this." She seized the phone from her father's hands and ignored the disappointment written on his face.

"Hello," she answered coolly.

"Uh...Vicki?"

Victoria pulled the phone away from her face and frowned at it. No one called her Vicki. No. One. Rocking her neck from side to side, she cracked a few stiff bones in her neck and then placed the phone back up against her ear. "Marcus, where in the hell are you?"

"I'm still in Las Vegas."

"Did you miss your flight? Did you forget that we were supposed to be getting married?" Her voice rose with every question. "How about, did you forget that we have over three hundred people here—waiting?!"

The phone line fell silent.

"Marcus?!"

"Um…no." Marcus cleared his throat. "I didn't forget. That's sort of why I'm calling. I, uh, I'm not going to be able to, um, marry you."

This time, she let the phone go silent.

"Vicki?"

"What is it with this Vicki crap?" she snapped. "Stop calling me that."

"Oh. Sorry."

"And what do you mean you can't marry me? Do you know how much has gone into this wedding? The time? The money?" She started pacing back and forth, wishing that he was actually there so that she could wrap her hands around his neck and squeeze it until his eyeballs popped out.

"Yeah. I'm sorry about that. But, you see, I met this wonderful woman out here and…well…we got married last night."

Victoria stopped pacing and, once again, the phone line went silent.

"Vicki— I mean, Victoria? Are you there?"

Frankly, she wasn't sure whether she was there or not. This certainly felt more like an out-of-body experience. "What do you mean, you got married last night?" she hissed so low that it sounded like she was pouring venom into the phone.

"HE WHAT?" her father roared.

Undoubtedly Marcus heard her father's roar because suddenly he developed a stuttering problem. "S-see. Wh-what had h-happened was…D-Delicious and I—"

"DELICIOUS? You're dumping me at the altar for some trick named Delicious? Have you lost your damn mind?"

"WHAT?" her father continued to thunder. "Give me that phone."

Before Victoria could really unload on her second-rate Urkel-wannabe fiancé, her father successfully grabbed the phone from her.

"NOW, LOOK HERE, MARCUS! Clearly you've either had too much to drink or you've smoked something that has cooked your brain. You must have forgotten who you're dealing with. From now until you're six feet under, I will take great pleasure in personally destroying you. Do you hear me, young man?"

Trembling with anger and humiliation, Victoria turned and stormed out of the master bedroom and went in search of a good stiff drink—or a whole bottle. At this point, it didn't matter.

The twins and her mother shuffled behind her. Each of them told her to calm down and tried to assure her that everything was going to be all right, while her father continued to rant and rave into the phone. Three quick shots of Jack Daniels later, her nerves started to settle down, but her fury was just getting started.

# Chapter 4

*One week later...*

Quentin Dewayne Hinton was rocking Eamon's last nerve. This simple babysitting project was backfiring more rapidly than he'd anticipated. Sure, he knew that his older cousin was a spoiled rich kid, but he was unprepared for Q's total disregard for reality. The man had managed to arrange his life to be one giant party. Since he'd arrived, he'd basically hired most of The Dollhouse's dancers to perform at his over-the-top private parties on the top floor of the Bellagio. Who in the hell rents the entire top floor of a casino?

Now Eamon was up to his ears with complaints from customers, because he didn't have enough women working the floor or the upcoming slew of bachelor parties. And where were his two brothers? Apparently nowhere since they were clearly dodging the fifty calls he made to each of them a day.

"I know that you're screening your calls," Eamon barked into the phone. "Call me back!" He slammed the phone down and then ground his back teeth together until he swore that he could taste powder.

*Knock! Knock!*

"What do you want?" he barked and then immediately regretted it.

The door slowly cracked open, but then just enough for Hayley to stick her head through. "Sorry to disturb you, but we have all the new girls ready to audition."

"You have their applications and had them fill out the questionnaires?" he asked.

Hayley bobbed her head and tried to flash a smile.

Sighing, Eamon climbed out of his chair and headed toward the door. "I guess the faster I do this, the faster it'll all be over with."

Hayley handed him a thick folder and then patted him on the arm. "See. That's the spirit, Boy Toy."

The meek smile that he was trying to force died as he cut her a look.

She just laughed.

The permanent marker that had been used on him at the Hendersons' bachelor party had been scrubbed with everything from soap, alcohol, makeup remover and at one point a few cotton balls of bleach. The lettering had faded significantly, but if anyone was to look real close, they would still be able to make out the words.

"It's not funny," he grumbled when Hayley's laughter refused to die out.

"I think that depends on who you ask," she volleyed back.

Sighing, Eamon picked up his pace. He had enough of everyone's cackling.

It being just a little past noon, there were just a few

people scattered about cleaning and stocking up the club. At the main stage in the center of the club were approximately fifty new girls, ready to audition. At first glance, the women were all very beautiful and their dancing outfits ranged from everything like the naughty nurse to the dominatrix police officer.

Pretty much the typical stuff.

Drawing in a deep breath, he pulled out a chair and plopped down. "Good afternoon, ladies."

"Good afternoon, Mr. King," they chimed back as though they had been practicing all afternoon.

Eamon smiled and opened the folder Hayley had handed him and immediately started delving into the women's head shots and applications. "Okay. First up, Regina Bailey?"

"That's me." Regina stepped forward, showcasing a smile that stretched from ear to ear.

Eamon looked her over. "Like the smile. Like the legs…" His eyes parked on her flat chest and then hesitated. "So how long have you been dancing?" he asked while he read her information as she answered him.

"Since I was six," Regina said, remaining chipper.

"Professionally?" he asked, even though he'd already made up his mind that she wasn't right for the club.

"No. Actually, I just moved out here from Madison, Wisconsin. It's always been my dream to become a showgirl."

Eamon arched a brow and eased back into his chair. "A showgirl? You know The Dollhouse is a gentlemen's club. This isn't casino work."

Regina fidgeted a bit, but her smile never faltered. "Yeah. I know, but…I haven't been able to land anything yet. And—" she snuck a quick glance at the other women behind her "—well…I sort of really need a job."

Eamon stared at the young girl for a long moment before he then glanced back down to see that she was just twenty-one. An innocent. "Have you ever done any waitressing?"

"Yeah. Actually, my daddy owns a restaurant back home. I grew up helping wait tables. Problem is that it's just as hard trying to find a waitressing job out here as it is trying to land a dancing gig." Her smile finally started to falter.

"Well, today is your lucky day. I just happen to have an opening. It's yours if you're interested."

Eamon watched as if he'd just lifted the world off her shoulders.

"Really?"

He nodded. "I'm sure as long as you keep flashing that pretty smile of yours. You'll rake in a lot of money in tips."

"Oh, thank you so much." She blew him a kiss and started bouncing up and down. "You just don't know how much that means to me. I thought I was going to have to go back home with my tail tucked between my legs. Thank you. Thank you."

"All right. All right. You're more than welcome." He turned toward Hayley and handed her Regina's picture and profile. "Will you take Regina here and make sure that she fills out all the necessary paperwork?"

Her eyes danced with amusement as she whispered, "I didn't know we had a position available. I would've had my cousin Gwen apply."

"When Gwen learns to walk and chew gum at the same time, you do that."

Hayley laughed and then escorted Regina to the back office.

For the next two hours, Eamon watched the rest of the girls audition. There were a few potentials, maybe one or two break-out stars, but the majority of them were rhythm and balance challenged. Just when he and the DJ were getting down to the last dozen women, the front door swung open.

Eamon glanced at his watch. "I'm sorry, but auditions are closed right now." He shook his head. Tardiness was a trait that he couldn't stand. But when he heard a pair of heels stab the hardwood floors, he turned his attention to his right. "I said…"

Nothing, absolutely nothing could've prepared Eamon for the tall, fiery divinity that was storming his way. Six feet tall, with long flowing brown hair and blond highlights, this woman commanded attention like no one he'd ever seen before. Though her eyes were hidden behind a pair of fashionable bumblebee sunglasses, Eamon took time to note her high cheekbones and her thick kissable lips. And her body was sick. Sleek shoulders, high D-cup breasts, slim waist and butt that had just the right amount of jiggle when she walked.

"Now, this is more like it," he said and then shifted in his seat to relieve some of the pain of his erection that was creeping down his right leg and threatening to escape his boxers.

"I'm looking for the owner," the woman announced with a thinly concealed attitude.

Eamon didn't answer. He was too busy taking in her tight, white-lace dress that hugged her body like a second layer of skin and just barely kissed the middle of her incredibly toned thighs.

Clearly impatient, his dream woman snatched off her glasses and proceeded to stare him down with her blazing green eyes. He froze, looking at her face and remembering.

"HELLO!" She snapped her fingers in front of his face. "Do you speak in English? *¿Habla inglés?*"

Eamon finally broke out of his trance. "I'm sorry, what?"

She huffed out a breath and she settled a hand on her hips. "I *said* that I was looking for the owners."

"Well, you're in luck. You just found one of them. What are you going to perform for me today, honey?" He couldn't stop the smile that was creeping across his face. The image of her slicked down with baby oil and swinging that incredible body around a golden pole had him feeling like a preteen schoolboy. He couldn't remember the last time he'd felt like this—if ever.

"Perform?" She whipped her head around and finally took notice of the other scantily clad women behind her. When she turned back around, she was bubbling with laughter. "You've got to be kidding me." She rocked her neck. "Do I look like someone who works a pole for a living?"

Eamon took the question as invitation to take another look at the incredible brick house in front of him. Apparently he was taking too long because she started clearing her throat.

"Are you done?"

Eamon's gaze sprang back to her heated stare. "I guess I am now." He leaned forward and planted his elbows on the table and then braided his hands together. "All right. I'll bite. If you didn't come here to audition today, then why are you here?"

Her lips spread into a tight smile as she reached inside her large purse and withdrew some folded paper. "I came to serve you this." She thrust the papers toward him.

He froze at the word *serve* and refused to take the papers from her. "What is it?"

His discomfort and mistrust seemed to amuse her further because if her smile grew any wider, she was going to look like the Joker after a while. "I'm suing you." She dropped the papers on the table in front of him. *"Honey."*

"What for?" He snatched up the papers and rolled his gaze over the pages. So entrenched in his reading, he didn't hear when Quentin entered the club, let alone him walking up to the table.

"Hey, cuz. What's up?"

"FIFTY MILLION DOLLARS!" Eamon roared.

"Congratulations. You can read," she said smugly. "Now, if you can write and add, I'll be expecting that check when we go to court."

Quentin placed one hand on the table and leaned over so that he could catch the fire-breathing Amazon's attention. "Aren't you a feisty one?" He flashed his woman-magnet dimples at her. "Please don't break my heart and tell me that you're dating my knucklehead cousin here."

She leaned away from Quentin, suspicious of his over-the-top charm and his seemingly X-ray eyes.

"Fat chance," Eamon barked. "She's suing us."

"Oh? Are you one of the owners of this—" she glanced around and drew a deep breath "—establishment?"

"Guilty. Quentin D. Hinton at your service." He looked her over again. "Have you ever thought about a career as a dancer?"

"What the hell is wrong with you two?"

Eamon popped up from his chair. "Q, would you mind finishing up the auditions? Ms.…." He looked down at the paperwork. "Gregory?"

She smiled. "You're still impressing me with those reading skills."

He frowned at her constant sarcasm. "Ms. Gregory and I will be in the office if you need anything. There are just a few more girls. I'm sure you're more than qualified to handle it."

Quentin saluted. "Yes, sir. It's a hard job, but someone has to do it." He shifted his gaze back to Ms. Gregory. "When you finish your meeting you know where to find me."

She simply stared at the handsome playboy like she had never met or even seen anyone like him before.

"This way, Ms. Gregory." He swept his arm in the direction of the back office.

She hesitated for just a moment, but then finally pulled her purse strap over her shoulder and then marched off toward the back.

Quentin cocked his head to check out her walk.

Eamon socked him on the arm.

"Ow. What?"

"Just…handle the auditions. Geez." He fell in line behind Ms. Gregory. But after a few strides, his head slowly started to tilt to the side as well while he twisted his face at the sight of that wonderful jiggle this woman had.

She reached the door first and turned.

Eamon fixed his face and pasted on a smile just a nanosecond before she busted him.

However, her hard green eyes narrowed like she had eyes in the back of her head.

Playing it straight, he just opened the door. "After you."

She hesitated again.

"Don't worry. I don't bite," he assured her.

"Too bad," she volleyed without missing a beat. "I do."

Eamon's brows jumped up at the response as she turned and crossed the threshold. "I'll definitely keep that in mind," he said and then fought like hell to keep his eyes trained on the back of her head. It didn't work. He snuck another peek.

"Let me guess," Hayley said from his assistant's desk. "Another new hire?"

Ms. Gregory started to settle her hands on her hips again when Eamon jumped in. "No. Ms. Gregory and I have business to discuss in my office." He opened his door.

"Aaah. *Business*." Hayley winked. "I gotcha."

Eamon shook his head. This was not one of those times to toss sexual innuendos around. He tried to convey that by casting a hard look at Hayley, but she gave him the same clueless expression as Quentin. "What?"

Sighing and rolling his eyes, Eamon finally entered his office and closed the door. "All right, Ms. Gregory. What's this lawsuit all about?" He walked around his desk and plopped into his chair.

"The fact that my name is *still* Ms. Gregory," she seethed.

Of course that answer only confused him more. He frowned and wrinkled his forehead.

She squinted and leaned forward. "Does your forehead say *boy toy?*"

Eamon coughed and then tried to bring the subject back to this lawsuit. "You want to explain what you mean?"

"It does," she persisted. "Why do you have *boy toy* written on your head?"

Propping one elbow on the desk, Eamon tilted his head and then slapped his hand across his forehead. "Can we stick to the subject here? The lawsuit?"

"It's all right there. The Dollhouse also runs a sideline company called Bachelor Adventures, right?"

"Yes. And?" He dropped his hand and then leaned back

in his chair. Clearly getting information out of her was going to be like squeezing water out of a rock.

"Well, Mr. King. You and your establishment hosted my fiancé's—my ex-fiancé's—bachelor party a week ago. And instead of him showing up the next day to marry me in front of my family and most of New York's elite society, just imagine how all warm and fuzzy I felt when Marcus called me and told me that instead of marrying me he'd married a lovely booty-popper named *Delicious*."

Eamon's mouth stretched open while his gaze stroked her curves again. "Marcus Henderson was *your* fiancé?"

"Ah. I finally dusted off a few cobwebs in that small brain of yours."

His brows jumped, but his chest finally started to rumble with laughter. "You gotta be kidding me. You're suing me for fifty million dollars because you were left at the altar? That's ridiculous."

"Is it? You lure men here for some wild fantasy night, pump them full of liquor and God knows what else while an army of naked women swing around on poles and seduce them into having a quickie marriage at a drive-thru chapel that you guys seem to have on every street corner around here."

Eamon heard the words but he couldn't believe that someone would be crazy enough to say them, let alone believe them. Not to mention he still couldn't square the circle on just how Marcus Henderson managed to land a vixen like her. He rolled the riddle around in his head while he stared at her.

She started fidgeting. "Well? Aren't you going to say something?"

"What would you like for me to say?" He rose from his chair with a smirk on his face. "Clearly, you're insane or at the very least bitter."

*SLAP!*

Eamon blinked while the sting of her hand lingered. "Feel better?"

Her hand whipped around again, but before it could make contact, Eamon stopped it in midair and then pinned it to the wall behind her. There was something about the way her electric green eyes widened in surprise or the way she smelled like jasmine and white roses. No. Who in the hell was he kidding? It was the way her mesmerizing breasts heaved up and down against his firm chest that proved to be one temptation too many. So he did the very thing that he'd been thinking about since she walked into the club: he kissed her.

# Chapter 5

Victoria didn't know what happened. One minute she was so angry that she was breathing fire and then in the next she was a dripping pool of wax from the heat of this stranger's kiss. Not only that, there must be something wrong with her brain because she could swear that she heard her sensors crackling and popping. Yet she didn't want him to stop.

He tasted like those wonderful bits of chocolate with the heady filling of cognac. His tongue probed inside her mouth and she had the embarrassing response of moaning as if he'd found an oral G-spot. While he kept her one hand pinned to the wall, the free hand took full liberty to slide up the back of her thigh and then cupped the back of her right butt cheek and squeezed.

She moaned again, but he swallowed it up while kneeing her legs apart. This must be what it felt like to be ravished. The way the heroes always did in those old black-and-white films. The ones she never understood in which the women were always willing to drop everything they ever knew and all that they'd ever wanted to be just so that they could ride off into the sunset with some man. In this one weird moment she understood those women perfectly.

Just when oxygen was becoming a distant memory, King tore his mouth away from hers and started setting little fires along the column of her neck and then was well on his way toward her cleavage when the door bolted open.

"Victoria, are—oh!"

Victoria's passion-drugged eyes finally popped open just as King's head lifted off her breasts. And when had she hooked her right leg around his hip?

At Grace's stunned face, Victoria suddenly remembered herself and became appalled. "What the hell do you think you're doing? Get off me!" With the strength of Super Woman she shoved Eamon back, but it was the shock of the sudden maneuver that sent him tumbling back and tripping over the corner of his desk. The next thing everyone saw was his hands and feet flying into the air. When he hit the floor, he hit it hard.

*BAM!*

"Oomph!"

Victoria winced and then leaned forward to peek over the desk to see if he was still conscious. He was and looking around like he was still trying to process what had just happened.

"Next time, keep your hands to yourself!" She snapped her head as if she'd just given him a really good piece of her mind and then jerked back toward her cousin. "Let's go!"

Grace's wide gaze shifted down Victoria's body and then pulled at her own top.

Picking up her signal, Victoria glanced down and saw that half her right breast hung out the low-cut V of her dress. Like a runaway brush fire, Victoria's entire face became enflamed with embarrassment. But she tucked herself back in, lifted her head and stormed out of the office like a level-five hurricane.

"Victoria, wait up," Grace called after her.

However, slowing down was the last thing Victoria wanted to do. She wanted to hurry and get out of that place as fast as possible. She burst out the back of the club only to be blasted by some hard-bass music booming from the surrounding speakers. She pressed her fingers into her ears and kept moving, but then the woman on stage in front of her caught her attention and her angry strides slowed.

The woman on the golden pole was amazing. She couldn't even begin to understand how it was even possible for someone to hold themselves upside down with one leg while twirling around. Then she stopped, folded herself back up while her legs split open into a perfect V. It was erotic beyond belief, yet at the same time graceful. Slowly, she glided down the pole until she gently settled down into the textbook full split. Then the dancer did something that she'd never seen before. Somehow she was able to make both butt cheeks pop, then one at a time.

"How in the world?"

Just then that Quentin character she met earlier turned his head and caught her checking out the show. He flashed those dangerous dimples at her and waved.

"Ooooh," Grace said from behind her. "Now, I wouldn't mind five minutes alone in the back with that one."

Victoria groaned as shame and embarrassment part *deux* washed over her with even bigger waves.

"Are you ladies sure that you don't want to audition?"

Quentin yelled above the music. "We're always looking for more talent." He winked.

"Let's get out of here," Victoria said and then turned for the door. After a few steps, she realized that Grace wasn't behind her. Rolling her eyes and huffing out a frustrated sigh, she marched back, grabbed Grace by the arm and dragged her out of the club before Quentin convinced her to jump on that pole and quite possibly break her neck.

"Oooooh. He was cute," Grace panted. "Did you see him?"

"Yes. I saw him. Beware of wolves in sheep's clothing." She shoved open the glass door.

"You mean sort of like that gorgeous wolf that pawed your breasts out of your dress in the back office?"

Victoria cut her gaze over at cousin. "So if I jumped off a bridge would you do it, too?"

Grace blinked.

"Exactly. Get in the car." Victoria rolled her eyes and opened her door. But before she could hop in behind the wheel, she saw King—she didn't even know which brother he was—jog out of The Dollhouse and head toward her. "Get in the car, Victoria," she mumbled under her breath and wasted no time doing just that.

"Ms. Gregory, wait up!"

Victoria slammed her door and locked it just as Eamon reached it and tried to open it.

"What took so long?" Iris asked, scooting up from the backseat and folding her arms on the back of their chairs. "Who is that? He's fine."

*You don't have to tell me.*

"Ms. Gregory!" He knocked on the window and then yelled, "We haven't finished talking."

"Is that what we're calling *talking* nowadays?" Grace snickered.

"Shut up." Victoria crammed the key into the ignition and started the car.

King tossed up his hands. "You're the one that came to see me. Remember?"

She shifted the car in Reverse. "You can talk to my lawyer," she yelled back and then jammed her foot down on the accelerator. He jumped back in time to save his precious toes from being run over and Victoria felt a stab of disappointment.

"You're not even going to tell me where I can find you?" he shouted.

Victoria shifted the car back into Drive and jerked the wheel to the right.

But while she was in the middle of making her getaway, Grace powered her window down and screamed, "We're staying at the Bellagio!"

"Grace!" She peeled out of the parking lot.

Her cousin whipped around in her seat, smiling like a peacock. "What?"

"Why in the hell did you do that?"

She crossed her arms. "You heard him. You guys haven't finished talking."

Victoria seethed as she took off like she was trying to qualify for the Indy 500.

Iris piped up again. "Okay. Does anyone want to tell me what's going on?"

"Trust me. I'll fill you in on every tantalizing detail when we get back to our hotel," Grace promised.

"I don't know why in the hell I asked you two to come with me," Victoria grumbled.

"Yeah. You would hate that about now. Though I wonder what would've happened if I hadn't walked in on you two. Lord knows how many carpet burns I saved you from. You should be thanking me. Not trying to take my head off."

"SHUT UP!" Iris popped them both on the shoulder. "Victoria was making out with that chocolate god back there?"

"Girl, it was like animal kingdom up in there," Grace laughed. "That brother had her pinned down and mounted."

The twins squealed with laughter before high-fiving each other like pro athletes.

Victoria continued to stew in her seat. *What in the hell was I thinking?* She shook her head, but the question kept looping inside her mind. By the time they pulled up to the hotel, she just had to admit the truth to herself. She wasn't thinking. She was just feeling—feeling things that she had never felt before.

*That's good enough reason to stay the hell away from him.*

She exchanged her key for a ticket at the valet and then waltzed into the casino's hotel.

"I say you forget about the lawsuit and hook-up with Mr. Tall, Dark and Handsome."

"I hardly think that he's a fifty-million-dollar lay," Victoria snipped.

The twins exchanged a look.

"You know I really hate it when you two do that," Victoria said as they stepped into the elevator. "If you've got something to say, I wish that you would just say it."

"It's just that…the lawsuit. You don't think that maybe you're overreacting?"

Victoria's mouth dropped open as she turned toward her cousins. "Overreacting? Have you forgotten how I was humiliated last week? My wedding announcement was in the *New York Times*. Three hundred of the most important people in New York show up for a wedding that cost my father a mint—only for my fiancé to fly to Vegas for a bachelor party and fall head over heels in love with a stripper named Delicious. Are you hearing me? Delicious. And you just calmly stand there and ask me if I'm over-reacting?!"

Grace shrugged and mumbled, "It was just a question."

"Then the answer is no. When I get through with Marcus and his hoochie momma—and even that lecherous club owner with the octopus arms—they're going to wish that I'd hired a hit man to take them out of their misery."

The elevator dinged on the thirtieth floor and Victoria, with her anger renewed, marched out with her cousins rushing behind her. "Victoria, we didn't mean to upset you."

"You know what? Don't worry about it. I'm just going to take a long shower, get some sleep and then we can just fly out in the morning," Victoria said, sliding her card key into the lock. "I'll just catch up with you two later."

"Wait."

"No. Really. I'm tired and I would really like to get some sleep." More like she was on the verge of crying again and wanted to make her escape before the first tear fell.

"Well…all right," Iris said, looking to her sister to see if she had any pearls of wisdom that would help the situation.

Before Grace could open her mouth, Victoria was slamming her door closed. It was a good thing, too. Not two seconds later, two fat teardrops seeped from her lashes and rolled down her face. Why did she expect anyone to understand where she was coming from? They didn't have every society page and blogger laughing and saying mean things about them.

"Billion-dollar Bride Jilted at the Altar."

"Slam-Dumped!"

"Runaway Groom!"

"Money Can't Buy You Love."

All she wanted was not to get hurt. She had been so meticulous and so careful that she didn't understand how this whole thing blew up in her face. Marcus was not ambitious, he was unassuming and everything pointed to low drama. No. She didn't love him. Love had nothing to do with their union. But she had thought that they'd grown fond of one another—friends, certainly. And that was the most important thing, according to her grandmother before she died. A woman's looks faded with time, and sex was overrated. The secret to a long-lasting relationship was friendship—companionship. She thought that at least she had that with Marcus.

Now she didn't even know where the hell he was. But she had a detective on it and as soon as he reared his head, she was going to ruin him. In the meantime, she would take her frustrations out on the people she could find: the owners of The Dollhouse.

Victoria closed her eyes and pulled in a deep breath. There was no point in getting herself all worked up again. But while she chugged in huge gulps of air, the image of Mr. King floated to the forefront of her mind and her body became all warm and tingly. He had to be at least six-four with the skin the color of a Hershey's milk-chocolate bar. Just remembering its rich and smooth texture had her one cavity acting up.

And his lips—not too big, not too small. They were just right and pillow soft. And the taste of his kiss…

Victoria's head drifted back while she emitted a long "Mmm." But as soon as she heard herself, her eyes sprang back open and she glanced around to make sure that she was indeed alone.

"Get a hold of yourself, Victoria." She exhaled and then leaned to each side to remove her high heels. But as she moved around the large suite, forgetting about her sexy King proved hard to do. She remembered vividly his surprising speed. The way he'd pinned her back against the wall. That one brief moment of helplessness and his pure dominance over her still had a way of stealing her breath.

When had she ever come up against a force that powerful? And why had that one act made her not only aware of being a woman, but conscious of a unique power she never wielded before? At a glance someone would've easily thought that he was in control, but she was certain that she was.

As Victoria entered the bathroom and turned on the hot water in the whirlpool tub, she analyzed everything that happened after she'd laid eyes on King. She remembered vividly how his eyes caressed her body. The glint in his eyes told her that he definitely liked what he saw. Clearly her years of veganism and five a.m. boot-camp workouts had paid off.

By the second time, his gaze performed a slow drag over her body, her heart was pounding, her nipples were hard as rocks and she was aching in between her legs. Long before King's cute cousin strolled in, there had to be enough pheromones raging between the two of them to ignite an orgy.

Victoria smiled as she removed her clothes, but remained in a dreamy state as she eased into the tub's hot water. What would've happened if Grace and that other woman hadn't barged in? Would she have allowed a complete stranger to do her up against the wall of his office?

The answer was obvious, but she lied to herself by shaking her head. The good, conservative girl within her said that she would have ended things before he had gotten the chance to ease his hand anywhere near her panties. But the bad girl in her said who needed a hand when she could clearly feel his hard erection pressed against her through their clothes. She knew exactly what he was working with and it had only turned her on more—not less. Plus, hadn't the man already laid claim to her butt? He was squeezing and caressing it as if it had been his God-given right. And wasn't his mouth just mere inches from popping her right nipple into his mouth? Where were her good sense and values then?

Her smile widened while she absently scrubbed her body. It wasn't long before she was wishing that their little interlude could've lasted just five more minutes. Five more minutes of that wonderful mouth, those talented hands and hard, thick rod that was poking her in between her legs, begging her to say the word. "Yes," she whispered, smiling.

In the distance, the hotel phone rang.

*The twins.* She sighed. *I told them that I wanted to be left alone.* She rolled her eyes and sank deeper into the tub. When the phone stopped ringing, Victoria smiled and went back to her memories of the sexiest man that she had ever met.

# Chapter 6

"Damn it!" Eamon disconnected the call and then pocketed his cell phone.

"Maybe it's just me, but I could have sworn that you were a lot smoother with the ladies," Quentin chuckled as he eased onto the bar stool next to him. "I certainly don't recall you having them run away from you like escaped convicts."

Eamon lifted a brow. "*You* want to give me advice on women?"

"Who better than a man who has been in the boxing ring with love?" Quentin volleyed without missing a beat. "I jabbed when I should've ducked and ducked when I should've jabbed."

"So you're an expert now?"

"Only enough to know that I'll never get into the ring again." Q winked. "But if you're just trying to lure these delectable creatures into your bed, keep the nights from getting too cold, then I'm your man. You'd have to talk to my brothers for that happily-ever-after crap. They seem to have that down pat."

Though Quentin maintained his smile, there was an underlying sadness in his eyes and a voice that he couldn't cover up. Why hadn't Eamon noticed before?

When Q grew uncomfortable with Eamon staring at him too hard, he patted him hard on the back. "Cheer up. Let me buy you a drink."

Eamon twisted his face. "We own the bar."

"Let's not get hung up on technicalities." He climbed out of his seat and went behind the counter. "What will it be, cuz? Bourbon? Jack?"

"Kamikaze," Eamon answered.

"Ahh. Vodka and triple sec." Quentin cocked his head. "Now, why doesn't that come as a surprise to me? A Kamikaze man is adventurous, bold and courageous."

Eamon laughed. "You're psychoanalyzing me based on the kind of drink I like?"

"Laugh if you wanna, but all bartenders know that it's an art as well as a science."

"You always did look at things differently."

"No. I think I'm on to something with this," Quentin said, reaching for the bottle of vodka. "Ask any bartender and they will tell you the same thing I am. You can tell more about a man by what he drinks than the clothes he wears."

"Is that right?"

"That is a fact," Quentin boasted confidently. "What any man or woman wears is for show. It's to proclaim a certain lifestyle or status, whether it's real or not is irrelevant. It has nothing to do with what's on the inside. But a drink is a little more intimate. I should know. I have drowned my sorrows in more than a few bottles."

*Amen.*

"So what's your drink?" Eamon asked.

"Whiskey sour." Quentin winked. "I let you figure that one out on your own."

Eamon laughed. He had to hand it to his cousin. He was definitely a charming guy.

"Here you go," Quentin announced. "One Kamikaze." He set the drink on the bar.

"Thank you."

Quentin corked up a brow. "What? No tip?"

Eamon twisted his face. "Add it to my tab."

"I'll tell you. No one ever appreciates a good bar- tender."

They shared a laugh while Quentin made himself a whiskey sour.

"So how long are you planning to hide out here?"

"Hide out? That's an interesting choice of words," Quentin said. "Is that what Xavier told you? He thinks I'm hiding?"

Briefly Eamon wondered if he said something that he shouldn't have, but he went ahead down this rocky road since his brothers had left him with very little to go on. "How would you describe it?"

"I would say that I was celebrating." His smile stretched a little wider.

"Celebrating?"

Quentin nodded as he turned up his drink. Once the contents were gone he immediately started to pour himself another. "I'm celebrating life, women and a hell of a lot of money that my father gave me."

"It must be nice," Eamon mumbled.

Quentin frowned. "The last time I checked you're not exactly destitute, cuz."

"No. But I'm not exactly a trust-fund baby, either.

Some people actually have to work for a living." That only seemed to amuse Quentin more.

"Is that the thorn in your paw between me and you? You don't like my carefree lifestyle?"

"I have a problem with a man who doesn't make his own way in the world." Their eyes locked, but Eamon continued. "You're a spoiled little rich kid who has never taken anything in life too seriously."

"And why would I want to do that?" Quentin challenged. "Who in their right mind would want to jump on some hamster wheel chasing after some vague definition of success? Is success money? I have money. Is success happiness? Five days out of seven I'm pretty happy. Maybe with love and family?" He shrugged his shoulders. "Believe it or not, I have those, too."

"What about starting your own family?" Eamon asked.

"Said one bachelor to the other." Q smiled. "Unless you're going to tell me that you have some little woman clubbed and cooking in your kitchen at home that you forgot to tell anyone about."

Eamon didn't know how he walked into that trap all willy-nilly. "Okay, you got me with that one."

Quentin laughed as he started in on his second drink. "People in glass houses…"

"Gotcha. You made your point."

Q floated for a minute, but then he seemed like he had discovered a riddle that he wanted or needed an answer to. "So why haven't you settled down?"

Had someone just switched on a gigantic interrogation light? Suddenly, the room felt incredibly hot and the tiny hairs on the back of Eamon's neck stood at attention. "I'll get there eventually," he said, hoping that would help kick the can down the road.

Quentin laughed. "Just not any time soon?"

Eamon shrugged. "Maybe…maybe not. I've been a little busy with The Dollhouse. Hands-on type of work." He tossed in a wink.

"You're starting to make me feel like you don't appreciate me and my little checkbook."

Eamon smiled, but he didn't answer.

However, Q wasn't about to let the subject go. "Anyway. The clubs are doing well and…"

The front door opened and a long procession of dancers entered the club, smiling and waving. "Hello, Q, Eamon!"

"You ladies ready to make some money tonight?" Quentin asked.

"You know it!" Cotton Candy held up two deuces and bounced her hips.

Q's smile sloped unevenly as he watched the women stroll toward the back room. He didn't miss a single bounce or jiggle. "You know you need to just go ahead and admit the truth."

Eamon frowned. Had he forgotten what they were talking about? "Which is?"

"Men like us can never settle down," Quentin said, matter-of-factly. "Just look at what we're surrounded with every day—beautiful smiles, long necks, big breasts, small waists, nice hips, apple bottoms and long, firm legs. I'm starting to think that it's just not natural for a red-blooded man to be able to choose just one."

"But you did," Eamon said before he could stop himself.

Q's eyes glanced back over to him, his expression unreadable. "Temporary insanity."

Eamon's brows leaped up again.

"That's my story and I'm sticking to it." He drained the rest of his drink.

Eamon was more than willing to let the subject drop. Hell, it was already beginning to feel a little *Twilight Zone*–ish. How was it that he was being counseled about settling down from a man who had no shame in shopping for sugar mommas when his father had cut him off? The man had probably submitted his own picture to the good folks at Webster's Dictionary to be inserted next to the word *manwhore*.

"Don't worry about me. I'll get married when the right woman comes along," said Eamon.

"In that case, just make sure you keep her as far away from your brothers as humanly possible."

Eamon tried to capture his cousin's gaze again, but Q was having none of it. Clearly, he hadn't meant to add that last part. The slip was a sure sign that he still hadn't forgiven his older brother. Maybe a little more time needed to pass. Before he could help himself, Eamon wondered if a woman could ever come between him and his brothers. His instincts were to doubt it, but he was old enough to know that life was strange and complicated. One should never say never because the truth was more like: anything was possible.

"Have you talked to Sterling lately?"

Quentin's eyes softened even though his back stiffened. It was clear that he churned the question over quite a few times before smiling back at Eamon. "We were talking about you. Not me."

"There's not much to say about me," Eamon volleyed. "I'm what people call a workaholic."

Q rolled his eyes. "I know. I have quite a few of your kind on my immediate side of the family. My father and both brothers, remember?"

Eamon nodded.

"Still." Quentin leaned over the bar. "We have a lot in common."

"You don't say?" Eamon couldn't stop his lips from curling in amusement.

"Trust fund and work ethics aside, I see us as two peas in a pod."

"Uh-huh."

"Look. We're two good-looking men, if you don't mind me saying so."

Eamon shrugged.

"We're both committed to this wonderful lifestyle called bachelorhood. Free from the strings that have tripped and entangled so many of our fallen brethren. Like I was saying earlier about the unlimited selection of women that surrounds us on a day-to-day basis. I'm now a firm believer that the old traditional notion of marriage—one man-one woman—is just downright antiquated. Women don't really *need* us anymore. That whole women's lib movement took care of that. They can bring home the bacon and fry it up in a pan, remember? Now we do need them, but not for cooking and cleaning." He laughed.

"I'm wondering if it's possible to evolve backward," Eamon said, hoping to cut off this stream of nonsense.

"Ha. Ha. All I'm saying is life is meant to be enjoyed and celebrated at every possible moment. You know what I mean?" Q started making his third whiskey sour.

Eamon laughed.

"Hold that thought," Q said. "I'm going to hit the john. This stuff is going straight through me." He rushed around the counter and then disappeared into the back.

Eamon shook his head and then continued to nurse his drink. It wasn't like he didn't know where his cousin was coming from. Unbeknownst to Q, Eamon had been in love once—a long time ago.

Slowly, his gaze lowered to his glass but his mind tumbled back through the years to land on a face that haunted its fair share of dreams. Her name was Karen Hayes, a light brown sister with green eyes and twin dimples. They met their freshman year of high school. Her family had moved from Compton, California, to Atlanta. Back then they used to call girls like her *fly.* To this day, he remembered that ridiculous but cute lopsided bob with the word *fresh* shaved into the back of her head.

Her style was short, midriff T-shirts with colorful baggy overall jeans like that hip-hop group BBD sported hard that year. Black Timberlands, bamboo earrings and gold roped chains, her whole ensemble was a trip, but was considered dope back in the day. It didn't take long for her to find a small clique to hang with and before anyone knew it, she called herself rapping in a small group that was determined to become the next Salt 'n' Pepa.

Every time Eamon turned around, the girl was spitting out a freestyle rhyme or busting out the latest dance steps that she'd learned off *Yo! MTV Raps.* Nobody could tell that cute girl nothing. She was convinced that she was the baddest girl on the block. And as far as a young Eamon was concerned, she was. In no time at all he was in love. He made sure that he was at every teen club or house party that she and her girls performed at.

He didn't think that she even noticed him. Mainly because he was incredibly shy. Smart as a whip but he was known to hang with the theater and music majors rather than any sports team. That came later on. Eamon was completely stunned and tongue-tied when she finally stepped to him. Someone had put it in her ear that he had a small studio in his grandparents' basement, complete with egg crates on the walls to help soundproof the place.

"Can't you speak?" she asked when all he'd managed to do was stare.

"Yeah. Yeah." He shrugged his pencil shoulders. "I can hook you up."

"A'ight, then. Me and my girls will be by your grandma's Saturday morning." With that she just turned and disappeared back into the crowd.

He didn't even ask her how she knew where his grandparents lived. He was just flying high that she had even talked to him. True to her word, they showed up bright that Saturday and Xavier and Jeremy witnessed him turning into a blithering idiot in front of her. They snickered and teased him, but at least they were cool enough to save the real embarrassing stuff until after Karen left.

The game plan was to help them make a demo good enough for them to get on *Star Search*. The result was them spending an awful lot of time together. Mainly because he was the only one they knew that had all the equipment—the microphones, the speakers, the sound board. Soon he was helping her write material. They hung out all the time and soon the high-school players took notice of him because of his association with the hottest girl in the whole school.

By the time summer came around, they were officially a couple. She rapped and he DJ'ed. It was a whole year before *Star Search* came calling and by then, the whole rap phase had passed and Karen's attention had turned toward fashion. She now wanted to be the black Coco Chanel.

In their junior and senior years they were crowned king and queen at the prom. College was scary since she was bound and determined to go to design school in Chicago while he attended the University of Georgia. But Eamon was determined to make it work so there were a lot of road trips and, if their parents felt sorry enough for them, occasionally airline fare.

Friends and family members weren't as sure that their long-distance love affair was going to last, but Eamon was determined to prove them wrong. To his family's surprise, Eamon remained true, never once in college was he even tempted to stray. By senior year, he managed to make believers out of them all. As graduation neared, he took on a third job to help buy an engagement ring.

Three thousand dollars seemed like a million to him at the time. It was a small gold band with a smaller diamond, but he promised himself as soon as he made it rich that he was going to replace the ring with something so big and gaudy that it would make all her girlfriends green with envy. The ring size really wouldn't matter with Karen, but it was a promise he made to himself nonetheless.

He never forgot the feeling he had when he walked out of that jeweler's store. Too bad that he never got the chance to see how it would feel to slide the ring onto Karen's finger.

"Now, you take that curvy brick house that came in here earlier," Quentin said, returning to the bar and acting like there hadn't been a break in the conversation.

"Do what?" Eamon asked, struggling to pull his mind back from the distant memory.

"Don't front. You know exactly who I'm talking about or you're not pitching on the same team that I am."

"Oh. You mean Ms. Victoria Gregory." As he said her name, Eamon's lips curled back upward.

"Yeah." Q nodded. "Now, there's a woman with a body for sin, but one look into those sharp green eyes and my head is screaming *danger*. Even though I was teasing her today, I know to steer clear away from that kind of trouble."

"You think so?"

"I know so. She's the kind of woman who can chew a man up and spit him back out to avoid indigestion."

Eamon had that impression, too, but that was the part of her that intrigued him more than anything else. "That's all right. Trouble never scared me much."

Q smirked. "All right. A hard head makes a soft ass. Don't say that I didn't warn you."

"Duly noted." Eamon finally drained the rest of his drink and stood up from the bar. "But don't worry about me. I'm a big a boy. I can handle Victoria Gregory."

# Chapter 7

"C'mon, Victoria. Nobody sleeps when they're in Vegas," Iris whined over the phone. "We're all dressed and ready to go party. You need to get this whole Marcus thing out of your system."

Victoria's eyes hadn't stopped rolling since she answered the phone. "I'm not in the mood to go party. You two can go ahead without me." She dropped her head against the pillows. If she could just hurry up and get them off the phone, she could return to her dreams about a certain club owner with the most incredible hands and lips.

"We're only going to be here for one night," Iris insisted. "Pleeeease? I don't like it when you mope."

"I'm not moping," she lied. "I'm strategizing my next move."

Iris huffed out a frustrated breath. "You're just not going to let any of this go, are you?"

Victoria grinded her teeth. "What do you mean, *let it*

*go?* You're acting like I've been on some type of rampage for the last year. This *just* happened to me a week ago! Can't you just let me be mad? Is that too much to ask? Am I not allowed to be pissed off about this? Why do I have to be magnanimous about becoming the laughingstock of New York? Would you be trying to take the high road if it was you? And before you answer that let me remind you that I was there when you keyed your last boyfriend's Bentley because you couldn't believe that it was his grandmother who'd called him the middle of night instead another woman. It wasn't until you learned that she really had broken her hip that night and needed a replacement that you even grudgingly apologized!"

Silence.

"Right. So now that I truly do get screwed over, your advice to me is to just get over it?"

"That's not what I meant."

"Oh? What did you mean?"

Silence.

"Uh-huh. Just like I thought. The truth is that you have no idea how I feel and you could care less. So please don't let me in get in the way of you and Grace going out and having a good time!" Victoria sucked in a deep breath. She was getting too heated and taking her frustrations out on the wrong people again. She sucked in a second breath and then forced herself to soften her tone. "Look. I just need an evening to myself. Is that too much to ask?"

"No."

"Thank you." Another deep breath. "And I'm sorry. I don't mean to take this out on you. Truly. My emotions are just all over the place."

"I understand," Iris said, easing up on all that whining. "I really was just trying to help."

"I know that. Really. Just…you and Grace go out

and have a good time. I want to be by myself tonight. We can just meet up for breakfast before we head out tomorrow."

"You got it. Night."

"G'night." Victoria finally hung up the phone and pulled the bedding all the way up under her chin. She waited for sleep to come or even wide-awake fantasies of her chocolate King, but instead she was just left to stare up at the ceiling and wonder what she had really accomplished by flying all the way out to Vegas. She couldn't find Marcus and serving those papers at The Dollhouse hardly gave her the sort of satisfaction she was hoping for.

Maybe she succeeded in making an even bigger fool of herself, seeing as how neither owners had any real reaction to her mega-million-dollar lawsuit. She might as well have told them what day of the week it was. Maybe women sued them all the time. Who knows how many potential marriages their wild bachelor parties had destroyed?

And given how easily King had handled her in his office, who is to say that's how he handled all angry jilted fiancées? That was what it was, wasn't it? He handled her.

Hours ago, she thought that she was the one that was in control in that office. Now, she wasn't so sure. After all, it had only taken one kiss and she had transformed into a dog in heat.

What was it that woman said outside his office? Hadn't she just laughed at the notion that they were going in there to discuss business? Did everybody know what was about to happen in there once he closed the door?

Victoria groaned and then rolled over onto her side. Beyond the sheer curtain, she easily made out the glowing Las Vegas lights. The city was like an adult playground.

Even she could hear the gambling halls and pulsing night clubs calling out to her. It was truly a magical city.

Without thinking she climbed out of bed and walked over to the floor-to-ceiling windows and pulled back the curtain. There was a ring of people watching the Bellagio's breathtaking fountain show. But her attention was drawn to the people walking down the new strip. They looked like a million ants from up there. But she fooled herself into thinking that she could hear them all laughing and singing as they trotted along from one hot spot to another. None of them, she imagined, had a care in the world.

A crushing sadness washed over her and before she knew it, a few tears leaped over her lashes and managed to get as far as the center of her cheeks before she wiped them away.

*Knock. Knock. Knock.*

Victoria frowned as her she whipped her head around. "Was that the door?"

*Knock. Knock. Knock.*

"Damn. I thought I settled this with Iris already."

*Knock. Knock. Knock.*

Rolling her eyes, Victoria stomped away from the window and then marched past the master bedroom, past the living room and minibar before finally reaching the door.

*Knock. Knock. Knock.*

"Grrrr." She unlocked the door and then jerked it open. "I told you that I didn't want to—"

Her King smiled. "You told me what?"

With one quick glance she took in his incredibly handsome face. His smile alone was postcard perfect for a toothpaste ad. In the back of her mind, she realized that she needed to say something—anything, but all she could do was run her gaze over the way his broad chest filled out his royal-blue silk shirt or even how it tapered down at his chiseled sides. From memory, she knew how hard and muscularly rippled his abs were. He probably even had that nice defining cut right were his hip and leg connected. By the time her X-ray gaze made it to his tailored black slacks a grand jury could have easily convicted her of sexual assault.

King cleared his throat—loudly. "Good evening. It's a pleasure seeing you again, too."

Victoria's face suddenly flamed with embarrassment and instead of responding to his slick retort, she simply slammed the door in his face. Afterward, she stood there for a mind-numbing second where she tried to convince herself that what just happened didn't happen.

"Umm…that wasn't exactly the reaction I was hoping for," King boomed through the door, and then added a little chuckle for good measure.

Victoria's eyes bugged while the muscles in her stomach rolled and twisted into tight knots, but for some reason, she couldn't speak.

*Knock. Knock. Knock.*

"Hello? I know that you're here," he continued to chuckle.

It was probably his amusement that finally got under her skin. "What the hell are you doing here?!"

"What do you think? I came to see you."

Silence, mainly because she didn't know what to do with that answer.

"If I remember correctly we didn't exactly finish discussing business in my office earlier."

His hands, mouth and his incredibly hard erection pressed high against her thigh flashed before her eyes like instant recall and she had a devil of a time swallowing a huge lump that was growing in the center of her throat.

"What—" She coughed to clear her throat. "Whatever you need to discuss, you just need to contact my lawyer. She'll do all the talking for me from here on out."

Silence.

Did he just turn around and leave? She wasn't sure so she leaned over and tried to see whether she could make out if she could see anything under the door. Of course, she couldn't. She crept toward the door and then slowly pressed her ear against it to see if she could at least hear anything.

"What if I told you that I didn't like lawyers?" he boomed suddenly.

Victoria jumped back as if the door had exploded. After clutching a hand over her heart and catching her breath, she said, "Then I would say that it was just too damn bad."

"Well. Forgive me, but I thought that since you went through an awful lot of trouble to deliver this nasty little lawsuit yourself that we could sit down and settle this between us."

*It's a trap. He's just going to try and seduce me again. Wait. Or had she seduced him?* She couldn't remember what her final verdict was on that hot episode in his office.

"Of course, I'd rather not try to broker this thing through the door like this. People are starting to look at me strange out here."

She remained silent though her hand itched to open the door.

*Knock. Knock. Knock.*

"C'mon. Open the door."

Victoria clutched at her clothes and only then realized that she was in her pajamas. "I'm not dressed."

"Granted, you're not wearing my favorite dress you

had on earlier, but the last time I checked, pajamas still qualified as clothing."

*He really is a smart-ass.* She turned away and rushed to take a look at herself in the mirror. Thankfully, she didn't look like a hot mess, but for good measure, she ran the brush through her hair a couple of times. As far as her clothes, King was right. There was nothing wrong with her two-piece pink pajamas. It wasn't sheer or risqué in any way.

*Knock. Knock. Knock.*

"Geez. Talk about being persistent." She rushed back toward the door, took a deep breath and opened it.

There leaning against the doorframe with arms crossed and wearing a crooked smile, stood her King.

*My King? Where the hell did that thought come from?* She shook her head clear.

"Mind if I come in?" he asked, sounding like a wolf that was bold enough to knock on Little Red Riding Hood's grandma's door.

Victoria wasn't a woman who was easily scared, but there was definitely a trickle of fear in her bloodstream as she looked this handsome devil in the eye and issued an invitation. "Come on in."

His lips kicked up an extra notch as he unfolded his arms and strolled across the threshold like a king entering his own castle.

The knots in Victoria's stomach managed to tighten more while her knees almost started to knock together. Just being around him again had her body teetering on the verge of mutiny against her lifelong habit of restraint and self-control (minus what happened earlier that evening). While he strolled inside, glancing around, Victoria closed the front door and stole another deep breath while she checked out his back view.

*Damn. This brother is fine coming and going.* Seriously. She couldn't find a bad angle on him anywhere. In a way that was annoying. It would help her immensely if she could find some flaw that would at least humanize him. After all, it's impossible to remain angry at a man who looked like a god.

"All right," she said, crossing her arm again. "Now what?"

King turned and lazily roamed his gaze over her. It was probably payback for the way she had gawked at him outright when she'd opened the door. "*Now*—you get dressed so that I can take you to dinner."

"Dinner?"

"Yes. It's this ancient practice we have around here where we sort of sit around a nice table, sometimes there's candlelight and soft music playing in the background."

Victoria cocked her head and pursed her lips together.

He just smiled and continued. "We have these people that are either called waiters or waitresses and we order what we'd like to eat. They scurry off to the back and tell this majestic cook—a master of all things culinary and whatnot. Next thing you know that waiter is placing our mouthwatering food before us and we just…dig in." At the end of his dinner description, his smile was so wide she could easily count all thirty-two teeth.

"Funny."

"Maybe I missed a career as a comedian?"

"You're not that funny."

"Or maybe not." He winked and then closed the space between them.

For the briefest moment, Victoria nearly panicked and stepped back, but at the last moment, her brain kicked in and ordered her feet to remain rooted where they were.

She didn't want to concede any ground to him. But that decision was damn near her undoing because the minute his seductive cologne wrapped around her senses, she started having visions of braided fingers, sweaty bodies and silk sheets.

"Now, about dinner. I hope that you like Italian because I made reservations at this wonderful spot away from the tourists but a secret jewel that you'll enjoy."

"I'm not going to dinner with you."

"Our reservation is in forty-five minutes."

One of Victoria's brows steadily climbed higher. "Thanks, but…I'm not hungry."

The mutiny started. Her stomach just had to pick that exact moment to start growling. And it wasn't just some small growl that she could laugh or ignore but it was this long, loud rumbling growl that would have put any hungry African lion to shame. And while her empty stomach was making a fool out of her, she was either crazy or bold enough to maintain eye contact with this grinning god.

Next, she tried to cut off the never-ending growl by pressing her arms flat against her stomach, but unbelievably that just made it worse—by making it louder.

A *full* minute later, the humiliation ended and King simply glanced down at his platinum MontBlanc watch and said, "Make that forty-four minutes. You better shake a leg."

Victoria thought about tossing another excuse his way, but why risk being caught in a second lie? "Fine. Dinner. But there will be none of that…other stuff."

A sudden light twinkled in his eyes. "Too bad. I sort of liked that other stuff."

She couldn't prove it, but the oxygen had somehow been sucked out of the room because she couldn't breathe.

Braided fingers. Sweaty bodies. Silk sheets.

He looked at his watch again. "Forty-two minutes."

She swallowed and somehow uprooted her feet so that she could creep around his mountainous body and escape to the bedroom.

King seemed content if not amused watching her squirm around him. Even after she managed that small feat, she could still feel his heavy gaze on her until she finally closed the bedroom door and then slumped against it.

"What in the world have I gotten myself into?" she sighed.

# Chapter 8

"What in the world have I gotten myself into?" Eamon asked, shaking his head. Even after Victoria had closed the door, he stood in the center of the main living room debating whether he was biting off more than he could chew when it came to dealing with Ms. Gregory. Where was that bravado he had when he told Quentin that he could handle the uptight and frosty temptress?

*An heiress.* He couldn't believe it when he did a quick Google search. But there it was: the daughter of one of the wealthiest billionaires being jilted at the altar. After reading just a few articles he could see why she'd been livid. The society tabloids had ripped her to shreds.

Though he had little doubt that he was having a strong effect on her, it wasn't like she wasn't doing a number on him. With no makeup and a simple pair of silk pink pajamas, she was still perhaps the most naturally beautiful creature he'd ever seen. And he doubted that he could ever forget the scent of jasmine and white roses without the image of braided fingers, sweaty bodies and silk sheets from flashing in his head.

Eamon sucked in a deep breath and then shook his head but it didn't do much good since the whole suite held on to her soft fragrance even as the minutes ticked by. "Get a hold of yourself," he said to himself and then straightened his shoulders in compliance with his command.

Perhaps it was wise if he just focused on dinner and the lawsuit. Of course, he knew that he didn't really need to respond to the lawsuit since it was silly on its face and so transparently ridiculous that it would be a travesty to the judicial system if it was ever litigated. So maybe just focusing on dinner would be the better option. He started walking around the suite while he churned that decision over in his mind, as well. Truth of the matter, he didn't really care whether the woman ate, though it was clear that her stomach had some complaints about it. Dinner was a ruse.

His sole objective was to try to re-create that heat and magic that they had exchanged in his office earlier that day. He couldn't remember ever feeling anything like it. Not even back in the day with his old high-school sweetheart.

"Trouble," Eamon repeated Quentin's words and for the first time the thought that his philandering cousin may have actually called this one right. He stopped before the floor-to-ceiling window and stared out at the city that had become his second home. It was never more beautiful than at night. It was also when anything and everything was liable to happen. "Just dinner," he sighed.

Maybe if he said it enough, he would actually start to believe it. But if he wasn't mistaken he could hear his subconscious laughing at him. It was like it and his body were in on a joke that they refused to tell him about it. But didn't he kind of know?

He sucked in another deep breath. Why did he feel like he was suffering from a mild case of stage fright? Then he remembered how Victoria's gaze had a way of slicing through him. He sort of liked how her eyes would narrow when she was angry or irritated or how they would flicker like green fire when he was seconds from kissing her sexy full lips.

Eamon closed his eyelids allowing the memory to play in his mind. He was just about to moan out loud when Victoria's voice floated behind him.

"Looks like you're thinking about something real hard."

Surprised that she had caught him unaware, Eamon whipped around but then had to fight like hell to prevent his damn tongue from rolling out of his head. Stunning in a simple green and metallic print dress that once again hugged her Coke-bottle curves like a second skin and showcased her stunning legs and metallic stilettos, Victoria settled a hand on her hip and waited while his gaze completed at least a third orbit over every curve and angle.

She looked good. Damn good. And what was worse, Eamon concluded, was that she knew it. She had even taken the time to pin her hair up, with the exception of a few wisps of curls that lay teasingly against her long neck. The green in her dress made her eyes pop, which only succeeded in drawing him into what felt like a Venus fly trap. The pendulum of power had definitely swung in her direction.

"If you stare at me much longer we're going to miss our reservation," she said, smiling.

Eamon blinked, but afterward he still felt like he was

caught up in some old black magic so he tried blinking again. It failed to work then, too. *I'm definitely in trouble.*

"Is there something wrong? Are your contacts giving you trouble?"

He laughed. "No contacts. I'm just… You look stunning," he admitted. There was no way of getting around the truth. But to his surprise, she blushed, staining her long neck and cheeks a warm burgundy. "Don't tell me that no one has ever paid you a compliment before."

She cut her gaze away. "Don't be silly." She suddenly got busy looking around. "Now, what did I do with that clutch?"

He watched her as she moved around the suite, not sure what to make of her sudden shift in behavior. But before he could say anything else, she found her clutch bag.

"Here it is." She smiled, but still managed to avoid his gaze. "I'm ready if you are."

Eamon smiled and then glanced at his watch. "We still have fifteen minutes. I'm impressed."

Victoria opened the front door as she found her sass again. "Of course you are. Look who you're with." She tossed him a wink and then strolled out of the room.

Eamon laughed as he strolled out behind her. The ride down in the elevator was filled with mindless small talk and when the door open, Victoria bolted out of the small box as if he'd lit a fire under her pointy stilettos. He smiled, certain that she was playing games to make sure that she didn't fall into any traps and lose her precious hold on that tiny pendulum of power swinging between them. But if she wanted that power, he was going to make her fight for it.

His long strides had no problem catching up with her sudden power walk and by the time they were strolling out of the Bellagio's elegant lobby, he walked beside her and pressed his hand against the small of her back.

"Henry." He nodded to the head valet.

The older black gentleman turned with a smile, but when recognition settled into his brown eyes, he really let up. "Ah, Mr. King. How are you today?"

"Never better, my man." Eamon removed his hand from Victoria's back to slap palms with one of The Dollhouse's regular patrons. "You're still doing that favor for me?"

"Doin' my best, but I have to tell you—" he shook his head "—your cousin is keeping most of us on our toes around here."

"I believe you." Eamon laughed as he handed over his ticket. Two minutes later, he and Victoria slid comfortably into the leather seats of his Aston Martin and then glided out onto Las Vegas Boulevard. Though he was content to just enjoy her signature scent mingle with the new-car smell, he felt pressure to break the ice. "Do you like jazz?" he asked.

She shrugged noncommittally. "It's all right. My father enjoys it."

Wry amusement twisted his lips. "Is that supposed to be a jab at my age?"

"No. I'm just saying." She shrugged again, but her lips were definitely twitching at the corners.

"Exactly how old do you think I am?"

Victoria crossed her firm thighs. "I'm sure that I don't know."

Eamon's robust laughter filled the sports car. "Ah. I see. You're real sly when you're trying to check a brother."

"Naw. I'm not trying to check you."

"No?" He leaned over toward the rearview mirror and started to examine his head.

"What are you doing?"

"I'm looking for that checkmark that you just put on my forehead."

She laughed, but not one of those fake ones that she tossed around from time to time. This one was a real belly laugh that was as infectious as it was melodious.

"You know you did it." Eamon moved away from the mirror and reached for the radio that was already on his favorite jazz station. As luck would have it, Miles Davis and John Coltrane's "Blue in Green" floated into the car and set the right kind of mood. After a few riffs, Eamon chanced a glance over at the passenger seat and caught the tranquility on her face. Eyes closed. Lips still smiling.

"You lied," he said. "You do like jazz."

Victoria lifted a slender finger and pressed it against her lips. "Shhh. Don't tell anybody."

Eamon's gaze drifted back toward the road. "Don't worry. Your secret is safe with me."

They fell silent as Coltrane's fingers danced over the keys and Davis worked his magic on the horn. When the song finally ended, he turned into the parking lot of Bella's. It was a small, quaint Italian restaurant a little distance from the casino strip, away from the main tourist spots, but still part of the city's nightlife and a secret jewel for the locals.

"This looks interesting," Victoria said, glancing around.

Eamon chuckled as he turned off the radio. "It's a little late to be worried about whether I've kidnapped you, isn't it?"

"It's never too late to worry about that," she said.

The valet opened their doors and Eamon waited patiently with a smile as she walked around the car and joined him before entering the low-lit restaurant.

"Ah, Eamon," Benito Boi, the restaurant manager,

boasted the moment they walked into the door. "I just heard that you would be joining us tonight. *Benvenuti!*"

They shook hands but like always Benito pumped with a lot of gusto for a man nearing his seventies.

"Ah. Now, who is this bella?" Benito's attention shifted to Eamon's date.

"This is the lovely Victoria Gregory. She has taken pity on me this evening and has agreed to be my date."

Victoria hiked up on her pencil-thin brows up at him.

"Ah. It's about time," Benito said. "It's no good for a man to eat alone, but—" Benito's gaze swept over Victoria's frame "—I'm afraid that you've chosen a woman that is considerably above your station, *amico mio.* You'll have to be on your best behavior."

Victoria's full lips stretched while her eyes danced. "You heard the man, *Eamon.*"

It was the first time that she had said his name and he had to admit that he liked the way her voice hugged each vowel. There was something incredibly sexy about it.

Benito grabbed two menus and then escorted them toward the back of the restaurant.

Victoria sucked in several deep breaths as she followed Benito. It seemed to her that the restaurant grew darker the farther they walked. Where were they going to have dinner, in a crypt?

"Here we are," Benito said, opening the door. "A nice secluded spot so you and your lovely friend can get to know each other."

Victoria stepped into the small room to the beautiful table with crystal, silverware and flickering candle light. "Out of the fire and into the frying pan," she mumbled under her breath.

"What was that?" Eamon asked.

She turned toward his honest face and sly smile and knew that he had heard exactly what she had said. "Nothing."

Eamon winked and then went to pull out her chair.

Her only option was to play along. She took her seat and pretended not to notice how Eamon's hand drifted along the back of her shoulders after he'd helped push up her seat.

When Eamon settled into his own chair, Benito showcased their bottle of Barbaresco to him and then quickly and masterfully worked open the cork with a soft *pop!*

Victoria watched as Benito splashed some wine into Eamon's glass and waited while Eamon swirled the red vino around in his glass before smelling it and tasting it.

*"Benissimo."*

Benito smiled and then proceeded to fill their large wineglasses a quarter of the way. "I'll be back with your fresh bread," he announced and then rushed out of the small room.

Victoria settled back in her seat and then languidly crossed her firm thighs. "Looks like it's my turn to be impressed."

Eamon corked one of his immaculately groomed brows. "Why? Just because I own a gentlemen's club you thought that I didn't have any home training?"

She paused for a moment, but then answered honestly. "Guilty." She almost sighed when his rich laughter rumbled around her.

"You know, I'm going to change my earlier assessment. You actually have many ways of keeping a brother in check. Slick, sly and direct. You're a regular heavyweight champion."

"In today's world, a woman has to be on her toes when

dealing with the opposite sex. But even a seasoned player gets knocked on their ass every once in a while."

"Ahh." He bobbed his head. "Mr. Henderson."

Victoria nodded while she absently crossed her arms and told herself to prepare for anything.

"You know, I'm truly sorry for what happened," he said with a genuine note of sincerity. "But you don't truly believe that I or even my club really had anything to do with Mr. Henderson's sudden case of cold feet, do you? Not to be tactless, but…these sorts of things do happen all the time."

She let that ridiculous statement hang in the air until he started to squirm. "Happens all the time?"

His expression changed as if he'd finally heard what the hell he'd just said.

"Marcus didn't get cold feet. He got married. Remember?"

He bobbed his head. "Yes. Sorry. Let me try again."

She held up her hands. "No. Please don't. I haven't even eaten anything and I'm already ready to throw up."

Eamon drew in a deep breath and eased back against his chair as if he'd realized that he'd just blown their tenuous truce to high hell and back.

Benito returned with a small, hot loaf of bread and a larger saucer of olive oil. Neither Victoria nor Eamon spoke while the older gentleman recited the night's specials as he ground fresh pepper into the olive oil.

Eamon asked, "Could you give us a few—?"

"I'm ready to order," Victoria announced.

"Ahh." Benito lit up. "Not only are you beautiful but you're a woman who is quick and decisive." He winked and then elbowed Eamon. "You might want to hang on to this one. I have a *good* feeling about her. And people around here will tell you that I'm never wrong about these things."

"Are these the same people who are on payroll?"

"One and the same," Benito boasted.

"Then I'll just pass."

"What can I get for you, *signorina?*"

"I'd like to start off with the *frietella di granchio*—I'm crazy about crab cakes."

"Ah. It's a weakness for myself, as well."

"For the main dish, I'd like the *branzino con finocchi e rughetta*. Please make sure that the sea bass is cooked all the way through. And for the *dolci*—"

"You already know what you want for dessert?" Eamon asked.

Victoria's laser green eyes shot up over the menu. "Is that a problem?"

"No. No. Not at all." He smiled awkwardly over at Benito. "Quick and decisive."

Benito gave his thumbs-up and gave her another wink.

"I'll have the tiramisu."

"Excellent." Benito took her menu and then turned toward Eamon. "And for you?"

Eamon just handed over his menu. "I'll just have what she's having."

"Excellent. Excellent. I'll leave you two alone." There was more winking and thumbs jutting up before the exuberant manager escaped their small room.

"Well. You've gone from not being hungry to being able to eat enough for a small minor-league team in less than an hour."

She smiled before she had a chance to stop herself. "Yes. I'm not what men would call a salad date. I hope that's not a problem for you."

"Why would it be a problem? I tend to have a healthy appetite myself." He locked on to her stare while he sipped his wine.

Victoria tried to pass off the weird fluttering in her stomach as mere hunger pangs, but it wasn't working. The way the flickering candlelight danced in Eamon's eyes put her on edge. How on earth was she going to be able to deflect a whole evening of sexual innuendos from the man when she was fighting not to sweep everything off their table and beg him to do her right then and there?

"I have a question," he announced. "It's something that has been bothering me since the moment we met."

She reached for her own glass. "Shoot."

"I remember Marcus Henderson rather well. Nice guy… but, uh…how in the world did you two hook up?"

Victoria blinked.

Eamon chuckled and shook his head while he set his glass back down. "No disrespect, but you two are like night and day. The heiress and the accountant doesn't quite jibe with me. What gives?"

"I don't think that I understand what you mean."

He locked down her gaze. "I think you do."

It was her turn to squirm in her seat. "I didn't realize that I needed to run my preference in men by the Eamon King committee."

"You're ducking the question."

"Just because you ask a question doesn't mean that you're entitled to an answer."

"Humor me and answer it anyway."

"No."

"Why not?"

"Because…" She struggled for answer. "I don't want to."

"Fine." Eamon shrugged. "Then you force me to give my own assessment. Care to hear it?"

"Do I have a choice?"

He cut his gaze away as if he was seriously considering the question but then delivered a quick "No."

She did, however, get a quick reprieve because Benito and a waitress delivered their appetizers, but they blew in and out like a Midwest tornado.

"Now, where was I?" Eamon asked. "Ah, yes. You purposely selected a man that you thought was a safe choice—nonthreatening."

"Don't be ridiculous." She unfolded her silverware and placed her linen napkin into her lap.

"Someone who didn't put on airs or was in the market for a trophy wife," he continued. "Probably even someone who wouldn't mind signing an iron-clad prenuptial agreement, either."

Victoria sliced into the tender crab cakes too hard and then jumped when the fork clanged against the plate.

"How am I doing?" he asked.

She refused to answer him.

"I'm not going to pretend that I grew up under similar conditions. My brothers and I grew up with more love than money. But my experience the last few years has introduced me to this phenomenon where it's difficult to judge whether people are around you for who you are and not what you have or possibly what you can give them." He paused for a moment. "But from what little I do know about you, I think you're selling yourself short."

During the next pause, her eyes slowly climbed from the gorgeous crab cakes to his maple-brown gaze.

"You're beautiful, smart and there's feistiness in you that is an incredible turn-on."

Victoria watched as his gaze went from hot to

smoldering within a snap of her fingers. She didn't know how long they sat there staring at each other, but it was long enough for their main course to arrive even though they had yet to taste the appetizer. Benito paused just long enough to refill their wineglasses and then directed the waiter to quickly set the food on the table. In another blink they were gone.

"All right," she said after finding her voice again. "Since you seem to know so much, what kind of man do you think I should go after?"

Eamon's lips sloped crookedly and in that instant, she decided that was her favorite smile by him. "That's a softball question."

"Then let me hear your easy answer." That damn candlelight continued to dance in his eyes, hypnotizing her effortlessly.

He reached across the table and captured her free hand within his. The electric connection jolted her. The small hairs on her arm and the back of her neck stood at attention.

Eamon's voice dropped to an all-time low register, "You need *and* deserve a man who is bold, adventurous and could take on that hot temper of yours with the same passion that you dish out."

There was no doubt in Victoria's mind that her Agent Provocateur panties were now soaked and the ache pulsing between her legs matched the hammering that was going on inside her chest.

*Braided hands. Sweaty bodies. Silk sheets.*

At the moment, she would've gladly substituted the silk sheets for an oak table.

Victoria swallowed and licked her lips. She felt a surge of confidence when she saw how his eyes tracked her pink tongue as it glided across her glossy lips. "That's an interesting list of qualities. You wouldn't happen to know anyone like that, would you?"

His slick smile returned as he nodded. "You're looking at him."

## Chapter 9

The small private room in the back of Bella's instantly went from a sauna to a raging inferno when Eamon stood up from his chair and swept his muscled arm across the tabletop and sent their dinner crashing to the floor.

Victoria was convinced that her heart had cracked through her rib cage as she stared up at Eamon like he was Mount Everest. Fleetingly, she thought that if she had any objections to what was about to go down she needed to speak now or forever hold her peace. She opened her mouth, but as luck would have it her vocal cords chose that moment to go out of service. The next thing she knew, Eamon's large and powerful hands were wrapped around her waist and she was airborne. It was a short flight before she landed onto their empty tabletop.

She might've had some concerns about the possibility of someone walking in on them, but the warning in her head was silenced the moment Eamon's hungry mouth found hers. She moaned like an innocent fawn, but she soon found herself too drunk from the heady, rich taste of Eamon's kiss. His silken tongue glided against her own and then started mating in a ritual that was as old as time.

At that moment, there was no real thinking on either of their parts. It was all instinct and feeling. She was vaguely aware of her dress sliding up and her silk-lace panties sliding down her legs, just as he hardly paid attention to the tiny scratches her long fingernails made as she tore at his shirt. Even above the music she could hear buttons ping and zing around the room like .38 caliber bullets.

With an extra yank, Victoria's dress flew over her head and she was left sprawled across the table with only her pink-lace bra with a black ribbon around the band and sweetheart-shaped cups and a pair of metallic stilettos. Eamon raised his head long enough to take in her erotic pose, while she feasted her eyes on his muscular frame and smooth chocolate skin. Every inch of him looked so rich that she was sure that she would get a cavity if she risked biting him.

When their eyes locked together again, their mouths followed suit shortly thereafter. It might've been a mistake for her to close her eyes, because the colors inside her head spun like a kaleidoscope on crack.

Dean Martin crooned "when the moon hits your eye" as Eamon's fingers skimmed her body, stopping briefly to circle her belly button. Even that hardened her nipples. Through the delicate lace, they looked like toy marbles, and soon started to ache the same way the rose-colored pearl did between her legs.

She needed some relief…and soon.

As if their mouths were connected through tantric sexual telepathy, Eamon's fingers were on the move again. Skating casually along the bottom of her flat belly and then dipping toward the soft fur between her legs. She didn't mean to, but she started to hold her breath the closer he came to dipping his fingers into her warm honey pot. Her lungs were probably grateful that she didn't have that long to wait.

The moment he pried her open and slid his middle finger inside of her, she pulled her lips away from his mouth and sighed like a deflating tire. He made small, teasing circles while he rained featherlight kisses down her long neck. It was enough to make her shoot off her fist orgasm in less than ninety seconds.

Eamon chuckled while her body quaked. "Something tells me that you've been waiting for that one."

Victoria wished that she had something smart to say to that, but she was losing brain cells at an alarming rate. And when Eamon started frenching her left nipple through the thin nylon of her bra while kneeing her to spread her legs wider, she was ready to start speaking in tongues.

Eamon was doing his own dance with insanity. At that moment, he would've sworn in a court of law that Victoria's heavenly breasts were either sprinkled with fairy dust or brown sugar. And since diabetes ran in his family, he needed to take it easy. If that wasn't enough, there was something dangerously wicked about the feel of the honey coating his hand.

She was slick, warm and soft.

He was hard, smooth and ready.

He fought a war as to whether to take his time or ravish her like a starving man before an all-you-can-eat buffet. His body and mind were split right down the middle. One thing was for sure, his new addiction wasn't waiting for him to make up his mind. She crested her second orgasm the moment he slid in another finger.

Just watching her expressions alone was enough to get

any red-blooded man off. She didn't hold back with her sighing, moaning and groaning. Her face was a colorful canvas of orgasmic emotions and it was simply breathtaking. Gone was the carefully constructed wall around her heart and the well-honed sarcasm and cynicism. She was simply and completely caught up in the moment.

That was what made Eamon decide to take his time.

He abandoned her sweet breast making a mental note to return to it later. This time when he traveled down her body, he used his tongue to roll straight down the center of her torso. No GPS was needed. He was locked on to his coordinates while easing her body down toward the edge of the table.

Victoria's head thrashed as her body started building toward her third orgasm. It was already a record-breaking night as far as she was concerned. But when she felt the first flick of Eamon's tongue hit the center of her Tootsie Pop, she bolted upright on the table.

But that didn't stop Eamon's feasting. If anything, he was just getting started. Once again, she opened her eyes, but became fixated at the sight of this black King buried between her thighs. Their gazes remained locked as his tongue twirled around her honey-coated clit. The faster it went, the lower her jaw sagged. Between his tongue and the steady pumping of his other hand, she was riding another orgasmic wave. This one was by far the strongest of the three and Victoria instinctively tried to back away from the explosion that was just seconds from happening.

Eamon was having none of it. If she moved an inch, he moved two and made sure that he held on to her creamy, firm thighs for dear life in case she tried to buck him off.

As it turned out that was exactly her next game plan. The power of her third orgasm had her babbling a one-on-

one conversation with the Almighty while she collapsed against the table, bucking and thrashing like a cowgirl at the rodeo.

"Mmm. That was good, baby. Did you enjoy that?" He peppered kisses around her inner thigh while reaching into his back pocket for a condom. "Hmm?" More kisses were planted around her lower stomach, quivering belly button and then around the valley between her breasts.

Only when he was close enough to her lips could he make out her faint whisper of "Yes."

He smiled at the sight of her messy hair and flushed face. This was definitely a vision he wouldn't mind spending his life gazing into. As quickly as the thought floated across his head, it disappeared like a wisp of smoke and he turned his attention again toward another slow suckling of her sweet breasts. This time, he peeled down the delicate bra and went for those beautiful brown nipples. Meanwhile, Eamon's steel-hard erection saw the corner of her right leg as a quiet request.

After thirty seconds, with no resistance or protest, he shifted his head to give the other puckered nipple some quality time while inching his hips and hard-on closer to her soft down.

She moaned. It was a clear sign that she was regaining her strength. Hard, ready and pressed against the apex of her sex, he found some reasonable amount of restraint to say, "If you want me to stop, say so now."

When she didn't immediately answer, there was a skip in his heartbeat while his brain tried to scramble for a plan B. Just when the warning bells were going off and his hips were about to retreat, Victoria reached over and cupped his face in her hands. Their eyes locked for another simmering connection while she thrust her butt downward and joined their bodies together. Once she did so, he was the one to gasp at the sudden snug fit. However, she had only managed to get him halfway in. To complete their joining, he lifted her up effortlessly and then allowed gravity and her body's sweet juices to ease him all the way home.

He groaned.

She moaned.

Now that they were joined, he didn't press her back down onto the table or even jack her up against a wall. Instead he sat down in a chair with her on his lap. The moment his bottom hit the chair, Victoria took the reins and started working her hips in a figure eight and even tossed in the occasional bounce.

Eamon continued groaning while burying his head in between her breasts. When it really got good to him, he locked his hands onto her hips while she rode him through the land of ecstasy where there were jasmine and white roses everywhere. He played every single mental game he could think of to extend the dizzy feelings that were coursing through him, but he was one trick short and the next thing he knew he was coming like a runaway freight train. It was just a stroke of luck that she came with him.

"Volare" floated like a lyrical dream from the overhead speakers while the newly minted lovers continued to cling to each other waiting to catch their breath. By the end of the three-minute song, both of them slowly started to take in their surroundings.

"Oh my God," Victoria said, pressing a hand against her kiss-swollen mouth. "Look at this place."

"Yep. It's a mess," he said rather amused.

At the sight of that cocky smile, she tried to scramble off his lap.

"Wait. Where are you going?"

"To get dressed. It's just lucky that Benito hasn't come back here and caught us…"

Eamon arched a brow while he kept her firmly locked on his lap. "Hasn't caught us what?"

She looked at him as if he'd just sprouted a second head. "Stop playing and let me up. This whole thing is embarrassing enough."

"Oh. You're embarrassed now?" he said, his amusement deepening. "You didn't look too embarrassed a few minutes ago. In fact…you looked rather breathtaking."

She stopped squirming on his lap. And he was sorry that she did. His dick was getting harder by the second.

"There you go blushing at compliments again. I swear I don't know what to make of you." He started nibbling on her neck and lower earlobe. At the sound of her sweet moan, his erection was back in full force. The speed with which he was able to reboot was impressive. Then again, she turned him on in a way that no other woman ever had. He was intrigued enough to want to keep her around a little while longer to get to the bottom of what he was feeling.

There wasn't anything wrong with that—was there?

She started to get up again, at least that's what he initially thought until he released her waist only to have her slide back down his ever hardening cock. When she tightened her vaginal muscles and rolled her hips, he knew that she wanted to play again.

"I guess that you're not so concerned about Benito anymore?" He lifted his hips as well and started meeting her soft thrusts with one of his own.

"We might have a few extra minutes," she reasoned between short breaths.

"We have longer than that, if he wants to keep his job," Eamon chuckled before zeroing in on her delectable right nipple.

Victoria stopped and grabbed the sides of his face. "What are you talking about? This is his restaurant, isn't it?"

Eamon frowned. "I don't remember selling it to him."

She released his face and then eased back in his lap. Once again, his arms locked around her waist to make sure that she didn't try to escape. "This is your restaurant?"

He bobbed his head and smiled. "It looks like I'm going to have to get your opinion on those crab cakes another time."

"So no one is going to come back here?"

"Not unless they want to reserve a spot on the unemployment line."

Victoria slapped him on the chest.

"Oww!" He blinked. "What was that for?"

"You could've told me," she snapped, but couldn't stop her lips from creeping even higher.

"Sorry, but, uh…" He tweaked her nipples. "I was a little busy."

"Were you now?" Her smile grew downright playful while her hips started making those wonderful figure eights. "Well, you haven't seen nothin' yet."

"Oh?"

She nodded. "Fasten your seatbelt, it going to be a bumpy ride."

## *Chapter 10*

Victoria hadn't even opened her eyes when a smile eased across her lips. Next, she stretched her long body across the bed as far as she could in the tangled sheets. Muscles and synapses hummed harmoniously like she'd just finished getting a long-overdue tune-up. She moaned and then sighed aloud at the feel of the morning sunlight caressing her skin. Despite her internal clock going off like crazy because it had to be well past her usual wake-up time, she snapped back into the form of a C to reclaim her position inside a warm and comfortable nook and hit her mental snooze button.

For a fleeting moment, she entertained the wild notion of just spending the day in bed. After the whirlwind of the past week, surely she was entitled to such an indulgence. The longer the idea lingered in her head, the more she warmed to it. She could order room service, fluff up the pillows and just get lost in an afternoon of soap-opera drama. It had been years since she'd sneaked a peek at what was happening in Pine Valley or Port Charles. Instead of Ferris Bueller, it would be Victoria Gregory's day off.

She chuckled against a muscled arm. Then another one slowly eased across her waist and enveloped her completely. The body heat solicited a moan. And when a pair of lips pressed against the back of her neck, she moaned even deeper.

"You want to share what's so funny?" a silky baritone asked.

Maybe it was because she liked the way the warm wall of muscles rumbled when he talked or how she savored the richness of his voice that made her smile inch wider.

"Hmm?" he persisted while his lips started traveling south.

"I was just thinking how nice it would be to spend the entire day in bed."

"Ahhh. That would be nice."

The arm around her hip moved slightly and the next thing she felt were these strong yet soft fingers gliding up her leg. "Mmm. That feels nice."

"Yeah? You like that?"

Why wouldn't she? The mattress shifted behind her while her legs were being nudged open. She was only too happy to oblige. The reward was those same fingers dipping inside her sleek rosy walls. Victoria's moans were now on a continuous loop.

Forget daytime talk shows or soap-opera dramas, *this* was the way she wanted to spend the day in bed. The soft pads of Eamon's fingers rotated slowly around the base of her clit. In no time at all, her body started churning.

"You're nice and wet this morning."

She couldn't tell if he was just stating a fact or giving her a compliment. Truth be told, she really didn't care.

All that mattered at that moment was making sure that he didn't stop doing what he was doing. To ensure that, she opened her legs a few more inches to give his magical hands full access.

"Is this what you really wanted to stay in bed for?"

Victoria sighed and nodded, but it became clear that wasn't enough for her morning lover.

"I didn't hear you, baby. Was that a yes?"

She wasn't prepared or able to form actual words, so all she managed to get out was "Uh-huh."

There was more shifting and before she knew it, she had rolled all the way onto her back and her legs were damn near pointing east and west. She still was unable to open her eyes. She could, however, feel Eamon as he positioned himself between her legs. Next, her soaking-wet lips were being pried open. For a second there was the cool kiss of the room's air-conditioning against her throbbing clit. But then it was quickly replaced by Eamon's warm breath as his mouth opened. By the time his talented tongue glided into her, she was already plunging down the rabbit hole to Wonderland.

Victoria's back arched so high it could've doubled as half of McDonald's golden arches. However, Eamon didn't give her another Midwest tornado performance. This time, he was giving her an easy Sunday-morning special. In a way, it was even more torturous and agonizing. She wanted to come so badly that she kept impatiently thrusting her hips and grinding. It didn't matter what she did, he wasn't going to change speeds.

Until recently—like in the past twelve hours—Victoria hadn't been a proponent of oral sex. The handful of lovers she'd had had never really shown much interest. And the two times her lovers did perform oral sex, she now realized that they didn't know what the hell they were doing. Hell, if she had known that it could be this damn good, she would've formed a fan club and served as president. She never knew that anything could be this intense and powerful.

Sometime later, after thrashing like a woman possessed, she came to rest on the bed with her head and shoulders hanging over the side. Despite the blood rushing to her head, she heard the unmistakable sound of a condom packet being ripped open. She smiled because she knew what was coming next—literally. Eamon's powerful hands gripped her by her waist and then dragged her body back onto the bed.

Victoria's eyes fluttered open at least a half an inch as she caught a glimpse of Eamon's lustful expression through her long fan eyelashes. She was struck by the fact that he looked like a chiseled god made of ebony porcelain or an African gladiator—proud and strong. There was no getting around that he was a visual orgasm, from his sinewy arms to his mountainous chest. A smile quirked at the corners of her lips a second before his hips surged forward and impaled her with ten inches of black steel.

The air escaped her lungs while sanity became a distant memory. When she turned her head around to get a glimpse of him behind her, she saw from the expression on Eamon's face that he was just as lost in ecstasy as she was. That knowledge gave her a sense of having a little more power, so she tried to exercise it by wrapping her long legs around his trim waist and rolling her hips forward.

He shuddered and then that sly smile that she loved so much splashed across his face. His maple-brown gaze was now the color of mahogany, a sign that their morning sex-a-thon was just getting started. What was it about him that triggered this response in her? How was it that she felt comfortable doing things with him that she'd never done before?

She'd never felt so uninhibited. She'd always thought being sexually modest was a part of her personality. Most of what she had done in the last twenty-four hours defied reason. It was as if she had become someone else…and she loved it.

Eamon planted his arms on either side of her head. She reached out and held on to them like they were black pillars of strength. Now anchored, she increased the speed at which she dipped and rolled her hips. It didn't matter that she could feel him thrusting in the center of her chest, she wanted him deeper. She would rather that than the puffs of air that she managed to get into her lungs between strokes.

When that glorious pressure started to build inside her, she lost sight of her beautiful King because she could no longer stop her eyes from rolling around in her head. The steady sounds of their bodies slapping together was like the bass to their duet of moans and groans. As she crested with yet another earth-shattering orgasm, she felt like the queen of the universe zooming from the sun to Neptune and then back again.

Her finale was a scream so loud and powerful it wouldn't surprise either of them if the entire floor heard her. Afterward, for what seemed like the longest minute, she just tried her damnedest to lie still. But her body's aftershocks made that impossible.

Eamon was smiling long before he opened his eyes again. Not only that, he was completely drained. And that was saying something coming from a man who competed annually in the New York City Marathon. He was amazed and yet frightened of this woman tucked under him. He enjoyed women—almost to a fault. But what he was feeling now was eroding the line of casual sex.

*Steer clear of this kind of danger,* a little voice in his head kept repeating.

Eamon cringed at Q's logic floating around in his head. Still there was something to his cousin's warning. He pulled in a deep breath, hoping that it would help clear his mind.

It didn't.

His ego took the floor in his imaginary courtroom and tried to convince him that he was just opening up a whole new world for his spoiled heiress, but his brain immediately argued not to buy in to last night's and this morning's dramatic performance. Only an over-emotive community theater actress could perform with that much passion and abandonment. *Don't get it twisted,* Eamon admonished. He knew he had skills, but could a woman really have as many orgasms as he'd counted last night?

Eamon rolled over onto his side, pulling Victoria's body against his for the requisite spooning. She was like a new toy that he didn't want to share or lose, at least not until he'd figured out how all the parts worked and what made her so special. That was what she was, his heart stated. *Special.* Hadn't he known it the moment he'd laid eyes on her?

He watched her as she dozed softly during her after-sex coma as more questions bubbled to the surface. The questions didn't scare him. It was the answers that might have him lying in a pool of his own sweat in the middle of the night. She looked nothing like the fire-breathing Amazon who'd stormed into his club less than twenty-four hours ago. The lightly applied makeup that she had on during dinner last night had long worn off and her hair looked as if it had been windblown during a category-five hurricane. Yet she was still stunningly beautiful.

The longer he stared at her the faster his heart raced, but he couldn't pull his eyes away. As the minutes ticked by, Eamon started etching every line and angle of her face into memory. Of course, it would be nice if he could wake up every morning to her face.

He frowned. Wasn't that the second time that rogue thought had drifted across his mind? Spooked, he shook his head and sat up. *No. This was just sex. Nothing more and nothing less.* He eased off the bed and then as quietly as he could, he headed to the bathroom and shut the door.

In the shower, the spray of hot water washed off some of the hazy feeling of sexual afterglow. Not all of it, but enough to get him to start feeling like his old self again. Sure, Victoria was a sexy-as-hell heiress with a major chip on her shoulder. Last night and this morning, she proved to be a woman of boundless passion with possibly a freaky streak. It was a heady combination for sure. But it didn't mean that he should be entertaining any notions of turning his life upside down to become a one-woman man. Those types of dreams were long gone.

"Long gone," he repeated as his amen chorus. By the time he stepped out of the shower, he had reclaimed his sanity. "It was just sex," he told his reflection as he wrapped a towel around his hips. When he marched back to the master bedroom, he was surprised to see Victoria sitting on the edge of the bed with the top sheet bunched around her.

"Good morning, Princess. Sleep well?" He traced an appreciative eye over her just-sexed look and smiled. His cock also started to stretch back down his leg. *Damn. I hope I have at least one more condom in my wallet.*

Victoria's gaze swung sharply toward him.

He found himself grateful that she didn't possess the ability to decapitate him with her mind. It looked like the other Victoria had returned. "Is there a problem?" he asked with his brows creasing the center of his forehead.

"We need to talk," she stated in a flat monotone.

"That doesn't sound too good when you say it like that."

Her glare softened a bit, but her jaw remained firm. "Look. It's probably best that I just come right on out and say this."

Eamon folded his arms. "All right. Shoot."

Victoria took a deep breath. "What happened last night was…just sex."

His eyebrows wrinkled comically in the center of his forehead at the sound of his own words being tossed back at him. To be honest, he didn't like it. "Is that right?"

"Yes. It didn't mean anything…and it doesn't change anything." Her gaze locked on to his. "Is that clear?"

*Damn. Was that how he sounded when he gave this speech?* "Actually, I'm sure that it is clear." He leaned back against the wall and studied her face. "Are you saying that you just used me for sex?" He almost smiled when a familiar shade of burgundy stained her face and neck.

"Don't be glib."

He unfolded his arms and pressed a hand against his chest. "Me? Glib? Never. I'm just curious. Do you make it a habit of doing this kind of thing?"

She jumped to her feet and just barely kept the sheet from falling to the floor. "Of course not! Don't be ridiculous! I've never done anything close to what happened last night."

Eamon cocked his head. "Come now. You're hardly a virgin."

Her mouth opened wide in shock. "You know what I

mean. I don't…" She lowered her voice. "You know—sleep around—or have one-night stands."

Chuckling, he folded his arms again. "It seems you and your ex-fiancé come to Las Vegas and do a lot of things that you two don't normally do."

Victoria's eyes bulged to the size of golf balls. "How *dare* you!"

"Me? I didn't wake up this morning and decide to become a raging…*witch* this morning."

There was one more gasp before she turned, picked up the clock radio and hurled it at him.

Eamon dodged out of the way. The clock smashed against the wall and left a large dent in the plaster.

"You take that back!"

He probably would have, if he could get himself to stop laughing.

"Take it back!" She turned around again, this time she grabbed the lamp and snatched the cord out of the wall.

"All right. All right!" He held up his hands but was still laughing. "I take it back. Don't hurt me."

With eyes flashing like emeralds and her chest heaving with anger, she was once again that powerful Amazon that had stolen his breath away the moment he'd laid eyes on her. He was fascinated by both sides of this complex creature. "Has anyone ever told you that you have one hell of a temper?"

The question worked as a mirror and she slowly lowered the lamp back onto the nightstand. "I'm sorry," she said meekly. "I…overreacted."

He nodded as a way of accepting the apology and took a tentative step toward her. "I apologize, too. I shouldn't have brought *him* up. That was tactless."

"Yes. It was," she agreed.

He grinned. "Does that mean that you accept my apology, too?"

She shrugged as her gaze lowered to the carpet.

"Wow. You're a real tough one, aren't you? You don't forgive easily."

"Are you going to whip out a psychology degree, too?"

"I have one framed at the house, if you'd like to see it. It was a waste of fifty grand but it looks good on my bookcase."

A smile cracked her face again. "Please tell me that you're joking."

He took another step. "I have a business degree, too. That one came in handy." When Victoria laughed, he used the moment to wrap his arms around her and pulled her into his embrace. Now that he had her, he was sure that he was halfway home. "Look. I don't want to fight. I thought that we were having a good time together."

She shrugged as her gaze remained lowered. "It was… nice."

Another laugh rumbled from his chest. "Just nice?"

"It was…" She fumbled around in her mind looking for another safe adjective. "Pleasurable."

"Pleasurable? I see." Eamon pulled his ego out of the trash bin and started taping it back together when it hit him what was really going on. "How would you rate me on a scale of one to ten? What would you give me?"

Her eyes were whirling around so fast that it was amazing that she managed to keep them in her head.

"I don't know. Maybe a…seven?"

It was a bald-faced lie and what made it so bad was that he knew it and she knew that he knew it. Instead of calling her on it, he pulled her even closer and announced, "Then we need to get back in bed if there's that much room for improvement." He moved his puckered lips in for a kiss, but she pressed her hands against his chest and pulled back.

"I don't think that's a good idea."

Eamon finally reached for her chin and gently forced her to look up at him. "Look. I can't have you going around telling people that I'm just a seven. Do you know what something like that will do to my reputation?" He gave her his sly smile. "I think that I deserve the opportunity to improve my score." He started peeling the sheet from her body. "It's only fair."

The sheet fell to the floor and Eamon's erection tented his towel. "Damn. Let's do this."

"Wait. Wait."

She pressed her hand against his chest again and it took every ounce of strength she had to pull back. "Problem?"

"I just want to freshen up first," she said, smiling. "It's not fair that you're the only one that smells like Ivory soap."

"Doesn't matter. I kind of like you dirty." He stole a quick kiss.

"No. Please. Just give me, like…ten minutes."

Despite the fact that his need to have her was so strong that he was just seconds from dry-humping her leg, he smiled and released her. "Ten minutes. If you're not out by the eleventh minute, I'm coming in there to drag you out—soaking wet if I have to."

"Deal." As she turned to head for the bathroom, he playfully popped her on her lush ass.

Giggling, she hurried out of his reach and slammed the bathroom door behind her.

Once she was gone, another smile exploded across Eamon's face as he mimicked her. "'It was just sex.'"

Never mind that those had been his words, too. He was already revising the sentence to add adjectives. "It was *good* sex. Better than good—it was *great* sex," he muttered to himself. "Spectacular…explosive."

*Face it. You just don't like the fact that she beat you at your own game.* Eamon rolled his eyes at his smart-ass ego. "That wasn't it at all," he argued back. "I just don't know where the hell she's coming up with that seven BS." Hell, just because he didn't like a whole lot of strings attached didn't mean that she couldn't give an experience like last night its proper rating. Frankly, he was willing to give it double digits. "And she will, too, when I'm finally finished with her."

He sat down on the bed and thought about striking a pose. *Too cheesy.* He sat up and looked around to see what he could do differently so that she'd be ready to jump his bones when she came out of the bathroom. While he was thinking, his stomach started to growl.

Damn. They never did get around to eating any real food last night. Eamon grabbed the phone and called room service. Maybe a hearty breakfast with a few roses was just the thing he needed to set the mood. When room service picked up, he ordered enough food to feed a football team.

He was so ready for the next round that he felt like a six-year-old trying to go to sleep on Christmas Eve. While he had a few more minutes on his hands, he started thinking about some of the questions that had popped into his head while he watched her sleep. Like how long was she planning to stay in town? Did she have any plans tonight? Of course, that meant leaving Quentin in charge of the club for another night. That might be risky. Right now he was just hoping the place hadn't been burned to the ground.

But if he could wrangle another night with Victoria

tonight, maybe he could introduce her to a few more things—nothing too out there. Maybe some warm body oil or silk scarves. That imagery pumped a little more blood to his erection. If he had been a wolf, he would be howling right now.

*Knock. Knock. Knock.*

"Wow. That was fast." He stood up from the bed and went to answer the door. "You guys really believe in fast service," he said as he opened the door. However, there wasn't a waiter standing on the other side. His memory kicked in and he recognized the face that had walked in on him and Victoria in his office yesterday, only there were two of them. "Oh. Hello, ladies," he greeted.

The women's mouths sagged open simultaneously, but then they took another glance at the number on the door to the suite.

"Is…Victoria here?" one of the twins asked.

"Actually, she's in the shower."

That answer made the twins' eyes triple in size, and was followed by a slow eyeroll down his body.

Belatedly, he remembered his erection and dropped his hands to cover himself. "Ah. Sorry about that."

From his left, he just barely made out this blur of color, next thing he knew it was rushing headlong toward them like a Tasmanian devil. The door was slammed in the twins' faces, and Victoria was plastered against the back of the door. Once again, her eyes were angry and her chest was heaving like crazy.

"What the hell do you think you're doing?"

"Uh…answering the door?" He half expected a buzzer to go off, alerting him that he'd given the wrong answer.

"Why in the hell would you do that? This isn't *your* room. It's not up to you to put all my business out on Front Street. Did it occur to you that maybe I don't want or need someone to see you in here dressed like that? They might get the wrong impression."

Both brows sprung to the center of his forehead. "And what *wrong* impression would that be? That we spent the entire night playing strip poker?" He settled his hands on his hips, exposing his erection again.

"Oh, God." Victoria slapped a hand against her forehead. "Look at you. Does that damn thing ever go down?"

"Keep talking and we'll see."

It was her turn to jab her hands against her hips. "I'm serious."

"I don't know what you are. I can't tell if I'm in the middle of a real argument or a slapstick comedy."

Victoria bolted away from the door, moaning continuously, "Oh, God." Then suddenly, "You've got to get out of here."

"What?"

She stomped over to him and grabbed him by the arm. "You heard me. I want you out."

"You've got to be kidding me. I just thought that it was room service," he protested as she pushed and shoved him forward.

"I don't care. Out!" She opened the door.

"But I thought that we were—"

"No! Out! It's over!"

Before he could seriously plant his feet still, Victoria rammed everything she had in her body against his back and propelled him across the threshold.

Eamon was shocked to find himself standing in the hallway, he quickly turned back toward the door, only to have it slam in his face. *What in the hell just happened?* He saw something move off to his right and he turned his head to see the twins still standing there with their eyes and mouths in the same position as when the door had been slammed in their faces.

Ignoring the fact that he was half-naked, he jutted a thumb toward the door. "Is she usually this grumpy in the mornings?"

*Who's Afraid of Victoria Gregory?*

## Chapter 11

Quentin sighed as he unbuttoned his jacket and made himself more comfortable. "My man should've counted his lucky stars right then and there and hit the road. If I could see that she was trouble, then any player worth his salt should've seen it, too."

"You didn't like Ms. Gregory?" Dr. Turner asked.

He bobbed his shoulders. "I liked her all right. She's definitely a beautiful woman. No doubt. But she was the type of woman who played for keeps, whether she knew it or not. She didn't strike me as someone you could just bed and walk away from. She's the type that puts invisible hooks in you while she's scratching your back."

Dr. Turner snickered.

Quentin glanced over his right shoulder and smiled. "Know a lot about that, do you?"

"We're not talking about me, Mr. Hinton."

"I thought that we already established that you were going to call me Quentin?"

A light twinkled in the doctor's eyes. "All right. *Quentin.* So what was it about this Victoria that you found so threatening?"

Frowning, Q shifted in the chaise. "I don't think that threatening is the right word."

"No?" She sounded surprised. "Victoria didn't *threaten* your newly formed boys' club?"

*Silence.*

"That is why you started hanging around your cousins, isn't it? To be around like-minded men—men who'd taken a vow of eternal bachelorhood, too?"

*Silence.*

Across the room, the image of Alyssa with her head angled to the side appeared. "Aren't you going to answer her?" the imaginary Alyssa asked.

Quentin clenched his jaw and rolled his eyes. *Why am I putting myself through this?* "Yeah…maybe," he finally answered. "I guess I can admit that. Two weeks after their explosive introduction, I thought maybe I'd been wrong. Eamon threw himself into work and Victoria went back to New York…"

# Chapter 12

*Two weeks later...*

Life seemed like it was getting back to normal. For the first time since her disastrous wedding, there wasn't a peep on Page Six of the *New York Post* about the jilted billionaire bride or her runaway groom. Surprised, relieved and even a little suspicious about the welcome change of events, Victoria paged through the newspaper to double check her good fortune.

In the days since she'd returned from Las Vegas, she spent little or no time thinking about her ex-fiancé and just about all of her waking hours wondering what and even who Eamon was doing. C'mon. Here was a man who owned a string of strip clubs, after all. Clearly anyone who was in Vegas was bound to lose their appreciation for clothing as well as their common sense. That was the latest excuse she told herself to explain her behavior in Sin City.

Hours after she had landed in New York with her twin cousins in tow grinning like Cheshire cats, she was actually starting to think that there was something seriously wrong with her. But after researching her symptoms on the web and practically every women's magazine she could find, she concluded that her body was just suffering from sexual withdrawal. It was silly, she knew, but she found several articles to support her theory. Now after two weeks of daydreaming and night-dreaming about the things Eamon had done to her body, she was either going to have to enroll in masturbation rehab or some frequent-flyer program so that she could get a weekly or monthly fix in Las Vegas. And that largely depended on whether Eamon wanted anything to do with her again, given how she'd treated him the last time.

There was a third option, Victoria decided. She could try to exercise Eamon out of her system. This was also the most logical solution. So she signed up for a five-thirty a.m. boot camp–like training session that she'd taken before and worked out with such a vengeance that it even stunned her trainer. After kick squats, front and reverse lunges and side-plank hip lifts, she ended each class looking like a sweaty mess.

A few of the regulars gave her odd looks, surprised at how much her endurance had increased.

"I like that hustle," her trainer praised as she headed toward the showers.

Victoria smiled. But the truth was, she still had enough energy to do another four-mile run. Maybe her plan to exercise Eamon out of her system wasn't working. On Friday of the second post-Vegas week, she caught sight of a group of women headed toward the workout rooms. It was probably their clothes that caught her attention. They seemed a little more flirty-slash-risqué than the usual gray-sweats types that hung around this particular gym.

It was her curiosity that made her backtrack and then follow the women to their class. To her surprise the workout room was equipped with a dozen silver poles. In front of the class was this cute, perky Dominican woman with a head full of micro-braids and a booty so thick she could put Nicki Minaj to shame.

"Ah. We have a new member with us today." The woman beamed and then rushed over to Victoria.

"Oh, no," Victoria said, shaking her head. "I just want to watch, to check it out. I've already worked out this morning."

"Awww. Are you sure?" she asked, cocking her head and dramatically curling her lips downward. "We would love to have you. Wouldn't we, ladies?"

The small eight-woman group readily agreed.

"Maybe next time. I just want to see what you ladies do in the class. Can I just watch?"

"Why, sure, you can." She thrust out her hand. "By the way, I'm Carmelina. I used to be a professional dancer. I still work out at Sapphire in New York part-time and before that at The Dollhouse in Atlanta."

Victoria's ears perked up. "You used to work at The Dollhouse?"

Her eyes widened. "Yeah. Truth be known, that was one of my best gigs before me and my husband moved out here. The King brothers were the best. Oh! I better get this class started. Welcome and I hope you eventually decide to join us." With that, she turned and headed back to the front of the class.

Victoria slowly stepped back to a corner of the room and watched.

Carmelina punched a few buttons and the room suddenly came alive with a few hard-hitting hip-hop beats. The women immediately launched into warm-up exercises.

Fifteen minutes later, Victoria was bored and was ready to head out, but that was exactly when things started to get more interesting. Though she kept a straight face, she was intrigued by the teasing and suggestive moves.

"Pace yourselves, ladies," Carmelina shouted. "Slow and easy. The keys to seduction are slow and graceful moves."

Victoria paid close attention to how the women exaggerated every move. As if on cue, the women reached for the poles, slowly dancing around it at first then leaning and stretching their legs up. They each performed one basic swing, followed by a few complicated twirls.

"Okay, ladies. Let's do the slap and tickle," the instructor yelled. "Turn your back to your man. Keep your legs straight and then *sloooowly* bend forward, look back, smile innocently and then stroke and lightly tap your bottom."

It was clear that all the girls were enjoying themselves while Victoria was taking notes. They went back to swinging around the pole, easily holding their body weight while upside down with their legs in a full split.

Victoria was sold and anxious to try out the moves. Until she had been to The Dollhouse, she had never given much thought to the athleticism required for the profession. The muscle control alone fascinated her. Seeing firsthand what was involved in the dance, she didn't understand why it wasn't an Olympic sport.

Her practiced stoicism melted away as her rapt attention caught Carmelina's eye. "Are you sure that you wouldn't like to give this a try? It's a lot of fun!" Just then, Carmelina flipped her body up, supporting herself with just the strength of her calves.

Victoria remembered the move from one of the dancers in Eamon's club. "All right," she said and walked toward a vacant pole. "I'll try it."

The other women paused to give her a round of applause.

Despite her sudden wave of shyness, her competitive nature wouldn't let her change her mind.

"Have you had *any* experience working with a stripper pole?" Carmelina asked in her the same chipper voice.

Victoria shook her head.

"Don't worry, we'll all work together to get you up to speed."

Forty-five minutes later, Victoria was sore in places only her gynecologist should know about. Strangely enough, she was invigorated by the end of the class and promised herself, as well as the group, that she was now their newest member.

Victoria kept her weekly Monday lunch with her cousins at The Garden in the Four Seasons Hotel. Dressed to the nines in a sea-green Prada dress and silver Christian Louboutins, she followed the hostess as she navigated around the marble floor and acacia trees to her usual table. To her surprise, her cousins had actually beaten her there. That had to be some kind of miracle. Her cousins were always late.

"Hello, girls." Victoria smiled and then took a few seconds to exchange their customary kisses on both cheeks. "I can't believe you two are already here."

"Three weeks without our Monday red snapper should be a crime," Grace said.

Victoria smiled.

"Are you okay?" Iris said. "We noticed that you were walking a little funny when you came in."

"Oh. It's nothing. I enrolled in a new class at the gym that's kicking my butt."

The girls nodded and then looked at each other.

*"Sooooo,"* Grace started. "When are we going to talk about *him?"*

"Oh, God," Victoria moaned. "Please don't ruin my lunch before I even get a chance to taste it. If I never hear the name Marcus Henderson again, it will be too soon."

The twins shared another look and Victoria caught the exchange over the edge of her menu. "Enough. Spit it out."

"Well," Iris said. "We weren't talking about Marcus."

Victoria settled back in her chair. "Oh." She supposed that two weeks was a pretty good record.

Grace leaned in over the table. "Yes. *'Oh.'* We've been dying to hear about the naked strip club owner you had holed up in your hotel suite."

"Yes. The sexy-as-hell Eamon King."

"What? You two hired a private investigator?"

"Please. There's this wonderful thing called Google." Iris smiled. "So give up the deets. How long have you two been doing the nasty?"

"The nasty?"

"I'm trying to keep it PC. Now stop stalling."

"I'm not stalling." Victoria tried to play it cool. "There's nothing to get worked up about. There's nothing to tell."

"Yeah. Right. And for future reference, there's no need to lie to us. *You just wanted to spend the night alone.*" Grace rolled her eyes. "You must've thought you really pulled one over on us. We're not oblivious to the need for an emergency booty call. Hell, I make them at least once a month."

"Once a month?" Iris said. "Please, you're in the minor leagues. I rotate some creepers on a weekly basis."

"Creepers?"

"Yeah. You know. Men you never introduce to your friends. You just creep around with under the cover of night. The booty-call role."

The twins giggled.

"Eamon was not a booty call."

The look her cousins gave her all but said *sell your BS somewhere else.*

"Look. Not everything is what it looks like."

"Well," Grace said. "It *looked* like you had a naked man in your suite. The same man I caught you trying to have *relations* with in the office of his strip club."

*"Relations?"*

"PC. Remember?"

"Yeah. Well. It's not a strip club, either. It's a gentlemen's club."

"You say tomato and I say tomahto," Grace challenged. "And you're still dodging, by the way. So come out with it."

The two leaned forward together and planted their elbows onto the table.

"I told you there're no deets. It's nothing."

"Did you sleep with him or not?" Iris asked.

The direct question made it impossible for Victoria to continue dancing around the truth. "A little bit."

Her cousins screamed.

Shocked, Victoria leaped over the table and slapped her hands over their mouths. "Have you two lost your minds? Look where you are."

The twins still wiggled in their chairs and stamped their feet.

"I can't believe you two are acting like children." She kept her hand over their mouths until she was sure that they were going to behave.

"Actually, we've been talking, and we think that it's great that you've finally let your hair down. It's *waaaay* past time for you to let go of some of that control."

Victoria frowned. "You two have been talking?"

"Well, it's just that you're always *sooooo*..."

"I'm always so what?"

"Honesty?" Iris said, timidly.

She definitely didn't like the sound of that. "Please."

"Well..." She looked over at her mirror image. "You're always so...*stuck-up*."

The statement hung over the table.

"Sorry," Iris finally added. "We love you though."

Victoria struggled not to let her shock and irritation show on her face. "I resent that."

"Resent it all you want," Grace said, less tactfully. "You just can't deny it."

This whole sexual-intervention-slash-tough-love therapy was starting to work Victoria's last nerve, but clearly her cousins weren't finished.

"C'mon. You have to know that you're a control freak, right?" Grace said. "Everything has its place. Every person fits neatly in a certain column. There's only black and white—no shades of gray. And while I'm on this honesty tear, you chose Marcus to be your husband before *you* asked him out on a date."

"That's true," Iris co-signed.

"And that was *after* one of your famous spreadsheet analyses of his character, his financial upside potential, a credit check and a criminal background check. Poor Marcus didn't stand a chance. He probably just choked."

Heat flushed Victoria's face. "Poor *Marcus?* You're taking *his* side after what he's done to me? Is that what I'm hearing?"

Finally Grace held up her hands and conceded. "All

right, maybe that was a poor choice of words—but my point remains the same. I actually love the idea of you easing off the brakes a bit. You're a successful investment banker in your own right. You balance an insanely cluttered social life with charities and supporting the arts. Now it's time for you to focus on your personal life. But you need someone who's going to help loosen you up."

"Yeah. And Marcus wasn't it," Iris testified.

"Definitely. Now, take someone like Eamon King…"

"Wow," Iris said. "Now, there was some serious heat being generated between the two of you. *Big time.*"

"Me and Eamon?"

The twins nodded.

Victoria wanted to dismiss their observations…but couldn't. "Anyway. Eamon is all wrong."

"Why, because he owns a string of strip clubs?" Iris challenged.

"No. And they're gentlemen's clubs," she reminded them again. "Plus he owns a couple of restaurants."

Grace frowned. "Please tell me that you haven't started another one of those damn spreadsheets."

Victoria refused to answer.

"Good Lord." Grace rolled her eyes. "Somebody save us from Microsoft Excel."

"Will you just forget about it? There is no Eamon and me. We're not a couple and we will never be a couple. So forget about it and let's move on." She reached for her glass of water.

"Does moving on mean that you're also going to drop that silly lawsuit?"

Victoria choked and then put her glass back down. "Now it's a silly lawsuit, too?"

Grace removed her elbows from the table just as the waitress arrived with their lunch. "C'mon, Victoria. It was always a silly lawsuit. Do you know how bottlenecked the courts would be if every woman started hurling lawsuits at strip clubs across America?"

"The judicial system would shut down. We could never get around to prosecuting murderers and rapists."

"Now you're just being silly. There's a difference between civil court and criminal court, you know."

"Yeah. Yeah. I watch *Law & Order*. Let's not get off the message. You just filed that lawsuit because you were angry. I get it."

"And I'm still angry and I'm pushing forward. End of story!"

"You're going to sue the man that you just had a fling with?"

"One thing doesn't have anything to do with the other."

"Wow," Grace said. "You really are a hardass."

Iris shrugged her shoulders. "I don't know. Maybe she has a point not wanting to settle down with strip-club owner. That's an awful lot of temptation to have around you."

Grace turned toward her sister. "It doesn't have to be a serious relationship."

*Are they really going to have this conversation like I'm not still sitting at the table?*

"I thought that we were just talking booty calls?" Grace said. "I'm not saying that she should introduce someone that's just a step above being a pimp into New York society. That would be a nightmare. Can you imagine the headline? The Heiress and The Pimp."

*Yep. They're going to just keep talking.* "Eamon is not a pimp."

"Yes. Yes. We know. He also runs a restaurant."

Victoria's head started to hurt. "You know what? I have to cut this short."

Grace and Iris turned. "Aww. C'mon."

"Don't be mad," Iris said. "We're just trying to help."

"I'm not mad," Victoria lied. "I just really have to go. I forgot I had this…other thing I have to do."

It was a bad lie and they all knew it.

Slowly the girls rose from their seats. The twins regretted that they may have hurt Victoria's feelings.

"All right," Iris conceded. "We're going to meet here next Monday, right?"

"That depends on whether we've moved onto a new subject," she tried to joke, but with a veiled warning. They kissed each other's cheeks again after which Victoria high-tailed it out of the restaurant as fast as her legs would allow.

Outside, she hopped into a cab and gave the driver her address. Alone in the backseat, her mind rehashed the ridiculous scene at the restaurant. She couldn't believe how her cousins had ganged up on her like that. Her personal sex life was none of their business.

"A booty call." She rolled her eyes.

"Ma'am?" the driver asked.

"Oh. Nothing. I was just talking to myself."

The driver nodded but gave her a strange look. *Great. Now people think I'm going crazy.*

For the next ten minutes, she just stared out of the window at the traffic while her cab inched along bumper-to-bumper.

*Booty call.* This time, she didn't roll her eyes. It would be kind of funny…and cool, if she just periodically picked up the phone and told Eamon that she wanted or needed to be serviced. Then again, who's to say that he wasn't already on someone else's short list?

She shook her head, but the term *booty call* was rooted in her mind like a California redwood.

"Ma'am?"

Victoria jerked out of reverie. "Huh?"

"We're here."

Victoria glanced out of the window of the cab to see that they had indeed arrived at The Centurion. "Thanks." She handed the driver his fare and climbed out. She flashed the doorman a smile and entered the softly lit, cream-colored lobby. As she headed toward the elevator, she saw the concierge point his white-gloved hand in her direction a second before a young man raced over to her.

"Uh, Ms. Gregory?"

She turned. "Yes?"

"I have something for you," he said, thrusting a thick envelope toward her.

"What's this?"

"You've been served."

"I'm what?"

"Have a nice day." He saluted her and then ran off.

Openmouthed, Victoria stood there like an idiot for a second and then quickly tore open the envelope. When her eyes raced over the documents, a lump of incredulity clogged her throat. "You've got to be kidding me. That jerk is counter-suing me?"

## Chapter 13

"I really appreciate you bailing me out of jail," Quentin said, patting Eamon on the back as they exited the Las Vegas Metropolitan Police Department. "I want you to know that I intend to fight these bogus charges. You should've seen how this creep was all over Crystal. I'm sure that you would've decked him, too."

"Somehow I doubt that," Eamon groaned as he squeezed the bridge of his nose, but it was too late. He could already feel the slow, throbbing sinus pain of a migraine coming on. Once he reached his Porsche, he scooped out his cell phone from his pocket and hit up Xavier on speed dial before climbing inside. He vowed if his brother didn't pick up this time that he would be on a flight to Los Angeles to wring his neck for putting him in this babysitting mess before the sun set.

He was in the middle of tourist season and he had his hands full with everything from horny college students to diva dancers and finicky liquor distributors. He didn't have the time to keep tabs on an overindulged, spoiled little rich boy. Quentin didn't actively go out and look for trouble, but it found him all the same.

"One party," Eamon muttered as he started up the car. "I let you host one party and next thing I know I'm posting bond and refunding ten grand to a customer who has to show up to his wedding with a black eye and fat lip."

Quentin waved off Eamon's complaint. "Refund? We don't do refunds," Q said.

"No. What we don't do is send paying clients to the emergency room." Eamon reached Xavier's voice mail. "Damn it." He hung up and tried his cell phone.

"I'm telling you. He was an asshole. Talk to the girls. They will back me up."

Eamon simmered while he waited for the line to connect. There was no use in talking to Q. He had his own way of seeing and doing things. Like screwing up the liquor orders, arguing with the health inspectors or firing half the limousine drivers, because he thought they should be replaced with some of the ladies he met at the Bunny Ranch.

"All right. All right." Quentin rolled his hand. "It won't happen again. I said it. Are you happy now?"

*Hardly.*

"I'm sure that once the judge hears my side of the story, he'll just toss the case right out."

More simmering. "Xavier, answer this damn phone."

"Hello."

Shocked to finally hear his brother, Eamon's voice stalled.

"Hello?" Xavier said again.

"I'm glad to hear that you're still alive," Eamon spat

out. "That means I can still take great pleasure in killing you myself."

Xavier chuckled. "It's good to hear from you, too. What's up?"

"Are you kidding me? Haven't you been getting my messages? You know what's up. It's your turn to start taking care of that little project you signed me up for."

Suddenly there was a loud blast of music over the line. "I'm sorry. What was that?" Xavier shouted over the music. "I can't hear you."

Eamon's simmering morphed into a boil. "Don't play," he warned. "I'm not in the mood today."

There was some loud chiming thing happening. "What are you doing? Clanging wineglasses together?"

"Shhhhhheeeeehhhhe. I'm sorry, but you're breaking up," Xavier lied.

"I don't believe this." Eamon punched the steering wheel.

"I'm going to have to call you back," Xavier continued.

"Don't do it. Don't you dare hang up this phone."

"Bye, bro."

*Click.*

"Xavier?"

*Silence.*

"Xavier!" Eamon pulled the phone away from his ear and stared at the small screen just to make sure that his brother had indeed disconnected the phone. "Son of a bitch." He tossed the phone onto the console and then punched the steering wheel again.

Quentin calmly folded his arms. "You know, that *little project* has ears. And even I can understand that weak-ass code you're transmitting."

"You don't say?" Eamon pressed his foot down on the

gas pedal. Twenty minutes, several car honks and few birds tossed at some very bad drivers later, they arrived at The Dollhouse. However, Eamon's anger was far from cooling.

Realizing that he had finally crossed some invisible line in the sand, Q tried to make some concession. "Tell you what. I'll reimburse the asshole personally."

"And the pending lawsuit that will undoubtedly be headed our way?"

"What? We don't just collect those?"

Eamon's jaw clenched tighter as he stormed into his office.

"That was supposed to be a joke, man. Lighten up."

Eamon dropped into his chair, resting his elbows on the desk. "We need to talk."

"Oh." Quentin frowned. "To think at one time I only hated hearing those words from women. Now I'm pretty sure I just don't like hearing them at all. It's never followed by good news."

"I think it's time for you to go home."

"What are you talking about? Las Vegas is like my second home. I love it here."

"I'm not too sure that it loves you back. Plus, I appreciate your wanting to help. I really do, but it's just not working out. Every time you do anything it means more work for me—and my plate was pretty full before you showed up. In case you haven't noticed it takes a lot of work keeping a place like this going. And believe it or not, it has nothing to do with drinking on the clock and making sure the dancers have plenty of baby oil in their stations. This isn't a game or an adult toy store. You are either going to have to start taking this place seriously or you just need to leave, cuz."

Quentin frowned. "I'm not going anywhere. I'm part owner, too."

Eamon tossed up his hands. "Then maybe it's just time for us to buy you out."

"Sorry. My share isn't for sale." Q folded his arms.

"Who are we kidding? You're always for sale." Eamon regretted the words the minute they came out of his mouth.

The blood seemed to drain from Quentin's face. The reference to Q's accepting money to marry the daughter of one of his father's business partners in order to reclaim his inheritance wasn't one of his finest moments and it likely cost him the love of his life. Had he not agreed to marry, then he would've won Alyssa's hand years before she'd fallen for his brother Sterling.

Eamon pulled in a deep breath. "I'm sorry. That was out of line."

"I don't know. It wasn't so much out of line as it reeked from the horrible stench of truth." He tried to flash a smile, but it fell flat. "But since we're mucking around in the truth, let me toss out some more of it. I'm not perfect. I've made mistakes. And here's a doozy. I don't need a babysitter. So you can stop paying valets, housekeepers and limousine drivers to keep an eye on me. I find it offensive."

Surprised and even impressed, Eamon leaned back in his chair. "All right. That sounds fair. But if you're going to stick around, I prefer that you really try to pull your weight around here…and I do take checks for that bail money I posted this morning." He smiled with a burgeoning new respect for his cousin.

"The check is in the mail." Q winked. "In the meantime, I suggest you get used to seeing me around, *cuz*." He marched toward the door and nearly ran into someone.

"Well, excuse me, *Ms. Gregory*. It's a pleasure to see you again."

Eamon's gaze shot up.

"I assure you that the pleasure is all yours," she sniped and then sidestepped him in order to enter Eamon's office.

Behind her, Quentin mouthed, *"Trouble"* and then got the hell out of there before she erupted. Judging by the smoke streaming out of her ears that looked like it would be any second now.

Like a light switch, Eamon's mood flipped. "Well, well, well. If it's not my favorite *pussycat*. It even looks like you've been sharpening your claws." He quirked his mouth into a wicked smile as his gaze caressed her curves. *Perfection*.

"Only so that I can scratch your eyes out."

"Aww. Now, do you really want to hurt me?"

Victoria planted her hands down on the desk and leaned forward. "More than you'll ever know."

Eamon followed her lead and eased forward until their faces were just inches apart. "You really shouldn't joke about something like that. I might take you up on it."

She literally growled.

"Tease."

Victoria jerked herself up and then pulled out a thick envelope from her monster-size handbag. "What is this? You're suing *me* now?"

"Looks like I'm not the only one who knows how to read. Not only would we have made beautiful babies, but they just might've made it to the thirteenth grade."

"You're trying to be funny?"

"Trying—but you're a tough audience."

She slammed the papers down onto the desk. "Defamation of character and *sexual* harassment? Sounds like our imaginary children would be extremely mentally disabled."

"Possibly. But we would have had fun making them," he said, refusing to be ruffled.

She blinked and shook her head. "This is just a joke to you."

"No. The bit about the children was a joke. I'm serious about the lawsuit," he said casually and then leaned back and kicked his heels up on the corner of his desk.

"Fifty million dollars?"

He shrugged. "It sounded like a nice round number."

"You're killing me."

Eamon cocked his head and blinked his woeful brown eyes at her in a way that put Puss in Boots to shame. "Now, is this the face of a killer?"

Victoria was clearly at a loss for words.

"Besides, I'm looking forward to airing out our grievances in court."

"This is not going to court. You're going to withdraw this stupid suit."

"And why in the hell would I do something like that?"

"Because the charges are a pack of lies and you know it. Sexual harassment. Please." Her eyes raked him up and down. "If anyone was harassed, it was me. The moment you brought me back here in this office, you had me pinned against the wall. No doubt it's a move that you've perfected in this sleazy strip joint."

"Ah. Ah." He waved a finger at her. "I run a classy establishment and I'm a pillar of my community. I doubt that you'll be able to find anyone in this beautiful city that will say anything less. You know, that comment just supports that character-defamation part of my claim. You should watch those insults that you hurl around. Some of them actually hurt a bit."

"And what if I dug up a few ex-girlfriends?" she asked, crossing her arms.

"Now, that might be a little stickier," Eamon conceded.

"Why am I not surprised?"

"Because you have very little faith in people?"

Her eyes narrowed.

"It was just a guess."

"I-did-not-harass-you."

"That's not how I remember it," Eamon said.

"And how do you remember it?"

"I don't know, but I'll have a nice little story put together by the time we're in court. I've been told that I have a very creative mind. I should've been a writer. I could've been a contender."

"I think you're fulfilling your destiny as a major asshole pretty well."

"Such language coming out of such a pretty mouth," he marveled. "Are you as turned on as I am?"

Charging around the desk, Victoria slapped his feet off the desk before leaning in and jabbing a finger into his chest. "I'm *not* going to let you make a fool out of me. You need to get that out of your head. I just got my name *out* of those snarky gossip pages. I'm not interested in going another round again."

He just smiled and stared. "Stunning. You really are just stunning when you're angry. All jokes aside, I'm really turned on." He got a kick watching her incredulity deepen.

"Are you a moron?"

"No." He shrugged. "Just horny. What do you say we close the door and do something about this sexual energy that's charging between us? I might even let you scratch my back if you let me pull your hair."

*Slap!*

Eamon smiled. "Help me out. Was that a yes or a no?"

*Slap!*

Before Victoria could register the stinging pain in her hand, Eamon's arm snaked out and jerked her into his lap. She gasped. Not because of his speed but because of his erection pressed against her firm bottom. Her body was overwhelmed with memories and everything started tingling and quivering. Her anger melted away and Eamon knew it.

"Ahh. You remember this position, don't you?"

She sucked in a breath, but didn't dare trust herself to speak just yet.

"Yes. You do." He reached up and brushed a few tendrils from the side of her face. "I believe the last time you were on my lap you were calling me a god or calling on God. Forgive me. My memory is a little hazy because…well. I was admiring *and* enjoying your riding skills."

Victoria started to say something but then his hands started sliding up her leg.

"You know, since I'm a betting man, I'm willing to bet that you're quite the equestrian, Princess." He didn't have to wait long for that familiar blush to rush to her face. "That is what ladies do in your high-society world, right?" Eamon's hands floated higher and higher. "Long legs. Powerful thighs. I bet you have a whole display case full of trophies you've won."

She pressed her lips together, but Eamon noted that she didn't deny his claim or try to climb out of his lap.

"So what do you say? Are you in the mood for a little afternoon ride?"

Victoria swallowed while her gaze followed his hand.

"It's okay, Princess. You can say yes. I won't hold it against you." His fingers disappeared under her skirt and he leaned forward to nibble on her right earlobe.

She closed her eyes and shivered.

Smiling, Eamon pulled back. "In fact, I'm willing to just let you use me however you like if it'll put a smile back onto those beautiful lips of yours."

Slowly, Victoria turned her head to see the sincerity in his lustful gaze.

"It's your decision." The tips of his fingers brushed against the seat of her crotch. "Do you want to stay and pretend we're just fighting over ridiculous lawsuits or do you want to do what you *really* came here to do?"

# Chapter 14

Victoria's gaze lowered to Eamon's lips while his invitation hung in the air. Her mouth started to water at the memory of his taste. One bite and she would be addicted again. She struggled to find that raging anger she had storming into his office, but it had vanished like a ghost. Now she was left vulnerable with her heart racing like a wild mustang.

It had been two weeks, or rather fifteen days, five hours and a little over seventeen minutes since she had the incredible pleasure. But it felt more like it had been forever. And hadn't she done everything short of fasting and having an exorcism to try and get him out her system?

The seconds ticked by as she stared into his smoldering eyes and his hands grazed her crotch. This may have been too strong a temptation for her to overcome.

"So what do you want to do? I'll respect whatever you

decide," he said. His voice dipped into a smoky baritone while that sexy smile sloped across his lips.

She twitched in his lap while her nipples ached. Somehow she managed to get her legs to work so that she could climb out of his lap.

Disappointment rippled across Eamon's face.

Victoria turned and walked toward the door, quivering like the last fall leaf on the first day of winter. When she reached the archway, there was one last desperate scream from the back of her brain. *Run!*

It was the voice of reason, she knew. But it was soon overthrown by desire. She reached for the door and then slowly closed it and locked it. Taking a deep breath, her nerves calmed.

"That's a good girl," Eamon praised. "Now, why don't you come back over here and give me a proper hello?"

Victoria faced him. *Damn, he was cocky as hell.* Then again, hadn't she known that? Didn't she like it?

Instead of obeying, she remained close to the door. There, she slowly lifted her hands to the back of her head and removed the pins from her hair. When her thick hair fell like a heavy curtain, she shook and slid her fingers through it so that it would splay across her shoulders.

Eamon's smile ticked higher.

Next, she took her time, reaching for the top pearl button of her silk blouse. *Slow and easy. Pace yourself. The key to seduction is slow and graceful moves.* So far it looked to be a good game plan because Eamon's gaze tracked her manicured fingers like a bloodhound. By the time she undid the last button and peeled open her blouse, Eamon looked like his tongue was ready to roll out of his head.

*I have the power now.* She draped the blouse over the empty chair in front of his desk. Next she reached behind her pencil skirt, undid the top button and then pulled the tiny zipper down. The skirt pooled at her feet and she calmly stepped out of it before adding it to the chair.

Excitement and fire glowed in Eamon's eyes as he eased back against his chair. "You have no idea how much I've missed you," he confessed while his gaze tripped over her hourglass frame.

"How much?" she asked, her confidence returned.

He patted his lap. "Why don't you come over here and let me show you?"

Victoria shook her head and then pivoted around giving him a full view of her sleek back and the peek-a-boo strings that hugged her hips and disappeared down the center of her well-toned ass cheeks. She didn't have to see him to know where his eyes were locked. She could feel them like a lover's caress.

"Hot damn," Eamon whispered with a small tremor in his voice.

Her confidence soared while she smiled at the closed door and reached for the small bra hooks. Two seconds later, it was added to her small pile of clothes. Pivoting back, the sight of her full breasts caused Eamon to inhale a sharp breath as if he'd been gut-punched.

Unbridled lust blanketed Eamon's face.

"Like what you see?"

"No." He shook his head. "I *love* it." He stood and walked around the desk. As he moved toward her, his gaze inched above her *Playboy* figure and settled onto her cover-girl face. "I still can't get over how beautiful you are."

"Has anyone ever told you that you talk too much?" she sassed. She reached for his shirt but didn't treat it with the same care that she had her own clothes. With all the strength she could muster from years of boot-camp fitness training, she jerked open his shirt with such brute force that it sent his buttons flying.

"We keep this up and I'm going to have to buy some new shirts," he joked.

Victoria jerked the shirt halfway down his arms and then gathered it tightly in one hand so that his arms would remain bound behind his back. She kind of liked the idea of him being helpless before her. Judging by his sly smile, they both knew that wasn't really the case.

"So what is it that you want to do with me, Princess?"

"I don't know. I'm thinking that if you keep talking, I'm going to have to gag you," she said.

"Ooh. Kinky."

"On your knees."

His brows did another jump.

"You heard me. On your knees." She pulled his shirt tighter, forcing his back straighter. "Now."

"As you wish." Eamon slowly bent his knees, though it still put him eye level with her cinnamon-brown areolas.

Another dose of power surged through Victoria. "That's better." She glanced over at his cluttered desk and then stole one of his moves by sweeping an arm across it and sending everything crashing to the floor. "Oops."

He chuckled.

Now with the desk cleared, she leaned back on the edge and then lifted her right leg and six-inch pumps off the floor so that she could drape it over Eamon's shoulder.

"You said that you missed me," she reminded him. "Why don't *you* show me how much?"

"Yes, ma'am." Grinning like a kid in Toys 'R' Us, he edged closer on his knees and then leaned forward to use his teeth to pull the thin crotch of her thong to the inside of her right leg. After that, he was face-to-face with her newly shaved pussy. He was pleasantly surprised by the new look.

"Are you going to make me wait all day?" she asked.

"No, ma'am." Without further ado, Eamon planted his face in front of her jasmine-and-white-rose-scented lips and tunneled his long tongue through her honey-drenched opening.

"Mmm," Victoria moaned as she leaned further back across the desk.

Loving her response, Eamon went in for another lick. Then a lick and swirl. Lick, swirl and dip. Soon, he was in full feast mode.

Victoria filled his office with the sounds of music— well, moans. But it sounded like music to both of them.

Eamon decided to change up and refused to let her climax before *he* was ready. Every time he sensed that she was getting close, he would pull back and start peppering kisses along the inside of her thighs. After a few seconds he would dive right back in.

*Lick. Swirl. Dip.* When she got close again, he'd pull back. After a while she was pleading, bucking and then trying to direct him by grabbing the sides of his head. Nothing she did could get him to unleash the tornado around her clit. Once he had her positively begging, he surged forward and gave her what she wanted.

Victoria climaxed and shuddered so hard, Eamon felt like he was between two mountains during an earthquake. To show her just how well he could follow orders, he shook off his shirt and then reached up and locked her back down in place so that the second tornado could touch down. A flood of honey surged against his open mouth. Still he remained rooted in place until it looked like she needed a tank of oxygen in order to breathe.

Now that he had allowed her to enjoy a little dose of

power, it was time for him to take back the reins. Eamon climbed back onto his feet and unzipped his pants. "My turn." He took her by the arm and helped her off the desk.

She came willingly, though it was questionable whether her head had stopped spinning.

Eamon turned her around and then bent her over the desk. He whipped out a condom like a gunslinger from the Old West, sheathed himself and eased his way inside of her. He had to take his time because her warm walls were still shaking and quivering with orgasmic aftershocks. Each time her walls pulsed, it gave his cock a tight hug. By the time he'd glided all the way in, a line of sweat had broken out along his forehead.

"You're so tight," he groaned while struggling to catch his own breath. It was important for him to be careful. The wrong move would have him coming *waaay* too soon. But he almost lost the war when Victoria started rocking back against him.

"Ah. You really did miss me." He slapped her on her butt.

Victoria continued to throw her hips back.

"All right. All right." He stood still and then folded his hands behind his head. "You go ahead and do you, Princess. Let me watch you get what you need." And that's exactly what he did. He watched her while she rode him from the side of the desk. "That's right, Princess. It's all for you."

Eamon slapped her ass again and smiled as it jiggled. It looked so good to him that he did again.

And again.

Soon her cheeks glowed red. "You like that, Princess?"

Victoria gasped and panted.

"How does it feel?"

She moaned as her pace accelerated.

Eamon's toes started to curl and his breathing started to shorten a bit, but he leaned forward and then wrapped her thick hair around his right hand. Gently, he tugged her head back until he had full access to the violin curve of her neck. "I asked you a question, Princess. How does it feel? Are you enjoying yourself?"

More panting and gasping.

"Is this really what you flew all the way here for? Hmm?"

Victoria added some moans.

"Come on. Tell the truth. Don't lie to me. This is why you came."

It was clear that she was trying to evade the question by the way she kept throwing her hips back. So he pressed his free hand against her butt and stopped her from being able to back it up. Not that she didn't try.

"Answer the question, Princess." He took a moment to stop himself from coming again. "Why did you fly back to Vegas, baby?" he said as he removed his hand and gave her one long thrust.

"Hmm?" Another thrust.

"Tell Daddy why you came."

*Thrust.*

He tugged her hair. "Did you miss this good dick? Hmm?"

*Thrust.*

Victoria couldn't dodge the truth anymore so she nodded.

"Sorry. I can't hear you."

*Tug. Thrust.*

"Y-yes!"

As a reward, she received three thrusts.

"Why didn't you just tell me that?" He gave her three more quick thrusts. "Were you trying to act all prim and proper?"

*Thrust.*

"Is that it?"

*Thrust.*

"Hmm?"

*Thrust.*

It was clear that she didn't know how to answer that question. So he came up with a solution. "When you're around me, there's not going to be any more of that bourgie stuff." *Thrust.* "There's not going to be any more pretending that you're all high and mighty. You got that?" *Thrust.*

"There's not going to be any more games between me and you. You want something, you just tell Daddy." *Thrust.* "You got that?"

*Thrust. Thrust. Thrust.*

With one hand still wrapped around her hair, he moved his free hand to reach around her left hip and then dipped down in between her legs. Her sighs climbed higher when the pads of his fingers started caressing her clit.

"You understand me, Princess?"

"Y-yes. God, yes!"

"Then let me hear you say it." He stopped thrusting.

Victoria tried to cheat again and wriggle her way back.

Eamon slapped her ass again. "What did I say?"

"I need you, Daddy! Please!"

She wriggled again, but since she had asked politely he let it go. "Now, that wasn't so hard now, was it?" He released her hair and then locked his hands onto her shoulders and turned his hips into a jackhammer. Lost in their own world, neither of them paid attention to how hard the desk was being bumped around the floor. There was a quick change in positions so he could enjoy watching her face as she lay across the desk on her back. Before the afternoon was over, they tried it against the wall, the floor and even on the fax machine.

By their final orgasm, Eamon hadn't even noticed that his guttural groans now sounded like a roaring lion. When he floated down from that last orgasmic high, he needed an oxygen tank and he was only mildly curious as to how they'd ended up under the desk. But one thing was for sure, they had completely wrecked his office.

Victoria rolled over and placed her head against his chest. He expected her to fall asleep in just a few seconds. Hell, he was going to sleep, too. While he waited for his heart to slow down, he felt the need to say something. But all the things he wanted to say, all the things he was beginning to feel for this extraordinary woman, scared the hell out of him.

## Chapter 15

The next two months passed by like a montage in a romantic comedy movie. At least that's what it felt like to Victoria before she tried pinching herself to make sure it was real. But every day, she kept waking up lying next to this incredible King and wondering how her life had changed so dramatically. At first she just accepted that there was just this powerful sexual energy between them that needed to work itself out. Clearly they were compatible and she loved discovering a whole new side of herself that she'd never known existed before, and somehow Eamon instinctively knew just how far to take it and when to steer clear of some things.

She was learning to read him as well, too. He was comfortable enough with his masculinity to let her take control sometimes, but then he knew just when she wanted him to completely dominate her. Sex. It was just sex, she kept telling herself.

Until it wasn't just sex.

When exactly that started to change was still a bit of a mystery. It could have been one of the many nights when they'd gone dancing outside on the Terrace at the Pure Night Club or took in the KÀ Cirque du Soleil show. Victoria discovered that despite Eamon's cockiness from time to time, and his enormous sexual appetite, that he was also musically gifted.

She couldn't believe her ears the first time he sat down at The Piano Bar in Town Square and started playing everything from Joplin to Billy Joel as if he'd been a musical prodigy. She even watched as he dueled with one of the club's piano players. Soon the place was packed with people shouting out requests in such a frenzy that Victoria didn't understand why the chords weren't catching on fire.

Eamon's quick sure fingers danced around the keys while he cracked jokes with the audience and shot wicked smiles at her. When they had made love later that night, he'd opened up about a time when he had seriously considered becoming a songwriter. He talked about a music group when he was in high school, but Victoria also sensed that he was dancing around something else, as well. If she trusted her women's intuition, she'd say it had something to do with a girl.

The first time Victoria got the tour of his North Shore estate, she soaked in the beauty of the white, three-level home with custom chandeliers, columns with iron and brass scrolls and extensive stone work, she could have sworn that she'd just stepped into one of her father's homes in Palm Beach. When they walked into the elevator that went from the ground floor to the upper levels, she saw that the back of the elevator was made of glass and overlooked a stunning lake with a private dock. Of course, the room that she was most interested in seeing was the master bedroom.

The moment she stepped onto the Brazilian hardwood floor and gazed at the California king–size bed she thought that she had died and gone to heaven. The French-Empire style appeared to be black oak with a crown of barely twisted columns and decorative moldings.

"So is this where the magic happens?" she asked, cutting her gaze at him and expecting a cocky answer.

"The only magic I feel is when I'm around you," he answered and drew her into his arms.

Victoria didn't know whether that was a line he'd honed over the years or not. She just knew that it made her heart melt and her clothes disappear. Actually, that happened a lot around him. The first morning she woke up in his bed she was alone. But before she had the chance to wonder where he'd disappeared to, she heard this incredibly beautiful music floating through the house. Curious, she climbed out of bed, wrapped the insanely large top sheet around her body and went to investigate. As she walked through the hallway to take the long staircase down, the beautiful music eased a smile across her face.

Victoria found Eamon in the parlor, sitting at a grand piano in just a pair of black, silk pajama pants. Maybe that was the moment when the possibility of Eamon being more than a sex partner took root. Smiling, she leaned against the parlor entryway and just watched his face while music poured from his fingertips. It was more instinct than knowledge that led her to believe that the song was an original piece and he was the songwriter.

Being a child of privilege, Victoria had been to and seen lots of beautiful things around the world, but none of it really touched her. She saw, but didn't see. Heard, but didn't listen. Read, but didn't comprehend. She was a woman of structure and order…well, at least she used to be. Somehow all that was changing right before her eyes. And she couldn't have been happier. Should she trust it?

Closing her eyes, she didn't want to answer the questions her heart posed. The answers scared the hell out of her. For the moment, she was content to finally let the beauty just soak in. By the time the music faded, her face was wet with tears.

"What are these for?" Eamon asked, gently wiping away her tears with his thumbs.

Victoria's dewy lashes fluttered open to see Eamon now standing before her with his concerned brown eyes gazing down at her.

"I know the song isn't polished, but I didn't think it was that bad."

She smiled. "You have to be kidding me. I think that was the most beautiful thing I've ever heard."

Eamon chuckled. "It's rather early for you to be trying to inflate my ego, don't you think?" He pulled her into his arms and snaked kisses down her neck. "The beautiful thing to me is when you're moaning in my arms."

His lips grazed a ticklish spot and Victoria giggled like a schoolgirl. "Stop it." She pushed him back and then locked gazes with him. "I was being serious. You're really talented."

"And so are you." He squeezed her bottom.

She struggled to keep a straight face, but she wasn't willing to let the matter drop. "Why do you do that? Can't *you* take a compliment—or does it always have to be about your sexual prowess?"

He sucked in a deep breath but finally managed to get serious. "Thank you. I'm glad and humbled that you enjoyed my music, Princess."

"More than enjoyed it. Baby, you should be doing

something with a talent like that. You're really good. Trust me. I have family members who have gone to Juilliard. I know talent when I hear it."

"Baby?" Eamon repeated, hiking up a brow. "Am I your baby now?"

Victoria enjoyed a few more seconds of some wonderful groping before she tried to get serious again. "Why do you keep trying to change the subject? You could be a huge success in New York with a talent like that."

The mood shifted and all the humor died out of Eamon's smile. "Is that what's important to you? For me to be accepted in your snobby New York society?"

She realized too late that she had insulted him. "That's not what I meant."

"No? Are you sure?" His hands fell away from her waist.

"Of course I'm sure." Victoria grabbed his hands and tried to put them back around her waist. "I don't care what you do for a living or…what type of people you hang around."

Eamon cocked his head as he studied her. "And what *type* of people do I hang around?"

Her shoulders kept bobbing up and down in an attempt to shrug off the foolish question, but she just ended up looking like she had developed some weird tick. "I don't know. Strippers…hookers or ladies of the evening, I don't know."

"Hookers?"

It looked like she was going to eat both feet for breakfast that morning.

"You know, just because prostitution is legal in this state, doesn't mean that I hire them as employees at my club where I'm their pimp. As for the people that I do employ, you'll never find a group of more decent hardworking individuals. They are nice people. They have nice families and they pay their taxes. Maybe they weren't born with silver spoons in their mouths or went to Ivy League schools, but we're good people. Some of us are even talented."

He tried to remove his arms again, but Victoria refused to let him. "I'm sorry. None of that came out right. I didn't mean to imply… I just…" She searched but her brain failed to find words to help her smooth this over so she just went with the truth. "I'm just a snobby bitch sometimes."

The confession surprised him and brought his smile back at the same time. "Tell me more."

Victoria rolled her eyes, but she smiled, as well. "First. Let's make it clear that just because I said the word doesn't mean that you get to. Got it?"

"Got it." Eamon lifted up one hand and covered his heart with the other. "The *B* word shall not cross my lips."

"Better not." Her smile widened before she admitted a few more flaws she was aware of that had come to her attention over the years. "All right. I admit that *sometimes* I might judge people."

He gasped with dramatic shock. "You? Stop it. Next you'll be telling me that you have a bad temper and slap people from time to time."

Victoria's gaze narrowed. "Second rule. Nix the sarcasm."

Eamon twisted an invisible key at his mouth and then tossed it over his shoulder.

"You're enjoying this way too much," she said. "Let's just suffice it to say that I know that I'm not perfect. And… I'm sorry. I shouldn't have said or implied that your friends and employees were hookers."

"Oh. I have a few friends that are hookers. They just don't work for me."

Victoria gasped.

"I'm just kidding." He threw his head back and laughed while she started punching him playfully on the chest.

After that morning, Victoria found it a whole lot easier sharing things with him, a lot of it she had never shared with anyone, not even the twins. Whenever she tried to figure out why that was, she could only guess that it was because Eamon didn't judge her. Would he tease her over silly things? Yes. But it wasn't like the withering, snarky comments and salacious gossip that circulated around New York society and Page Six when you wore something two seasons in a row or snubbed the right people at the wrong time or the wrong people at the right time. Friendships were as solid as haystack houses during hurricane season.

Life in Las Vegas was remarkably simple compared to the big city, so much so that she couldn't remember when she gave serious thought to returning to New York. Now that she was experiencing what real happiness felt like, she didn't want to let it go.

"I just want to know when you're coming home," her father barked over her cell phone. "Two months is a long time for Las Vegas. Your mother and I are really starting to worry."

Victoria scrambled out of Eamon's bed and grabbed one of his T-shirts that was tossed on the floor. She didn't know what possessed her to answer her phone. "Daddy, there's no reason to worry."

"Really? Then why are you whispering?"

Victoria glanced over her shoulder to make sure that Eamon was still fast asleep while she tiptoed to the master bathroom. "I'm not whispering," she said in an even lower whisper. Once she made it into the bathroom and closed the door, she cleared her throat and spoke a little louder. "I…I was just waking up. That's all."

"Just waking up?" her father's voice rose. "Isn't it noon there?"

"Yes. It's…well, I've been keeping different hours."

"I'd say. You've always been an early riser now you're telling me that you just slept the whole morning away?"

"Well, I don't know what to tell you, Dad. Vegas is all about the night life. You go to bed early in the morning and you get up late in the afternoon. It's no big deal."

Mondell Gregory fell silent.

"Really, Daddy. Everything is fine," she assured. "I'm having a good time."

"Apparently. This new lifestyle of yours wouldn't happen to have anything to do with Eamon King, would it?"

Victory's spine stiffened as she gripped her cell phone tighter. "How do you know about Eamon?"

"Is that a real question?" he asked, chuckling.

"You've been spying on me?"

"I've been acting like I always have—like a protective father," Mondell stated flatly. "I had every right to be concerned when shortly after you were left standing at the altar, you fly down to Vegas and get yourself involved with some pimp that owns a chain of strip clubs."

"He's *not* a pimp, Daddy. You shouldn't be so judgmental and closed-minded about people. If memory serves me correctly, I believe that you spend quite a bit of time in *gentlemen's* clubs, too."

"Only to conduct business with investors," her father defended.

Victoria rolled her eyes. "Yeah right, Dad. I'm not five."

Her father's voice continued to rise. "I don't care if

you're five or thirty-five. You're still my daughter, who is with a man I don't know from Adam and I doubt that you do, either."

"You had him investigated, didn't you?" she accused.

"And you didn't?" he shot back. "That doesn't sound like the logical, pragmatic daughter I raised."

The accusation stung, mainly because it was the truth.

"Look, Victoria. I completely understand that you went through something very traumatic. I couldn't believe that Marcus would do something like that, either. We were both taken by surprise. On paper I saw what you saw—a nice stable man with great financial potential. I was all set to move him up in the company, bump in salary—the works. What can I say? He pulled one over on us."

"*Us?*" She started pacing the floor. "It wasn't *us*. It was me! *I* was humiliated. *My* name was dragged through those stupid tabloids. And you want to know what? I'm *glad*."

"What?"

"Yes. I'm thrilled," Victoria shouted and then jumped when her voice echoed back. But damn if that didn't feel good to say. "Marcus did me a huge favor by not showing up that day. I know now that I would've just been miserable being married to him. There wouldn't have been any *passion* or excitement. He wouldn't have challenged me to do things that I've never done before."

The line went quiet again.

"If you don't understand what I mean, then…" She sighed. "Then I just don't know what else I can tell you. Other than I'm fine and you can call off your spies."

Silence.

"Daddy? Are you still there?"

"I'm here, sweetheart," he said, evenly. "I just don't know what to say."

It was hard to tell whether he was mad or not and she wasn't even sure that she cared. She just wanted him to hear her and back off.

"I hope that you don't think that I'm the bad guy in this," he began. "I was just trying to do what I thought was best. On your wedding day, I thought that I was the one who had dropped the ball, that I should have been the one to have prevented you from getting your heart broken."

Victoria walked over to the sauna tub and sat down on the edge. "It wasn't your fault, Dad. And my heart was just fine. It was my pride that took a few blows." She exhaled as if the weight of the world had finally lifted. "I don't think one can truly protect themselves from getting hurt," she said. "It doesn't matter how many walls we put up or how carefully we step. I'm starting to believe that you just have to take the risk. You know? If it happens, it happens."

"We're not talking about Marcus anymore, are we?"

She shook her head against the phone. "No."

"So you're really falling for this Eamon King?" he inquired softly.

That was a huge question. *The proverbial elephant in her heart.* "Let's just say that it's a strong possibility," she admitted.

"And how does he feel about you?"

*The other elephant.* "I don't know, Daddy. I'm just flying with my eyes closed."

## Chapter 16

Eamon swam toward Victoria in his outdoor pool. "You've never been to Disney World?"

"No." Victoria had stopped to rest against the edge of the pool, and to steal a few minutes just to drink in his heavenly form. There was nothing like the sight of Eamon in the afternoon, the sunlight making the water glisten off his chocolate skin like white diamonds. She could watch him all day and never get tired.

"Disneyland?"

She shook her head. "I don't see what the big deal is."

He grabbed her legs and lifted them up in the water. "The big deal is that it's Disney!"

"Big deal," she said, still holding on to the ledge behind her.

Eamon took a step back, threatening to pull her away from the ledge and dunk her upper body into the water.

"Don't you do it," she warned.

"Or what?" He laughed and took another step back. "What are you going to do? File another lawsuit?"

"Ha. Ha." Victoria rolled her eyes. Now that sufficient time had passed, she could see the humor in her ridiculous idea to file that lawsuit. "Laugh it up, Joke Boy. But this time it's going to be a hundred million dollars."

"A hundred?" he gasped with feigned dismay. "I guess I should really be scared, huh?"

He took another step back, causing Victoria to just barely hold on. "Stop it!" Her protests probably would have had more power if she wasn't laughing. She tried to kick her legs free from his iron grip, but it was no use. "You play too much."

"Nooooo. You don't play enough," he corrected her. "I'm going to remedy that, especially now that I know that you've never ever been to the happiest place on earth. I don't even know how that's possible, Ms. I've-Been-Around-The-World."

"Whatever."

"My brother and I used to be obsessed with that place when we were little. I think it took my parents, like, two years to save up enough money to take us. Epcot, Sea World. You just don't know what you've been missing." He gave her legs a final tug and laughed when she came away from the ledge screaming. It was quickly silenced when her head hit the water and she was dunked about a foot deep.

Not waiting around for revenge, Eamon turned and took off, hoping that he had been quick enough to have a jump start on her by the time she sputtered back to the surface, but he was wrong. One of Victoria's talents seemed to be that she could swim like a fish. In fact, she was so fast he checked her feet a couple of times to make sure that they weren't webbed. This time when she caught him, she leaped onto his back and shoulders and successfully dunked him a couple of feet.

She tried to hold him down, but when it came to the strength department, he still reigned supreme.

"Now what are you trying to do?" he asked, lifting her clear out of the pool and then tossing her in the air.

Victoria screamed and kicked in the air for a full two seconds before landing back in the pool with an enormous splash. The resulting wave almost drowned him. It was worth it though just to get his revenge.

An hour later, they finally dragged themselves out of the pool and played one last game of tag as they raced toward the back of the house.

Eamon was impressed by the fact that she was just as fast out of the water as she was in. "Maybe I need to do a Google search on you," he said. "I'm starting to suspect that I've been duped and you're secretly some gold-medal Olympian who gets her kicks beating mere mortals in sports."

"Please. You just need to face the fact that you're just slow as hell, that's all." She followed him through the sliding glass door and then squealed when he suddenly whipped around and grabbed her by the waist.

"Who are you calling slow?"

"You, slowpoke." She tried to push herself away from his chest, but as she had discovered on many occasions, he didn't let her get her way.

"Now, what are you going to do if this slowpoke decides not to make lunch?"

Victoria twisted her face in mock confusion. "Why would you stop doing the one thing that you're good at?"

"Ooooh. You got jokes today?" He released her but gave her a good smack on the ass.

"Hey!"

"Hey, yourself. Watch that mouth, *missy*."

She laughed and strolled away. There was no need to look back because she knew that he was checking her out in her nude bikini. She washed her hands at the sink and then took a seat at the marble-topped island counter.

"So what do you say to fennel-and-onion risotto?" he asked.

"Sounds delish."

"Then risotto it is." He walked over to the sink and washed his hands.

"You never did tell me how you learned to cook so well," she said, reaching into the fruit bowl and grabbing a banana.

"Ah. That would be my mother."

"She's a good cook?"

"The best. In fact, it's the reason my father claims he married her."

"Really?"

Eamon shrugged. "Either that or because she was the most beautiful woman he'd ever seen. It depends on what day you ask him as to what he'll say."

Victoria chuckled while she peeled the banana. "Are they still together?"

"Yep. Forty-five years this Christmas."

"Wow. Impressive. They have my parents by ten years. At least you have siblings. You're lucky in that way."

"Oh?" Eamon started taking out the ingredients.

"Yeah. I always wanted a brother or sister. I think it would have been nice—at least less lonely."

He looked over at her and she flashed him a small smile. She didn't know why that had popped out.

"I guess growing up I didn't think of my brothers as a blessing. Trust me. It's not until after you're older, and if you're lucky, that you really appreciate them. Back then I just wished they would leave my stuff alone and stop tattle-telling."

"Which was which?"

"Xavier was always *borrowing* my stuff and Jeremy thought that he was a cub reporter."

Victoria laughed.

"All in all, I love those knuckleheads, even though they talk me into things I don't want to do—but don't tell them that."

"My lips are sealed. But tell me more about them."

"Well there's not that much to tell really. Xavier is a former heavyweight fighter. Growing up, I always knew it was only a matter of time before he would climb into the ring."

"Why is that?"

"Because he was always trying to fight somebody, Jeremy in particular, since he never knew how to keep his mouth shut. Plus, he was a big Mike Tyson fan back in the day. Frankly, I thought he had a real chance to go all the way. But he shocked the hell out of us when one day he just up and said he was tired of getting hit in the head." Eamon shrugged. "It's probably best, since he never really had that much in it."

Victoria chuckled. "Yeah. I'm really feeling the love."

Eamon laughed. "We tease each other all the time, but we don't mean anything by it. All in all, he's a really good guy—smart and a bit of a rascal. I think you'd like him."

"You think so?"

Eamon nodded.

"What about your younger brother, Jeremy?"

"Uh…Jeremy is a little more complicated." He pulled out an onion from the refrigerator, found a chopping board and a knife and brought them over to her. "Here, make yourself useful." He set them down in front of her.

Victoria looked down at the items. "Uhhh."

"Don't tell me that you don't know how to chop onions."

"Don't be silly," she said, frowning. "I mean, how hard could it be?"

He laughed. "A woman who can't cook. We're going to have to fix that if you're ever going to meet my mother."

Her eyes jumped up at the comment, but Eamon had walked away to resume prepping the meal, leaving her to wonder what he'd meant by that. Had he even realized what he had said?

"Like I was saying," Eamon continued. "Jeremy is another good guy. A little short though."

His mouth curled up and she suspected that she wasn't in on the joke. Under normal circumstances, she probably would've asked him to explain, but she was still wondering what he'd meant about meeting his mother. Could it be that he also thought they were moving in a new direction in their relationship? And why was she feeling hopeful?

"I still think you're lucky to have brothers." Victoria peeled the crinkly yellow skin away from the onion and then took two minutes trying to decide which way to make the initial cut. It really came down to an eeny-meeny situation.

Finally with more gusto than was probably necessary, she sliced the knife downward like a karate chop. When the onion split open, she smiled proudly.

"I need it diced," Eamon said.

"Oh." She looked at her magnificent work and then made another dramatic chop into one of the halves.

Eamon folded his arms and just watched her.

By the third round her eyes started burning and tears

rolled down her face. "Oh, God. I don't know if I can finish this. Ah. It's normally this strong?" She tried to slice again, but then just put the knife down and backed away so she could rinse her eyes out.

"If I didn't see that for myself, I don't think I would have believed it." He walked over to the island and in less than a minute, he had the whole onion chopped and diced.

Victoria already knew that he had quick fingers, but it was like lightning. Did the man's talents never cease? "Is your mother also why you got into the restaurant business, as well?"

"Yep." He started chopping the fennel. "She used to say that her mission in life was to make sure that her boys knew how to take care of themselves just in case we couldn't convince a girl to feel sorry enough for us to marry us."

Smiling, Victoria returned to the island now that her eyes were clear.

Eamon sighed. "So I cook. I clean. I even know how to sew and…"

"You know how to sew?"

His glanced back at her quizzically. "Don't you?"

The question caught her off guard. "I—I have a pretty good tailor?" The minute she said it, she realized how silly she sounded. Why didn't she know any basic household skills? Hell, maybe because she'd never needed to. She had a chef, a maid and a tailor. Instead of housework, she was a member of MENSA, and at the top of her class at Harvard Business School. She could understand complicated algorithms and could even recite eighteenth-century poetry at the drop of a dime. Why did that make her feel silly?

Shaking off her insecurity, she stood up and joined him at the kitchen counter.

"Show me how to cook."

Surprised, Eamon glanced over at her and noticed the firm tilt of her chin. "Are you sure, Princess?"

It was the first time that the nickname bothered her. "I'm not a Princess."

He hitched one side of his mouth. "I don't know about that. I kind of like thinking of you as my princess."

*A princess and a King.* Victoria smiled.

"All right," he announced. "You want to learn how to cook? Then let's get started."

For the next forty minutes, Eamon walked Victoria through the simple recipe. Victoria was impressed by the way that he could gauge measurements just by looking. But since she was new to the whole process, he used measuring cups. Her favorite part was when Eamon stood behind her and wrapped his arms around her so he could show her how to properly chop and dice. It was really kind of a turn-on.

"You must make your mother proud," Victoria said when they finally sat down at the dinner table to eat.

"That's what she says every time we talk. I think that she's just required to say that."

Victoria watched him while she took a few bites. Finally she just blurted out, "There's gotta be something wrong with you."

Eamon choked while he was taking a sip of his beer. "Come again?"

"You heard me. There's gotta be something I'm missing. How is it that you're still single? Every woman in this town should have been trying to pull every trick in the book to get you down somebody's aisle."

He laughed.

"I'm serious. You're a successful businessman with a chain of nightclubs and a wonderful Italian restaurant. You have a beautiful home. You're financially secure. You're an excellent pianist. You cook, clean *and* sew. And…" She shrugged. "You have some pretty decent skills in the bedroom."

His brows jumped at that bit of news. "Does that mean that I'm finally getting rated higher than a seven?"

Try a twenty. "Can we please stick to the subject? Why aren't you married?"

There was an odd look that crossed his face before he finally dropped his gaze. He tried to cover by giving her another dismissive shrug. "Maybe I've just been waiting for the right woman?" His gaze swung back to her.

"Have you—"

"You are asking a lot of questions today."

Even though it sounded like he was joking, there was something in his voice that suggested that he wasn't.

Victoria sensed that she had hit a nerve and she wondered what it was. Had he been married before? Why hadn't she ever asked that question before now? "All right. All right. I'll drop the subject. For all I know some male stripper ran off with your fiancée at her bachelorette party and I'm sitting here being totally insensitive."

Eamon laughed. "I should've known that you couldn't just drop it."

She gave him one of her mischievous looks. But she'd learned that Eamon was a master at changing the subject and that's exactly what he did.

"What *I* want to know is, what sort of fun did you have while you were growing up? Clearly Disney World wasn't on the list."

"Disney. Disney. Disney." Victoria rolled her eyes. "Will you give it a rest, already? Not everyone thinks Mickey is adorable, you know. *Some,* I'm not saying who, might think that he's a little bit…creepy."

Eamon almost choked again. "Mickey? Creepy? I think that's blasphemous!"

"He's a big *rat!*"

"Let me get this straight. You were actually *scared* of Mickey Mouse?"

"What part of him being a big rat don't you understand? And one that sings and dances and wants to play with little children." She shivered as if the thought gave her the heebie-jeebies. "It's weird. Strange. *Creepy.*"

Eamon roared with laughter. After a full minute passed and it appeared that he wasn't about to stop laughing anytime soon, Victoria leaned back in her chair and crossed her arms and tried to wait him out. When another minute passed and tears were streaming down his face, she decided that she'd had enough. "Ha. Ha. Chuckle it up. It's not nice to make fun of someone's phobia."

"H-how is Mickey Mouse a phobia?"

She tossed up her hands. "Hello? Big! Creepy! Rat! That big face and…weird eyes. If you ever lived in New York, you'd understand. That's our real immigration problem."

That didn't help. Eamon laughed until his sides started hurting. At last when he caught sight of her face and realized how annoyed she was, he tried to pull it together and reached for her hand.

Victoria snatched her hand out of reach.

"C'mon. Don't be like that. I've just never heard of anyone being afraid of Mickey Mouse. Emphasis on *mouse.*"

"Rat," she insisted.

"We have to get you over this, Princess. Tell you what. On your next birthday, I'm taking you to Disney World. I can't have you walking around being afraid of…"

Her eyes narrowed.

"A cartoon character," he substituted. "Besides, there's

more to the place than just Mickey. I think what you need is the opportunity to let your inner child out. The one you put in a cage waaaay too early in life. So, do we have a date? Your next birthday—no matter where we are in the world—I'm taking you to Disney World—or Land— whichever is closer."

"I think that's almost impossible."

"Why?"

"Because my birthday is tomorrow." Victoria realized that her smugness was premature when Eamon's eyes lit up.

"Then tomorrow it is!"

## Chapter 17

Quentin's neatly groomed brows dipped in confusion. "Let me get this straight. You're taking the week off so you can take your girl to Disneyland? Did I get that right?"

Eamon signed the electronic clipboard and handed it back to the deliveryman before turning his attention to his cousin. He should've known that Q was going to have something to say. He'd been shaking his head about him and Victoria for a while now. "Do you think you can handle everything while I'm gone or not?"

Q ignored the question and looked over at Hayley just as she squatted down on a stool next to Eamon at the bar. "Are you hearing this crap or do I need a Q-tip?"

"What? Does he have another excuse as to why he needs to take time off again this week?"

Eamon frowned. "What is that supposed to mean?"

"Take a guess," Hayley volleyed.

"Get this," Quentin said, leaning over the bar counter.

"He wants to take the weekend off so he can take her to… wait for it…*Disneyland*."

Hayley's mouth dropped open as she swiveled her head toward her boss. "You gotta be kidding me?"

"What's the big damn deal? She's never been before and it's her birthday tomorrow."

Hayley cocked her head. "Awww. How sweet. I wanted to go to Disneyland…when I was *ten!*"

Quentin cracked up. "You guys are going to look hella crazy trying to cut in line at Small World."

Eamon rolled his hands. "Go ahead. Get it out of your system. But I get the sense that Victoria didn't really get a chance to be a kid growing up. Sometimes I get the sense that she was incredibly lonely."

"Poor little rich girl?" Hayley asked.

"Something like that." Eamon looked up at Q. "You should know something about that, cuz. Did money make you happy as a kid?"

"Extremely," Quentin answered without missing a beat. "And it still comforts me at night, right along with a few naked ladies and a few cases of Cristal."

Eamon rolled his eyes. "I should've known."

"I'm a simple man, cuz. Love me or hate me. But I still find it extremely funny that your idea of a good time is to take your woman from an *adult* fantasy land—like this wonderful city in the desert—to a *children's fantasy land*. I might not be the brightest color in the crayon box, but I know enough to know that we can never go back and get the childhood we wanted. Ask M.J. God rest his soul."

"We're going to visit the theme park, not *buy* it."

Q shook his head.

"I don't know," Hayley said, studying Eamon. "I'm starting to think it's kind of sweet."

"Thank you, Hayley." Eamon winked and then hopped

off the stool. "At least one of you can see where I'm coming from."

"Oh. I see where you're coming from just like I know where you're heading, too," said Q.

"What's that supposed to mean?"

"It means that you drove off that cliff and don't even know it," Quentin added.

"Amen to that," Hayley said and slapped Q's hand for a quick high-five.

Eamon frowned. "How fast the tide turns."

Hayley laughed while she shrugged. "Sorry, boss. I just call them like I see them. Your butt is lost. Soooo lost a GPS can't help you."

"Whatever. Just hold the place down while I'm gone." He looked at Quentin. "That also means try not to get arrested."

"Go. Have yourself a good time. Hayley and I got this. We have for a while now."

"Now, what is that supposed to mean?"

"It means that you've gone from working ninety-plus hours a week to pulling part-time hours like a high-school teenager. Don't get it twisted, there's nothing I like more than a good bachelor party. But it's been a while since you hosted one, now, hasn't it?"

Eamon had a hard time trying to shrug that one off. "We have plenty of people to host. That's the point of hiring competent employees, present company excluded."

Q brushed off the barb, dusting his shoulders. "Sticks and stones. The point is your ass is pussy-whipped."

Hayley snapped an invisible whip.

"Funny."

"It is," Q agreed. "You don't see too many brothers who fall in love with a woman who was trying to sue them into the poor house."

"C'mon on, man. Cut her some slack," Eamon said. "She dropped that case a while back. She was just lashing out because she was hurt." He shrugged. "I can't fault her for that."

"Of course not. Water under the bridge."

"Of course, I don't understand how her fiancé could have ever left a woman like her standing at the altar, either."

Q and Hayley shared an amused look before she cracked the whip again.

"Funny."

Quentin snickered. "Well. He must've had some kind of swag because he married Delicious. You got to watch these geeks. They're going to rule the world one day."

Hayley cut in. "Please. Delicious had that marriage annulled, like, two days after it happened. It wasn't anything serious. She gets married all the time."

Eamon frowned. "What?"

"Yeah. She doesn't see what the big deal is. Married on Saturday—annulled by Monday. Trust me, they are real familiar with her name down at the courthouse."

Eamon rolled that information around in his head for a minute but dismissed the idea of Marcus Henderson popping up one day looking to win his ex-fiancée back. "How come I didn't know about that?"

"I don't reckon you know much about anything. You haven't been paying too much attention to a whole lot of stuff since your billionaire heiress had you calling her name like her own little pep squad back in your office."

Eamon didn't get embarrassed too often, but this was one of those times. "I, uh, didn't know that you heard that."

"Are you kidding? I think everyone in the state of Nevada heard you," Hayley laughed. "And don't think that you were slick when you had to purchase a new office desk and fax machine. We know you two wrecked the place. You weren't foolin' nobody." Her gaze raked him up and down. "I might have to send my man to you so you can give him some tips, though."

Quentin puffed out his chest. "You can send him my way, too."

Hayley laughed. "Please. I don't need him taking lessons in 'ho-ism'."

"Ouch." Eamon held up his hand so that this time he would get the high five.

Q looked at his watch. "I thought you had somewhere to be, Mr. Whipped."

Eamon squinted and leaned in close. "You know, green really isn't your color."

"Don't play yourself. Nobody's jealous. I leave all that relationship BS to the fools who don't know any better. I'm riding the bachelor life until the wheels fall off this bastard."

"Whatever." Eamon waved him off. "Nobody said anything about turning in their bachelor card. I'm just taking the girl to a theme park. Calm down."

Once again, Q and Hayley exchanged looks and then said at the same time, "Denial."

"Why am I wasting my time with you two?" Eamon asked himself and turned away.

"Denial is the first step," Quentin shouted at Eamon's back.

Eamon just held up his hand and flipped his cousin the bird.

"Fine!" Q yelled as Eamon moved closer to the door. "You and Minnie skip on down the road. I'm going to go ahead and pencil in your bachelor party now!"

Eamon left the club just as the DJ was coming in to get set up before they opened.

Hayley looked over at Quentin. "Do you really think that he's going to marry that woman?"

He shrugged. "Only if she'll have him."

Bright and early the next morning, Eamon crept out of bed so that he could sneak down to the kitchen to make breakfast in bed for Victoria. He'd hoped to make her special day one that she would never forget. He was particularly anxious to get her to California for her day at the theme park. Most of his excitement was because of the simplicity of it. What exactly does one get a billionaire heiress?

Was it possible that he was looking forward to this day more than she was? After washing his hands, he quickly got started slicing and dicing, whipping and baking. Today's breakfast was a baked omelet with a bowl of fresh fruit and a mimosa. In the center of the tray, he placed a single red rose. Smiling like a Cheshire cat, he took the elevator up to the second floor and entered the bedroom singing "Happy Birthday."

It proved to be perfect timing because Victoria was just stirring in the lush pile of pillows and rubbing her eyes. When she heard him singing, her hands fell way from her face, as she blinked in total surprise at the approaching silver tray.

"Oh, my God. I don't believe this. You didn't have to do all this." She sat up as Eamon settled her breakfast over her lap and then leaned over for a kiss. "I wanted to do it. Happy birthday, Princess."

"Thank you." Her eyes misted with tears as she slid her arms around his thick neck so that she could deepen their kiss.

"Make sure that you make a wish," he told her.

Victoria smiled at the single candle placed in the center of her baked omelet. Closing her eyes, she wasn't sure what she was going to wish for but then it suddenly bubbled up from her heart. *I wish that we could always be this happy.* She leaned over and blew out the candle.

"What did you wish for?"

"If I tell you then it might not come true."

"Well, we can't have that, now, can we?"

Victoria shook her head and then quickly dived into her brunch. She knew before the food hit her taste buds that it was going to be good, and she wasn't disappointed. Closing her eyes, she leaned back against the pillows and emitted a long-winded moan.

"You know, I can't decide whether you moan louder when you're eating or when we're making love."

"It's a tie." She wiggled her brows at him and then finally noticed the card leaning against the rose vase. "What's this?"

"Why don't you open it and find out?"

Victoria picked up the card and tore it open. She nearly laughed out loud at the sight of a glittery Disney card with a collage of every Disney princess that had made it to film, with Princess Tiana taking center stage. "Aww. It's so beautiful. Thank you."

She leaned over again and rewarded him with a kiss.

"Wait. You didn't read it. 'Prepare for magic, Princess. Today a King will treat you like a Queen.'"

She glanced up. "Aww. How sweet."

Eamon puffed out his chest and shoulders. "I do what I can."

"Cheesy…but sweet," she amended, unable to resist the jab.

"Uh-huh. Eat up, Princess. We have a plane to catch."

Victoria's brows dipped. "Where are we going?"

"Disneyland. It's closer."

"What? You were serious? You're taking me to a theme park?"

"Absolutely. I'm a man of my word. And today, Princess Victoria, you are going to get your chance to be a kid." He turned toward the door so that he could go and get his own breakfast and then remembered. "Oh. And don't worry," he said, spinning back around to see her still sitting there in shock. "I will protect you from any and all unsavory-looking mice. If Mickey wants to get you, then he's going to have to go through me first."

"Okay. Now you're just being silly."

"Yeah. Just a little bit." Eamon shrugged and then tossed her a wink.

Two hours later, Eamon and Victoria boarded a private jet to Anaheim, California, bound for the Disney theme park. One look over at Victoria and he could tell that her excitement level was steadily increasing. Once she was inside the fantasy world she did indeed transform into a kid, especially when they hit the Adventure Park. Never had Eamon seen anyone so giddy to be in a bumper car—or anyone so lousy at driving them.

He had known for some time that she was a screamer, but absolutely nothing could have prepared him for the mighty wails she released as they sailed, dipped and whipped around on roller-coaster ride after roller-coaster ride. By the time the fireworks went off behind the iconic castle, Eamon was convinced that they had to have walked at least ten miles.

The priceless moment came when Victoria spotted the Mickey Mouse character from about twenty feet away. She froze instantly and then grabbed Eamon's hand and led him in the opposite direction. He laughed so hard he damn near split his sides.

It was close to midnight by the time they arrived back at his house. Victoria was so exhausted that Eamon literally had to scoop her out of the passenger seat of his Porsche and carry her into the house.

"Thank you so much for a wonderful birthday," she moaned, softly squeezing his neck, but lacking the energy to press a kiss against his face. "I had so much fun."

"Probably not as much fun as I had watching you."

He heard her sigh while he struggled to open the door, but once he made it inside it was smooth sailing getting her up to the bedroom.

"You're just too good to be true," Victoria moaned as he settled her onto the bed and began pulling off her shoes.

"I can't tell you how many times I tell myself that same thing." He tossed her a wink and then helped strip her out of her clothes before quickly joining her in the bed. The minute he was in, she curled up toward him and settled into her regular spot tucked underneath his arm.

Fleetingly, he thought about ending the night with them making love, but that was right about the time she started yawning. Once that happened, he knew his eyelids were struggling to stay open. That was all right though. He'd come to love just holding her as much as making love to her.

*Making love.* He'd been saying that a lot lately. When had their just having sex transformed into making love? And how much longer would this tranquility he felt with her last?

# Chapter 18

Victoria had transformed Eamon's study into a small office for herself. While he darted around town between the club, the restaurant and Bachelor Adventures, she still put in work for her father's company off-site. It was easy, since in her profession, all she needed was her trusted laptop. Her hours were a little whacky, because it was usually late when Eamon came in and of course she wanted to spend time with him, too. So she focused more on the Asian markets since she was just climbing out bed when there was only about an hour left in the trading day in New York.

That satisfied her father a bit, but he still pressured her to tell him when she was coming back home or whether she was moving to the West Coast permanently. So far, she'd managed to dodge having to give him a straight answer. But she would need to soon—for herself as well as her father.

Around midnight was when she really started to miss Eamon. She tried not to think of what went on in a gentlemen's club night after night because it was the only way to control any doubts about him falling to temptation. But what if he did? What then? It wasn't like they had discussed them being an exclusive item, right? She was pretty sure that she was the only one he was seeing. Hell, she had moved into his house, really. He came home every day and called constantly when he was away to check on her. So what was the problem?

*The problem is that you're playing house instead of holding out for the real thing.*

Frustrated, Victoria decided she needed to draw herself a bubble bath so she could try to relax. But no sooner had she sank into the hot water did she hear something in the master bedroom. "Eamon? Is that you?" She got a little excited about the idea of him coming home early tonight.

"Yeah. It's me!"

She squeezed her eyes and clenched her fist victoriously. "Yes," she whispered. But then when he was quiet for so long, she feared that he'd just simply rushed in and rushed back out to work. "Sweetheart? Whatcha doing?"

A second later, the bathroom door flew open and Eamon strolled in in his robe. It was a good thing that it was such a large tub because it looked like he was about to join her.

"What do you think you're doing?" she asked when he headed toward her.

Eamon dropped his robe and then struck a pose. "What do you think?"

Victoria howled with laughter, but that just encouraged Eamon to strike a few more poses.

"Don't front. You know you love it." He flexed his arms to showcase two boulder-size muscles in his biceps.

"Not bad. Not bad," she finally conceded. But when he turned all the way around and clenched his butt muscles for a backside pose, Victoria nearly drowned because she was laughing so hard.

"Sticks and stones, baby. Sticks and stones," Eamon said, stepping into the tub and easing down on the opposite end of the tub. He sighed like he was starring in an old Calgon commercial. "Now, this is the life," he said, scooping bubbles up against his chest. "I can get used to this."

"Uh-huh. You know, I like to think of my bubble baths as my *me* time," she hinted.

"Go ahead. You won't even notice that I'm here."

"Somehow I doubt that. That's kind of like trying to ignore an elephant in the room." She flicked her hand and sent a spray of water toward his face.

"Hey! Don't you see that I'm in the middle of my beauty regimen?" He paid her back by slapping his large hand into the tub. A large wall of water smacked her in the face.

Victoria sputtered and spat water and bubbles out. "Whoa. I didn't try to drown you." She tossed more water at him.

"Oh yeah?" He reached over and grabbed her foot.

"There you go, always playing dirty."

"Is there any other way?"

"C'mon. Stop playing."

Eamon's smile split from ear to ear, but he didn't release her foot. Not yet anyway. Instead, he started tickling the bottom of it, knowing full well that she was ticklish.

Victoria went wild, splashing water everywhere while laughing and trying to pull her foot back. When she finally succeeded, there was just as much water on the floor as there was in the tub.

Eamon had the nerve to try to scoot into a corner and act innocent, which was impossible to do wearing a Cheshire cat grin and having enough bubbles in his hair to make it look like he was wearing a Colonial-era white wig.

Her eyes narrowed, wishing that she could think of a way to exact revenge.

"Look, I'm just going to sit over here and mind my own business," he reasoned now that the damage was done.

Victoria retreated back to the other side of tub.

Eamon smiled and leaned back, but he quickly started more mischief when he looked over to the tub's edge at her collection of beauty products. "What's this?" He lifted up a spa-gel mask. "Ooh. I'm Zorro."

She rolled her eyes, but laughed when he strapped the mask on. "You look ridiculous."

"Not sexy?"

She hesitated. "Maybe a little of both."

"Ahhh." He waved a finger at her and started singing and shaking his hips. "You think I'm sexy."

"Take that off." She moved toward him and snatched the mask off his face.

"Hey!" He went back to pretending to be offended. "Didn't your parents ever teach you how to share?"

"Didn't yours teach you how to not be annoying?"

He thought about it and then simply said, "No." Eamon's attention went back to the counter. "Damn. I didn't know that it took this much work for you to look as good as you do. What's this green stuff?"

"Put that down," she snapped.

Eamon dropped the bottle and raised his hands in the air like the bathroom police had just raided the place. "Yes, ma'am."

"Did you come home just so that you could annoy me?"

"Absolutely not," he answered, as he contradicted himself by nodding.

It was hard for her to pretend that she was annoyed when she was happy to see him.

"It looks like you have everything in here but one thing," he said.

"And what's that?"

"You need a good back scrubber." He winked. "Come here."

She looked at him suspiciously. "You've gotta be kidding, right?"

"C'mon. I'll be on my best behavior."

She didn't move.

"Promise," he added, crossing his heart.

Victoria didn't miss that he also folded his arm behind his back. No doubt so that he could cross his fingers. But it was hard to resist such an irresistible face. He was too handsome for his own good. "All right. But if you try any funny stuff, I'm going to get you back when you least expect it."

"Deal."

She held out her hand for him to shake on it, but he frowned. "What? My word doesn't mean anything to you?"

Victoria rolled her eyes, not believing that she was about to give him the benefit of the doubt. When she settled in between his legs, Eamon laughed like a mad scientist.

"Now I have you in my trap." He wrapped his arms around her and then started blowing raspberries against the column of her neck.

Victoria squealed.

"I got you and I'm never letting go," he exclaimed. Soon

after, his laughter died when his words bounced back off the bathroom tile. *Had he sensed that she didn't want him to ever let her go?*

Silence hung between for a long time before Victoria looked back at him over her shoulder. "So are you going to wash my back or is this just a cheap way for you to cop a feel?"

Her sly smile succeeded in pulling Eamon back to reality. "Would it bother you if I said yes to both?"

"Not at all."

They laughed and Eamon got busy. He took his time, washing her back. Every once in a while, he'd bend forward and plant kisses among the soapy bubbles. Once she was cleaned to his satisfaction, he instructed her to lean back so that he could now concentrate on the other side.

She complied without complaint.

He started at her shoulders, got lost in a trance when a stream of soapy bubbles raced through the valley between her breasts and beyond. Before long, he glided the sponge lower. It went around the valley, over her quivering flat abs and then disappeared into the water.

Once he was in the zone, he released the sponge and instead plunged his fingers through the opening of her legs. Victoria moaned and turned her head up toward him. In response, Eamon lowered his head and captured her soft lips into a kiss while his fingers continued to rock back and forth inside of her.

It didn't take long for her to start squirming and thrusting her hips. That only encouraged him to deepen the kiss. He loved her taste and how their tongues danced erotically together. Her squirming gave way to quivering. When she hit her pinnacle, Eamon swallowed her orgasmic whimper.

After they climbed out of the tub, Eamon retrieved the towels and took time to pat her dry. The bedroom was already lit with candles. "I'm a man who plans," he said with a wink.

She was surprised at seeing towels on the bed, but when he picked up a bottle of warm baby oil, she understood.

"Why don't you just lie down right here so I can show off another talent I have?"

"Gladly." Victoria lay on her stomach and folded her hands underneath her chin.

Eamon climbed onto the bed, straddling her with his thick thighs. When the first drop of oil hit her skin, Victoria jumped a bit but he kept pouring a steady stream down the center of her back. After he capped the bottle, he massaged the oil into her soft skin with all the practiced ease of a professional masseur.

"That feels so good."

Again Eamon got caught up in making languid circles across her back.

The oil slowly started to warm up to a nice body-temperature heat. Victoria couldn't help moaning again. By the time Eamon had worked his way down to her lower back, she was as limp as a wet noodle.

"Does it feel good, Princess?"

"It feels divine."

He liked hearing that. Eamon continued kneading her body, determined not to miss a single inch. He moved his hands over the nice curves of her butt and for a brief moment he imagined his brick-hard erection sliding down the center. It looked like an erotic picture of a hot dog and bun.

He smiled, but he kept the juvenile thought to himself. Instead he reached for the bottle of oil again and poured two streams of the liquid over each cheek and even on the back of her thighs before massaging the oil into her skin. Trying to remain a good boy was becoming increasingly hard. As his hands worked in between her thighs, his fingers grazed her pussy.

Victoria quivered, causing her lush booty to jiggle a little bit. So of course, he did it again. This time his oiled fingertips eased inside of her and then mixed with her own natural lubrication.

"Mmm."

"Looks like you're getting wet again, Princess," he said as he worked a second finger inside of her. She was even wetter. The room came alive with the sound of her rapturous moans and the soft sound of his hand sloshing around in her jar of honey. But nothing was getting him harder than the sight of her butt bouncing in front of him.

"Oh God," she cried, panting.

Eamon knew that she was seconds from another orgasm. He bent down and tattooed her ass with small kisses. "You want me to go faster or slower, Princess?"

"F-faster," Victoria answered, rolling her hips.

Following orders, Eamon slid in another finger and then gave her exactly what she asked for.

In no time, she released a high-pitch squeal and he watched with amusement when she clenched her butt cheeks tight as wave after wave crashed over her. Picking up the massage-oil bottle, Eamon finished rubbing down the rest of her while she collected herself.

"Are you relaxed now?"

Victoria slowly rolled over and smiled up at him. "You have no idea. I swear, I don't know what I'll do if something ever happens to your hands."

He smiled. "I guess that makes two of us."

Victoria sat up and grabbed the bottle from him. "My turn."

"Ah," he said, catching the glint in her eye and recognizing that her competitive nature had just kicked in. "All right. Let's see what you got."

They quickly exchanged positions, but when he lay on his stomach, she threw in a curve.

"No. I want you to lie on your back."

Eamon turned around and looked at her.

She was serious.

"Okay. It's going to be that kind of oil job, eh?"

"Like yours was sooo aboveboard. Now turn over," Victoria ordered.

"With pleasure," Eamon said, rolling over and tucking his hands behind his head.

Victoria smiled and climbed on top, her thighs straddling him.

While she dribbled oil onto his chest, Eamon's eyes settled on the sight of her pretty pink pussy peeking out from her open legs. "Now, this is what I call heaven."

Victoria ignored the comment and started working the oil into his skin.

Smiling, he liked the way her slender fingers slipped and slid across his chest, he also liked the sight of her breasts swaying as she moved, as well. She inched her way down, gliding over his waist, but he nearly came unglued when his cock snaked between her legs, glided through the center of her pussy and bounced straight up in the air in front of her as she eased farther down his body.

But whatever disappointment he felt for the missed opportunity, it disappeared when her oily fingers wrapped around his fat cock and proceeded to slide down its thick length. Shuddering, Eamon sucked in a breath.

Victoria smiled. "It looks like I have your undivided

attention." She circled her hand around the fat head and then slid it back down the growing length. "I kind of like that."

He opened his mouth to respond, but she picked that very moment to increase her hand's speed. Of course, he forgot what the hell he was about to say. The sight of her caramel skin racing along his glistening black dick not only increased the speed of his rising nut, but also caused his toes to curl and his stomach muscles to quiver.

"Ah. Looks like somebody is about to come," Victoria teased. "Is that what you're about to do, sweetheart?" She leaned forward so that she could ease his glossy cock in between her breasts. Once she had him snuggled between her full D-cups, she pressed her hands on either side of her breasts and squeezed them together. When she started sliding them up and down, Eamon's breathing became chaotic and pearl-shaped drops of pre-cum oozed from the head of his cock and drizzled down like cake icing onto her caramel-colored breasts, making them look like a beautiful erotic dessert.

"Aw. Yeah. You're about to come," Victoria teased. "Aren't you, sweetheart? But, you know, maybe I should stop." And she did. "I mean. You're always playing too much," she said thoughtfully.

Eamon's eyes doubled in size. "N-no. No I don't."

She cocked her head. "I don't know if you deserve to come."

"W-what? Stop playing."

"Oh. But I thought you liked playing." She slid her breasts down for one good stroke and then stopped again. "Isn't that what you like to do?"

Eamon tried to cheat by thrusting his hips, but when he did that she removed her breasts from his cock. "Wait.

Where are you going?" he asked, sounding like a man disoriented with fever.

"What? You want something?"

"Aw. Don't do this."

A smile exploded across her face. "Don't do what, baby?"

"All right. All right. I'll stop playing so much."

She hitched up a brow. "Is that right?" She eased him back in between her breasts for another breaststroke. "Is that a promise?"

Eamon sighed with instant relief.

"So from now on you're going to stop when I tell you to?"

He moaned as his eyes fluttered closed.

She stopped. "I asked you a question."

His eyes flew open. "Yes. Yes!"

"It looks like we have ourselves a deal." She gave him a few more breaststrokes before adding, "I think that deserves something a little extra special."

Eamon hardly had time to process what she said before she leaned her head down and stretched her mouth over the head of his cock.

Every ounce of air flew out of Eamon's lungs, partly because he was surprised and partly because of the feeling of glorious ecstasy. In the four months that they had been together, he had never asked or expected her to reciprocate his love of oral sex. He just assumed that was something that she wasn't into and accepted it. But now feeling his cock gliding back and forth in her warm mouth was damn near bringing tears to his eyes.

Her breasts sprung away from his shaft while she adjusted herself so that she had more room to suck him deeper. Occasionally, he would hit the back of her throat and he would hear her gag a bit, but that didn't stop her flow.

In no time at all, Eamon's nut was rushing through him like a freight train. He bolted upright and then tried to pull her loving mouth away so that he could have just a little bit of time to slow the train down. But it was far too late. A bright, white light flashed before his eyes, momentarily blinding him as a roar tore through his throat.

Victoria's lips popped off his cock just as he exploded like a volcano.

"Oh, God." He shuddered and then plopped back down onto the bed, trying to catch his breath. He closed his eyes and must've dozed off for a second because the next thing he knew Victoria was lovingly cleaning him up with a warm wet towel.

"That was amazing," he praised.

Victoria smiled and climbed up to snuggle next to him. "I'm glad that you enjoyed it, but I'm holding you to our deal."

"What deal was that?" he asked, faking amnesia.

That just got him a hard slap on the chest. "Play if you wanna, but that will be the last blow job you get from me."

"Oh, yeah?"

"Yeah." She reached over for a pillow and then smacked him dead in the face.

"All right, now. Go ahead with that."

*Pow!*

"Say something else slick," she dared, smiling.

"Please. I know you can't resist all this sexy chocolate." He stretched his chest and tried to flex his muscles.

Victoria rolled her eyes. "Oh, brother, please."

Eamon curled toward her and peppered kisses along her neck. "All I have to say is Princess, baby. Can Daddy come play in your funhouse?"

She giggled, mainly because he was being silly and his lips tickled.

"You know what you're going to say?" he asked and then started mimicking a female voice. "Oh, sure, Big Daddy. You can come play."

Victoria howled. "Please. I don't talk like that."

"Go ahead and say it. '"Oh, sure, Big Daddy.'"

Still laughing, she weakly pushed him away.

Eamon remained persistent. "C'mon. Say it."

"No. Stop."

"I'm not going to leave you alone until you say it." Then he got her with a sneak attack by tickling her sides.

Victoria screamed and lost her grip on her pillow. After that, Eamon was straddling her again while he tickled her mercilessly.

"I'm waiting. Say it."

She held out for as long as she could, but it came down to making a decision between being able to breathe or winning this silly standoff. "All right! *Oh, Big Daddy.*"

"No. No. Say it right."

"Oh, sure, Big Daddy— Oh. I can't breathe."

"Oh, sure, Big Daddy what?" he asked, refusing to give an inch.

"Y-you can come play in my funhouse."

Finally he stopped tickling her sides and pumped his fist into the air. "Now who's the King?"

Victoria pulled in a deep breath, grabbed a pillow and then swung it so hard, it knocked him back over to his side. "Big jerk."

He laughed and pulled her back up against him. "Yeah, but you *love* this big jerk, don't you?"

It wasn't a question that he'd meant to ask, but there it was—hanging in the air between them. For a few seconds, though, it felt like a lifetime as they stared and searched into each other's eyes. He didn't even realize that he was holding his breath while he waited for an answer.

"Yes," she said. "I do."

## Chapter 19

*She loves me.*

Eamon really knew that he was in trouble. The only thing was he couldn't figure out whether it was the good kind of trouble or the bad. He had focused his entire adult life trying to succeed in businesses that, at times, even he thought were impossible. During those years, he believed that the kind of love he had experienced with Karen so many years ago was something that could only happen maybe once in a lifetime—and that was if you were lucky. Most of the evidence around him supported that theory. There were some exceptions. For example: his parents. Even then it was easy to ascribe their marital bliss to their being part of a different generation.

It had taken so long for him to recover from that devastating heartbreak over Karen that he just couldn't ever see it happening again. *Just like Quentin.* Eamon dragged in a deep breath and shook his head. Maybe it was time to admit that he had been wrong about his cousin, as well. Yes, he was a spoiled rich kid, but there was definitely more to him than met the eye.

*Just like Victoria.*

It was time to stop trying to rationalize, dismiss or shrug off what was clearly happening to him all over again. What was the point? According to Q and Hayley, he wasn't fooling anyone. Somehow, somewhere and some way he had gone from being a man who couldn't be dragged away from work to being a man who dreaded going to work. He dreaded leaving Victoria's side for fear he'd miss a joke or a smile or a laugh.

His once-treasured bachelor pad had been invaded with more and more of her stuff. Half of his wardrobe had been relocated to another closet. His bathroom counter was littered with what looked like a mini-mall of makeup and perfume bottles. He even noticed her adding little decorating touches around the place to give it more of a feminine feel. Before she arrived, he would've thought that would've freaked him out or, at the very least, pushed all his panic buttons. Instead, he liked that she was making herself at home.

Eamon loved waking up next to her as well as teasing her about her need to compulsively organize everything. Plus, she had a fierce competitive side. Really. Would it really hurt her to let him win a swimming race every now and then? Then there were her lousy attempts to learn how to cook. A couple of nights ago, she insisted on cooking a meal by herself. It was generous to say that it was edible— but he ate it, smiling the whole time and wondering if he'd paid that month's healthcare premium just in case he would be needing to see the doctor that night. Then this morning, she was so proud of sewing a line of buttons on one of his shirts—all crooked, but at least they were on there.

"That's wonderful, Princess." The lie was worth the beautiful smile she gave him.

It was time to face it—everything was better when Victoria was around. It wasn't one-sided, either. He was convinced that he was good for her, as well. Gone was that huge chip on her shoulder. She smiled easier, laughed harder and every time they made love...*made love*. There was that word again. When had sex with no strings attached become making love?

Searching his mind, he struggled to think of any one particular moment. It was more like a slow, steady progression, if he had to guess.

When they were together, he was certain that he had discovered all her secret G-spots. He sensed when she wanted to be dominated and when she craved a more cherished, intimate connection or she simply wanted to play.

Today, he played hooky from The Dollhouse again to take Victoria on a romantic gondola ride on the canal, snaking through the Venetian Hotel. It was like taking a trip through Venice, floating under bridges and balconies while a singing gondolier paddled behind them.

"Tell me more about your brother Jeremy. Was he ever into sports like Xavier?"

"And risk messing up his pretty-boy face?" Eamon laughed. "Hardly."

"Oh? Is he *that* good-looking?"

Eamon's face twisted. For a split second Quentin and Sterling's spat over a woman rushed to the forefront of his mind. "No. He's butt-ugly. We kept him hidden in the basement so that he wouldn't scare everyone in the neighborhood."

Victoria slapped him on the chest. "Be serious."

"What makes you think I'm not?"

"Because I already saw a picture of him in the house. You and your brothers look a lot alike. I was just teasing you."

"Yeah…well, don't be getting any funny ideas about trading me in for a younger version. I don't think that I can handle that."

She thrust up her chin and cut her eyes away. "I'll make no such promises."

"All right, now. Don't get tossed into this canal for getting sassy." He pulled her up against his chest.

Victoria snuggled close. "But seriously. Tell me something about him."

"Here's a little story about my little brother Jeremy. Once when he was about six, he'd found this box of puppies out in the woods. Anyway, he brought the puppies home. But our dad said that we couldn't afford to keep them and that we would have to either take them to the pound or maybe try and find someone who would adopt them.

"Jeremy didn't like that so he decided to run away with the puppies. It sent the entire family into an uproar. My parents went on the local media and pleaded to the community to help find him. I remembered being terrified that they would never find him. After all, he was so small and so trusting. He was gone for, like, two days before his best friend, Roy, dropped dime on him and confessed that he was living in his backyard in his tree house."

"You're kidding me," Victoria interrupted.

Eamon shook his head. "When he came home, all the adults showered him with tears and kisses. Me and Xavier had different reactions. Once we got him alone we tackled him to the floor. Xavier beat him up a little bit for scaring him so bad and I think I went the whole summer refusing to talk to him for the same reason." That was Eamon's earliest memory of experiéncing the loss of a loved one. He hated that overwhelming sense of helplessness. It paralyzed him.

"Like I said before, he's a good guy. He and Xavier have sworn to be lifelong bachelors. 'Too many women and not enough time' is one of his favorite sayings."

Victoria hitched up a dubious brow. "Only Jeremy and Xavier took this vow of singlehood? What about you?"

"Me?" he stalled.

"Yeah, you." She poked a finger in his chest. "Is that the real reason you're not married? You've taken a vow?"

Eamon shook his head. "Naw. You got me all wrong." He paused and then confessed, "I wanted to get married once."

"Oh?" Surprise lit her eyes. "When was this?"

For a moment, Eamon regretted that he'd turned down this road. "It was a while back. Right after college." Maybe he should've left it at that, but Victoria's patient silence had the truth spilling out of him. "She was, uh, my high-school sweetheart. We bonded over music. She wanted to be a rapper and I thought that I was going to be a songwriter or a producer or something."

Victoria nodded.

"Anyway. We dated all through high school and then split up when she went to college in Chicago and I stayed in Georgia. After we got through our freshman year, when everyone thought that we'd break up, we realized that there was a real possibility that we could make it work. So that's what we did. We took turns visiting one another, which was very hard since we were broke as a joke. By the time graduation day neared, I knew that I wanted to make her my wife." A lump started growing in his throat.

"So what happened?" Victoria asked.

"I, uh, took out a loan. Bought this beautiful engagement ring that if you got up real close and squinted your eyes just right, you could see the diamond chip in it."

Victoria laughed.

"Hey. It was all I could afford at the time," he joked.

She smiled. "Sorry. Go ahead."

A couple of seconds later, Eamon's smile faded. "Then…came graduation. Since both of our schools were doing their ceremonies on the same day, we were going to miss seeing each other's commencement ceremonies. But the good news was that she was going to be driving down right afterward. So we were going to see each other soon. No big deal. I got up, packed up a picnic basket, put the ring in my pocket and went over to Karen's parents' house to pick her up."

He fell silent again.

Victoria tried to wait him out, but he was silent for so long, she thought he wasn't going to finish the story. Yet it was too big a cliffhanger for her to just let it go. "She turned you down?"

He released a cynical chuckle. "That would've been easier to deal with."

Confusion blanketed her face.

"I would've even preferred it if she had just decided not to show up but…" He sucked in a deep breath. "Anything would've been better than to have her father tell me that his daughter didn't make it home because she was killed by a drunk driver."

Victoria gasped. "Nooo."

A tear skipped down Eamon's face, but he quickly chased after it and wiped it away. "I stood out on that stoop with that diamond ring in my pocket for I don't know how long. Hell, to this day I don't even remember how I got home. I just knew that…she was gone."

"Baby, I'm so sorry." She leaned up and planted a kiss against his face. "I can only imagine how hard that must have been."

It was horrible and though he'd healed considerably since that time, he knew that Karen would always have a place in his heart.

Victoria squeezed his hand.

Eamon glanced down and stared at it for a long time. There was a certain kind of magic in her touch that truly made him feel that everything really was going to be all right—and that there was a possibility that there was room in his heart for two women.

His gaze roamed from her hand and climbed up to her beautiful face only to see her eyes glisten with tears. "Hey, there's no need for these."

"It's just that I didn't have any idea."

"Of course you didn't. You couldn't have." He wrapped his arm back around her and then tucked her in the crook of his arm, the place where she belonged.

# Chapter 20

*May, New York*

"I do have to admit that you seem much happier," Grace said, staring at Victoria over lunch at The Garden.

Beside her, Iris studied Victoria with the same intensity. "Yes. There does seem to be a bit of a glow about you. Las Vegas agrees with you." She lifted her champagne glass. "To finally getting your pipes clean."

Laughing, Grace and Victoria raised their glasses, as well.

"I'll drink to that." Victoria tapped their glasses, but she only managed a small sip before they dove straight in for the dirt.

"So does this mean you're finally returning to New York, or is this a temporary thing?" Grace asked. "I have to tell you that things haven't been the same here without you. It's wedding season and we have received a slew of—"

Iris gave Grace a quick elbow-jab.

"What? Oh." Grace lowered her gaze to her food. "I'm sorry. I forgot."

Victoria waved off their concerns. "Please. I'm hardly sensitive about the idea of people getting married. You can say Marcus's name around me, too, if you want. I'm so over that period in my life."

The twins glanced at each other, undoubtedly to exchange another round of telepathic messages.

"Forget about it. It's a long story. All you need to know is that I'm happy now—truly happy." Victoria couldn't stop smiling. It was on the tip of her tongue to tell them that sometimes happy didn't really seem like a strong enough word. Hell, at any given moment she wanted to break out singing old love songs.

"To answer your question, I'm just visiting for the weekend. I figured that should be long enough to assure my father that I'm fine and I'm not being held hostage in Vegas."

"He's just concerned," Grace said. "Hell, we all have been to tell you the truth. You just up and left. That was sooo not like you."

Victoria smiled. "Maybe it is the new me."

The twins' brows leaped in curiosity at the same time.

"What was it that you called me again?" Victoria lifted her head and tapped a finger against her chin until suddenly snapping her fingers as if she'd recalled the term. "An anal control freak. That was it."

Grace's face reddened. "I guess that was a bit harsh."

"A little bit," Victoria agreed. "But you were right. And I'm not saying that I've changed *completely* but I think I've changed a few things that matter."

The twins continued to smile at her, but Victoria could

see that they were anxious. She sighed and leaned back in her chair waiting for the next round of attack. She didn't have a long wait.

Grace leaned in first. "I'm just concerned about whether any of this is...*rational*."

"Rational?"

"Yes. I mean...to just up and move in with a man that you hardly know."

"I know him now. I've been living with him for the last six months."

"And that's another thing," Grace continued. "I never pegged you for the type to move in with a man. I know we're modern women and all, but like my grandmother out in the country says, 'Why buy the cow if you can get the milk for free?'"

"Women aren't cows."

"But you understand the metaphor, don't you?"

"Look. I really appreciate everyone's concern, but I know what I'm doing. Eamon and I are very happy. Isn't that enough?"

"So you guys are officially an item? Boyfriend and girlfriend?" Iris asked.

"Well, we're not putting any labels on it."

The twins looked at each other.

"We are in an exclusive relationship."

"Mainly because you just moved into his house," Iris said.

"Because I just know. He's not seeing anyone and I'm not—"

"Why not?" Grace interrupted. "With all the men roaming around in Las Vegas, why Eamon King? You just dropped everything in your life to go chase after a man who runs a chain of strip clubs? He's not seeing anyone? There's like twenty to thirty women who work for him that run around naked every day. That's way too much temptation."

"Eamon is not like that."

"He's a man, isn't he?"

Victoria clenched her teeth and shifted around in her seat. The pessimism of New Yorkers. How could she forget? She just tossed up her hands. "You know, let's just drop the subject."

Grace ignored her. "All I'm saying is that I was all for you loosening up and letting your hair down every *once* in a while. I didn't mean for you to totally lose your grip on reality."

"Wow. Okay. Clearly you two can't handle the fact that I have moved on and have found someone who completes me. I'm sorry about that, but it's your problem, not mine. I don't have to justify *anything* to you."

"Victoria, I didn't mean—"

"Yes, you did." Victoria struggled to remain cordial. "I really, *really* want to believe that your concerns are coming from a good place. That is the only reason that I'm not cussing you out right now. That, plus that would have been the old me. Now I just want to sit here and enjoy my lunch with my favorite cousins and hear about what's going on with you two lately."

Before either of them had a chance to respond, a familiar voice spoke from behind her.

"Well, I'll be damned. Look who has decided to return to New York."

Victoria didn't bother to turn around. She just rolled her eyes and mentally counted to ten. "Hello, Lolita. Fancy meeting you here today."

Lolita reached the table and smiled snidely at her. "Well, they say it's a small world, after all." She circled the table with her fake green-contact-lens eyes, and gave Grace and Iris the same wintry smile. "Hello, ladies."

The twins just nodded and folded their arms.

"My, my, my. Clearly money can't buy you class—or manners."

"But you keep trying, don't you?" Victoria asked.

The twins snickered.

Lolita's jaw twitched as her evil gaze focused on Victoria. "Cute. I'm just glad that your pimp in Las Vegas finally gave you time off to come and visit your family and friends. Clearly he's quite the slave-driver since it's been six months since anyone has seen hide nor hair of you in polite society."

"How would you know? Have you been listening under the bathroom stalls again when you should've been cleaning the toilets?"

"Damn," Grace said. "It looks like the old Victoria is still in there after all."

Lolita opened her mouth to unleash another attack, but Victoria held up a single finger to cut her off.

"Let me stop you right now before you write a check your ass can't cash. Don't think that just because we're up in the Four Seasons that I won't snatch that horsehair off your head. I will. And you might as well stop rocking your neck at me because you're looking like a bobble-head to me right now.

"Listen up because I'm going to say this *one* time. We are family, but we sure as hell are *not* friends. So I'm about to make you a deal. You stay the hell out of my life and I'll stay out of yours. I don't care if you see me walking down the street, walk on by and keep my name out of your mouth. Anything other than that, then we are going to have a problem. You got that?" Victoria's heated gaze melted Lolita's frosty one. "Good. Have a nice life."

Lolita stood there for a half a second, looking like she wanted to say something, but clearly wasn't sure whether Victoria would make good on her threat.

"Don't make me count to two," Victoria said.

"Whatever." Lolita tossed her head back and stormed away.

"Well," Iris said, reaching for her champagne again, "You still got it."

Victoria shrugged the incident off. "Only for special cases, and Lolita is definitely a special head case."

"Still," Grace hedged. "She's not the only one who's been talking."

"Please. And I don't care what people are saying anymore. I truly don't. I've made the decision to live my life the way I want to live it. I can't begin to tell you how liberating it is to finally not care about what other people think." She stopped for a brief moment to draw in a deep breath while she searched for the right words. "You know, I never told you girls this before, but do you remember my ninth birthday party? My mother put together this huge, over-the-top circus."

Iris nodded. "Yeah. I believe so."

"Remember around about halfway through it I went to my room and refused to come back out?"

Grace nodded. "Yes. It was a real diva moment. You wouldn't even come out to open up your presents."

"I wasn't being a diva," Victoria said. "I was upstairs in my room crying my eyes out."

"Why?"

Victoria sucked in another breath. "I'd gone to use the bathroom, but I stumbled on Tracy Hickman and her mother having a little argument. Tracy was whining and complaining that she wanted to go home because she didn't want to be there and she didn't like me."

"I never really liked Tracy Hickman," Iris said. "She is really a bitch."

"Amen," Grace agreed. "Not to mention that she's been married four times already. I mean, damn. I'm starting to think that she just does it just to have a wedding."

Victoria had thought the same thing. "Anyway, I would have been fine with it being just her. But it was her mother's response that really shook me to the core."

"What did she say?" Iris asked.

"She knelt down to Tracy's eye level and told her firmly that *nobody* liked me and that the only reason everyone came was because my father had a lot of money."

The twins gasped. "That bitch!"

Victoria nodded. "I was crushed. There I was thinking that all these kids came because they were my friends and it turned out that it was all a lie. It didn't help that I was a chubby kid and already had a complex because Tracy was calling me fat all the time. And then there was David Benson."

"Humph!" Iris frowned. "Never liked him, either."

"My first boyfriend in high school. We got into some silly argument that I don't even remember what it was about, and in a fit of rage, he shouted that if it wasn't for my father that nobody would even have anything to do with me. It hurt like hell mainly because for a long time I thought it was true. It was the confirmation that I needed to build up my defenses, protect myself—and my heart the best way I could. I started keeping people at a distance. I became very good at deciphering who was around me because they were truly my friend or who was there because they were trying to climb New York's social ladder. I'd rather have no friends than fake friends. I went overboard trying to control everything, including who *on paper* would make a good husband. Marcus didn't turn too many heads in the looks department, which I foolishly thought meant there was little chance of him running off with another woman." She rolled her eyes. "But we were never in love. At least, I wasn't."

The twins reached across the table and covered her hand with theirs.

"We are your friends…as well as your family."

"Yes. You are. And I cherish you more than you'll ever know. Look, I realize that I have been fortunate to be born into a lifestyle of privilege. I'm just saying that money doesn't buy you friends, and it certainly doesn't buy you love."

"And that's what you have with Eamon?" Grace asked.

A smile finally returned to Victoria's face. "Yes. I believe so. You told me that I should let loose and take chances. For the first time in my life I've done just that. I've jumped off a cliff with my eyes closed. And for the moment, it just feels like I'm flying. It's not just because he's handsome, or that he's financially secure in his own right or even that he really knows how to turn me on in bed."

The twins squealed with delight and Victoria jumped out of her seat to slap a hand over their mouths. Nevertheless, that didn't stop them from clapping their hands and stomping their feet under the table. When they finally calmed down, she removed her hand.

"I swear I can't tell you two anything." But she tossed them a wink while her face heated with embarrassment.

"Please, please say you're going to kiss and tell," Iris said breathlessly.

Victoria glanced around. "Now, you know I don't normally do this," she whispered. "But let's just say that he really knows how to get my body to feel things that it has never ever felt before."

The twins started to squeal again, but at Victoria's narrowed gaze they slapped a hand over their own mouths.

When Grace removed her hand, she pointed. "Are you blushing?" Then her eyes lit up. "Oh, my God, you are! What on earth has this man done to you?"

"Let's just say that he has made me a woman," Victoria confessed. "Totally and completely, in every way that a man can."

"Geez. We just thought that he would make a good booty call."

Victoria shook her head because she thought that she wasn't getting through to them. "It's not just the sex. We laugh together. I mean I *really* laugh. And he's smart… and romantic. He's teaching me how to cook. I've learned how to sew."

"Oh, my God. He has turned you into his maid," Grace gasped.

"Don't be silly." Victoria waved her off. "I *wanted* to learn how to do these things. In fact, I was a little embarrassed that I didn't know how already. It's really sweet to see him eat my food even though I know it tastes awful and he praises me when I sew buttons on his shirt and they're far from being straight. But the most important part is that I don't think he gives a damn about my money or who my parents are. He just loves me."

Iris cocked her head while she continued to smile with big moon eyes. "Aww. That sounds so romantic. Is that what he told you?"

Victoria shrugged. "Well, not in so many words." She lowered her head.

The twins looked at each other.

"C'mon. Don't do that. He loves me."

"But he *hasn't* said the words?"

"He doesn't have to."

The twins picked up their forks simultaneously and started picking over their meal.

Victoria watched them, wanting to continue to argue her point. But for the first time, doubt pricked her armor of confidence. So she shut up and ate her lunch.

By the time Victoria and the twins parted ways and she was headed out to her parents' estate, her mind churned with questions. She had only been in the city for a couple of hours and she could already feel herself reverting to her old ways. Outside the window of the cab, she watched the world's largest melting pot flit around like they were late in responding to a three-alarm fire. She might have missed a lot of things about New York, but its hectic pace wasn't one of them.

She missed Las Vegas's easy and laid-back atmosphere and she missed Eamon.

"Oh, there you are," her mother, Ceyla, sang, opening her arms. She quickly pulled her daughter in for a tight hug and then rained kisses across the side of her face. "I can't tell you how much we've missed you. Your father is going to be so happy to see you." She closed the door behind her. "I think if you stayed away another day your father and I were going to be on the next thing smoking to Las Vegas."

Victoria laughed as she peeled out of her jacket.

"I'm not joking. Your father had mapped out an entire plan as to how to kidnap you."

"Yes. I sensed that talking to him over the phone yesterday."

Her mother pulled back and stared at her. "Oh, my. I hate to say it, but Las Vegas agrees with you."

"I keep hearing that.

"Well, you look different." Ceyla captured Victoria's face in her hands so that she could study her. "There's a certain glow about you. It couldn't be that you're in love, could it?"

Victoria blushed all over again, but this time she decided to be more cautious in bragging about the virtues of love and happiness, especially now that she had a few more questions. "Maybe it's because I'm getting a bit more sun."

"Is that what you young people are calling it these days?" Her mother winked. "I don't know who this Eamon King is, but he already has my vote if he's making you this happy."

Victoria hadn't realized how much she needed to hear that until the words flowed out of her mother's mouth. It instantly cleared up a lot of the damage her doubting had caused. "Thanks, Mom." She delivered a quick peck on her cheek.

"Is that who I think it is?" Mondell Gregory thundered, strolling out of his study. "Well, I'll be damned. That woman right there looks like my little girl." He stopped and cocked his head. "Yeah. I believe that's her, but it's been so long I'm not sure."

"Hello, Daddy."

"Come here, little girl." He threw open his arms and gave her an old-fashioned bear hug. "Oh, sweetheart. Don't you ever stay away that long again."

"I won't."

"That better be a promise." He planted a kiss on the top of her head and then released her. "So. Where is this Eamon King? I have a bone to pick with him for keeping my daughter away for so long."

Victoria frowned. "Uh. There must be some misunder-
standing. Eamon didn't come with me."

Mondell's brows dipped. "And why the hell not? Is he
afraid to meet me like a man or something?"

"Actually, I didn't think to invite him," she admitted.

"Then maybe you're the one who doesn't want me to
meet this gentleman."

"Is that true, Victoria?" her mother asked.

"No. I just didn't think that you guys wanted to meet
him." Well, it wasn't *exactly* true. It was more like she
didn't want to scare Eamon by suggesting that she'd like
for him to meet her parents. That sort of thing tended to
freak men out, especially since they technically hadn't
established that they were an item.

Her parents exchanged looks much like the way the
twins did during their telepathic messaging thing.

Mondell slid his hands into his pockets and rocked back
on his heels. "Now, that doesn't make a lick of sense, baby
girl. Why wouldn't we want to meet the man that you've
been shacking up with for the last six months?"

Victoria tried to smooth things over by smiling wider
and leaning against his side. "Dad. This isn't the sixties.
They don't call it shacking up anymore."

"I don't care if it's the year three-thousand. You know
how I feel about all that sexual liberation talk."

"Now, Mondell. Remember your blood pressure."

"I'm fine. I took my medicine this morning," he said
to Ceyla. "I'm trying to make a point here. A man and a
woman should not live together without getting married.
Excuse me if I'm old-fashioned. But what is the incentive
for a man to buy a ring when he's getting all the benefits
without it?"

Victoria sucked in a deep breath. This looked like it
was going to be a long afternoon.

"I guess it's too much to ask whether you two are sleeping in separate rooms?"

Her mother gasped. "Mondell!"

"What?"

"I'm not about to let you stand there and interrogate her about her love life."

"She shouldn't be doing anything that she can't talk about. She keeps reminding me that she's grown."

"Daddy, can I at least come in and sit down before you give me the third degree?"

Despite him looking like he wanted to argue his point some more, her father stepped back with his lips pressed together.

"Don't pay your father any attention. We lived together a year before we were married."

"Ceyla!"

"What? It's true." She wrapped her arms around Victoria's waist and led her out toward the back patio.

"You're supposed to have my back. I'm trying to make a point here."

Victoria and her mother snickered as they walked away arm in arm. They convened out on the patio. Her parents' butler, Aaron, smiled and welcomed her back home before serving them tall glasses of lemonade.

However, it just took ten minutes before her father was ready to dive back in. "So when will we get a chance to meet this young man? Mind you that my patience is wearing thin."

Ceyla opened her mouth, but her father cut her off.

"And don't tell me that I'm being unreasonable. You've been pacing around here, wondering the same thing yourself."

Her mother snapped her mouth shut and then looked over at Victoria guiltily.

With her one remaining wall of defense crumbling, Victoria had to come up with some real answers. "You'll meet him, Dad. I promise."

"When?" he pressed.

"Soon" was all she could come up with. "You'll meet him when the time is right…and we're comfortable and clear where we stand with each other."

Mondell frowned while her mother reached for her hand again.

"Is everything all right?"

"Everything's fine. We're still just in the getting-to-know-you stage. Meeting the parents comes later when we know exactly where we're headed. That's all."

Her father shook and grumbled under his breath. "Well, I was going to tell you this later, but I might as well go ahead and put it out there."

"Mondell—" Ceyla warned and shook her head.

"It's all right," he said, ignoring her warning.

Victoria frowned at the awkward pivot in conversation.

"You'll never guess who I ran into the other day," he said with a sudden false cheerfulness in his voice.

Since it could be a million different people, Victoria shrugged.

"Marcus," he boasted, thrusting out his chest.

At first the name didn't render a reaction. She couldn't imagine her father bringing up *that* Marcus.

"Marcus who?"

He eased on a wobbly smile. "Don't tell me that you forgot him already? Marcus Henderson."

*Did I just step into the* Twilight Zone? "And exactly why should I care that you ran into him?"

Mondell drew in a deep breath and leaned closer to her to take her other hand. *Is this an intervention?*

Her father met her steady gaze. "I know that you still may be hurt…and even angry with Marcus. You know that I was, too, for a long time. But, you know, time can heal a lot, and I sat down and heard his side of the story. Did you know that he had his marriage annulled, like, days after that whole fiasco happened?"

"Good for him."

"Well…I think that you know by now how things can get a little crazy in a place like Las Vegas. I mean with you living there and all. And when you're in that small bubble, things have a tendency to get out of hand. You do things that you don't normally do."

Victoria eased her hand back. She didn't like where this was going. "Dad—"

"Wait. Hear me out. I was just as angry as you were for what happened. I felt that I was as much to blame for what happened."

"Don't be ridiculous, Dad. I told you—"

"I don't like it when my little girl is hurt. And I wanted to do all I could to make it right. I wanted to find his scrawny butt and wring his neck with my bare hands. *But*—like I said, I heard him out and—"

"Daddy—"

"Please, please. Let me finish." He took another breath. "He just had too much to drink. Somebody probably slipped something in his drink at that club."

Victoria's back stiffened. She suddenly knew what this was about. Her father didn't just suddenly forgive Marcus. He just thought that he was a better choice than Eamon.

"Maybe if you could just talk to him?"

"No," she said firmly.

"He still wants to marry you."

"You're not listening to me," she pressed. "I don't care if he's sorry. And I certainly don't like the implication that

Eamon is running some shady enterprise to make bachelors run off and marry his employees. That's insulting, and I can't believe that you actually believe that yourself."

"How do I know what to believe? It's not like I've ever met the man myself. I can't vouch for someone's character by proxy. Marcus is a good man. He screwed up, but he's still a good man with a lot of potential. We both did the research and spreadsheet. It's all in black and white."

Victoria slammed her eyes close and counted to ten. Hearing that *rational* logic being echoed back to her made her really see how ridiculous she had been. After taking several deep breaths, she opened her eyes and smiled. "Dad, I love you. You are the best father that a girl could ask for. But I don't want Marcus. I don't *love* him. I never did. Had we gotten married, I would've been miserable. Do you understand?"

Tears glossed Mondell's eyes.

"Can you explain your love for Mom on a spreadsheet?"

His eyes crept over to Ceyla. Tears streaked down his face as he shook his head.

"*That* is what I feel for Eamon. He's a good man. Someone that I never really thought existed out here. But he does and he makes me feel so alive and so loved. I don't care if he never says the words or ever puts a ring on my finger. I just know that I want to be with him…always."

Ceyla cupped her face in her hands as her tears freely flowed down her face. "Oh, that's so beautiful."

Mondell reached for his daughter's hand again and squeezed it affectionately. "I understand. And in my biased opinion, he would be a fool to ever let you go."

He opened his arms and she slid easily into his embrace for an old-fashioned bear hug. "I love you, Daddy."

"I love you, too. And I really hope that Eamon King knows what he has."

*That makes two of us.*

# Chapter 21

"Welcome to The Dollhouse, Las Vegas," Eamon King shouted, raising his glass to the raucous bachelor party as they entered the V.I.P. section of his exclusive Las Vegas club. Trey Songz's silky smooth baritone floated over the crowd while thirty excited men whooped and hollered over the loud pulsing music like children after inhaling a bag of Halloween candy. It was the usual bachelor-party crowd of married men seizing a night to revert to behaving like drunken college kids.

After Eamon's greeting, the men let up a loud whoop and held their drinks high in the air.

"Let's get this party started!" someone shouted.

"Don't worry, that is exactly what we're about to do. And trust me, you're all going to leave with smiles on your faces," Eamon promised.

That answer received another shout and a few fist pumps in the air.

"First, I need to know, where's the lucky groom?" Eamon asked.

"Here he is!" the men hollered and proceeded to push a young brother, who, in Eamon's opinion, looked like he was just barely of legal age to be in the club. But there was a cockiness about him as he approached Eamon with his hands held up in the victory sign.

"All right, Mr. Boykin," he boasted. "I want to personally guarantee you as one of the owners of this establishment that tonight will definitely be one that you will *never* forget!"

"Whooooo!"

Eamon had to stick his finger in his ear and jiggle it to regain his hearing. He hadn't expected such a loud voice to come from such a small body. After that he finished his usual spiel of introducing the V.I.P. hostesses and then the dancers. He tried to muster as much enthusiasm as he could. But the truth of the matter was that his heart just wasn't really in it.

He missed Victoria. Granted, she was only going to be gone for a weekend. And so far it had only been twenty-four hours, but he couldn't stop feeling as if there was just something missing. Not to mention every five minutes, he was looking at his cell phone to check to see whether she had called. The only call he received was one letting him know that she had arrived safely.

Despite the sound being crystal clear, he felt every mile that separated them. When Victoria had first mentioned that she needed to go back to New York to see her family, he was fine with it until he realized that she hadn't extended the invitation to him to come with her. He waited a day or two and by that time he felt awkward, too awkward, to hint that he'd like to come and meet her parents. They were in this awkward place where neither of them was truly ready to admit that they were a couple or that they were still in just a "wait-and-see" phase.

For the first couple of months that they lived together, Eamon had chalked his role up to being the rebound guy. Just something for her to pass the time with until Victoria was ready to really jump back into the dating arena. But then there was the night he'd gotten her to admit that she loved *this big jerk*. That sort of spooked him a little bit. It wasn't that he didn't feel the same way. It was that in that moment, it confirmed that what he was feeling was really real. No more speculation. This was the real thing. So why was he so scared?

*Because what if it's snatched away again?*

Eamon's heart tightened in his chest so painfully that he almost missed a step coming off the stage as Delicious made her grand entrance. Of course, he played it off and eased his way through the V.I.P. crowd while they cheered on their good buddy as his best dancer put them all in a trance. As he neared the exit of the V.I.P. room, he caught sight of his brother Xavier propped up against the wall.

"What are you doing here?"

"I came to check to see how you were doing. What do you think?" he said, pushing away from the wall. "I haven't received any more threatening phone calls so I hopped on a plane to make sure that you hadn't killed our charming cousin. You're too good-looking to end up in jail."

Eamon rolled his eyes. "Yeah. I should sock you in the mouth on general principle, but I might break my hand on that brick you call a head."

Xavier held up his fist and pretended to bob and weave. "You're more than welcome to try, but I still got a few good moves left in me."

"Whatever, man." Eamon waved him off and then took another glance around the loud room.

On the stage, Delicious was twirling the tassels on her nipples while a few brothers stuffed dollar bills wherever they could in her skimpy outfit. Before he knew it he was heaving out a sigh. He really missed Victoria.

"Sooo," Xavier said, drawing his attention. "What's up with you, big bro? How are things going?"

Eamon managed a shrug while he reached into his pocket and scooped out his cell phone. *No calls.* What was she doing? Why hadn't she called back? Eamon couldn't ignore this underlying fear that once Victoria was home, she'd start to miss her old life. After all, her family and friends were there, her job and her own apartment. Who's to say that she wouldn't walk in the door and decide to stay in New York? The only thing that was tying her to Vegas was him. Was he enough?

"Yo, man," Xavier said, snapping his fingers in front of his face. "Am I boring you or something?"

"Nah. Nah. It's just I was seeing if anyone called." He put the phone back into his pocket and sighed again.

"Ah…because you look really preoccupied."

"Nah. Nah. I just got a lot on my mind right now." He breathed out a heavy sigh. "You know how it is."

"A lot of work and everything?"

"Yeah. Yeah." Eamon scooped up the phone again and looked at it. *Is this damn thing even working?*

"It's funny that you mention work," Xavier said. "I called here a few times looking for you and you have hardly been here."

"I was probably at the restaurant or something." Eamon turned and headed down the club's stairway and then onto the main floor. One glance and he knew that it was at nearly full capacity.

"We're running low on Grey Goose," Hayley informed him as she threaded her way through the crowd.

"What? We should've just gotten a few new cases."

"Are you sure?" she asked. "You have been a little pre-occupied lately." She cocked her head. But then she noticed Eamon's brother. "Oh, Xavier! I didn't see you come in."

Xavier smiled. "Hey, Hayley. How have you been?"

"Same old, same old. Which one of you do I need to hit up for a raise?"

Eamon and Xavier pointed at each other.

"Whatever," Hayley laughed. "Eamon, could you double-check on whether you made that order? It might be time to look into getting a new distributor. Those guys are always forgetting something."

"That will make the fifth distributor this month." He huffed out a frustrated breath. "I'm on it," Eamon said, sliding the phone out of his pocket again to check his screen.

"It's good seeing you again, Xavier." She smiled and winked. "If I wasn't married, I'd swear the three of us would make a good T-Bone sandwich."

Xavier was not the one to tease. "What does your man have to do with me?"

Hayley laughed and sauntered off with her tray.

"I wasn't joking," Xavier called after her, but then turned back around, laughing. "She's a mess. Whoa!" He stopped suddenly. "Is that Q?" Xavier asked, pointing across the club to the third station bar.

"Yep." Eamon's smile stretched.

"He's actually working? How in the hell did you manage that?" he asked, stunned.

"It wasn't me. It seems like he just naturally found his calling in life," Eamon laughed.

"You're telling me. Look at him go." Xavier started toward their cousin's station.

Quentin, smiling and laughing with the crowd, was putting on quite a show. "What's your pleasure? What's your pleasure?" he asked, picking up a bottle and spinning it around his hand before pouring the liquor into the glass and topping it with another spinning bottle of mixer.

Xavier stopped just before the bar and stared openmouthed. "I feel like I'm seeing a miracle or something."

Quentin continued to juggle, toss and spin the bottles around—all without wasting a drop of liquor anywhere. He drew a big crowd with all the patrons shouting different drinks, trying to stump him. But so far there wasn't a drink that Quentin didn't know how to make. The waitresses loved Quentin. His performances made for a dramatic hike in tips, and the tip jar he had was turned over to the girls to split among themselves.

"I'm speechless," Xavier said.

"I was, too, the first time I saw it. Goes to show you, everyone has some kind of talent."

"I gotta get him back out to Atlanta."

"Oh. *Now* you want to take him."

"Well, I didn't know that he would actually be useful." Xavier laughed.

"And what if I say that you can't have him?"

"Then I'll just have to play the best-friend card. He's coming back to Atlanta."

"That is so wrong in so many ways." Eamon shook his head and pulled out his phone again.

"Man, who on earth are you waiting to hear from, the President of the United States?"

"Huh?" Eamon glanced up.

Xavier crossed his arms and stared at him. "What's really going on with you, bro? You're definitely not acting like yourself."

"Uh, nothing. Nothing. Like I said, I just got a lot on my mind."

"Like a certain woman that you have stashed at your crib for the past six months that you haven't told me or Jeremy about?"

Eamon started to give another flimsy excuse when Xavier stopped him with a look.

"C'mon, man. It's me. Tell me what's really up with you."

Eamon's large shoulders deflated a bit. "All right. Let's go into the office."

"I'm right behind you," Xavier said, pushing ahead so that he could go first.

A few minutes later, the brothers entered Eamon's office and collapsed into the appropriate chairs.

"All right. I'm all ears," Xavier said. "Lay it on me. Who's the woman that's got you looking at the phone every five minutes?"

"Her name is Victoria Gregory."

"Local chick?"

"Nah. She's out of New York. She's an investment analyst, very smart…very beautiful." He smiled. "But she's a lousy, *lousy* cook."

Xavier's brows hitched up. "Damn. She must really have got you twisted. I haven't seen you smile like that since…"

Eamon nodded. "Yeah. Since Karen."

A silence drifted over them for a moment before Xavier said, "Then I'm happy for you, big bro. Truly. And if you don't mind me saying so, it's about time."

"What do you mean 'about time'? I'm a year older than you and you have never been in a serious relationship."

"True. But I'm not wired that way. I've always enjoyed the single life—me and Jeremy. You, on the other hand, are like Pops. I've known that since Karen passed away. You've been trying to be something that you're not—all because you're trying your best not to get hurt again. Remember, I was there. I know how much it crushed you to lose her and I saw how you changed. You've always been driven, but…after that situation it was like you just doubled down on the workload."

"Expanding the club was your idea."

"But then you opened a restaurant. Trying to just run one big business would work the average person into the ground. I didn't expect you to run around here like you were Superman."

"Well, you'd be pleased to know I've cut back my hours considerably."

"Because of this Victoria?"

Eamon nodded.

"Then I already love her. In fact, I can't wait to meet her."

"Well, right now she's back in New York, visiting family." He pulled the phone out again. "She left yesterday."

Xavier laughed. "Ah. So *that's* why you're checking your phone like a teenage girl? Ha! Classic."

Eamon just listened.

"Between you and me, I've been counting the days until you stepped up to me and Jeremy telling us that you want us to buy you out or something."

Eamon's eyes widened in surprise. His brother had hit the nail on the head.

"Now, the restaurant—that's you. And even your music, especially your music. You're a one man, one woman kind of brother. You should be married to a nice woman producing me some nieces and nephews somewhere. And if some of the things that I've been hearing about and seeing for myself—" he gestured toward the phone "—is true, then it looks like you've already found her."

Eamon stared down at the phone. His brother made it sound so easy.

Xavier leaned forward and whispered, "Here's an idea. Why don't *you* call her?"

"She's probably busy."

Xavier cocked his head. "You're scared."

"Man." Eamon cocked an awkward smile and shook his head. But that act wasn't fooling anyone.

Xavier stood up. His large frame monopolized half of the office. "I'm going to leave you with this: Quentin waited too long to make his move and another brother stepped in. You don't want to make that same mistake. It looks like you've been given a second chance with love. Take my advice and don't screw it up."

## Chapter 22

No way was Victoria going to last an entire weekend away from Eamon. After just one afternoon, she was literally starting to feel sick. The rest of the evening with her parents went well, especially after she got her father off the topic of discussing her and Eamon's relationship. A few more family members had stopped by, Aunt Brenda and even Aunt Fiona.

Victoria could tell by the way Fiona's mouth was pinched that she must've talked with her daughter Lolita. But she really didn't give a damn, and after exchanging a few withering glances, she was sure that her jealous aunt got the picture. At least when the women started pressing her about Eamon, her father had her back in changing the subject. True, she didn't really care about what other people thought and said anymore, but it didn't mean that she was going to just supply material or give oxygen to the gossip. Aunt Fiona was as big a gossiper as they come. In fact, she wouldn't be surprised if she learned that Fiona had the editors for Page Six on speed dial.

By the end of the evening, Victoria knew that she was heading back to Las Vegas. Not Sunday, but now.

"Are you?" her mother said after she told them what she was going to do. "You just got here."

"I know, but—"

"My, my, my. You really are in love." Her eyes glistened. "I can't tell you how happy that makes me."

"I'll be back—and the next time, I'll even bring Eamon."

"Now, that better be a promise, too," her father said, coming in on the tail end of their conversation.

"It is." She turned to her father and exchanged hugs and kisses.

But her mother was already starting to fret. "Are you sure that you're going to be able to get a flight this late? Maybe you should wait until the morning."

Victoria recognized the stalling tactic for what it was. If her mother could get her to wait until tomorrow morning, then she would try and press for tomorrow night. "I'm sure it's fine. I'll just fly on standby." She smiled sweetly at her and then went in for another hug. "Don't worry. You'll see me soon."

Their goodbyes were drawn out, but finally Victoria left her parents' estate with their driver. Even then they continued to wave to each other as the car pulled off. They made a quick stop at her place back in the city so that the driver could get her bags.

As luck would have it she got there in time to take the last flight out. It would be a little over a five-hour flight, but given the three-hour time difference, she would be there about two hours later Vegas time, she reasoned. Her stomach twisted with excitement. After rushing through the security check-point, she heard her cell phone ringing. Quickly, she dug it out of her purse and saw Eamon's name on the screen.

She was just about to answer the call when a better idea hit her. *Maybe I should just surprise him?* Victoria bit her bottom lip to tamp down the excitement at pulling off a good surprise. If she answered the call now, he would definitely know she was at the airport.

"I'll just see you in a few minutes, baby," she said under her breath and then returned the phone to her purse.

Eamon heaved out a disappointed breath and snapped the phone shut. It was hard to stop his mind from racing with a thousand possibilities for why Victoria hadn't answered her phone. He'd narrowed it down to either her being kidnapped to her being with another man. Anything was possible. It wasn't like they had had that monogamy talk. And right now he was kicking himself for it.

"Have you made a decision, sir?" the blue-suited salesman smiled kindly from behind a jewelry counter.

"Yes. I'd like to see that one," Eamon said, pointing to a three-carat emerald-cut diamond that was sparkling at him in the center of the glass case.

"Ah. You have an excellent eye, sir," the salesman praised before opening the cabinet with his gold key.

When he set the diamond on top of the glass, Eamon's lips were already starting to curl. He lifted it by the platinum band and accepted the loupe that was handed to him in order to check the cut, color and clarity. Once he was satisfied, he started to feel a familiar anxiousness twisting around in his gut. It was the kind that scared him, just the one letting him know that he was really about to make a big move.

"I'll take it," he announced.

"Excellent, sir."

On the drive home, Eamon turned on the radio and surfed through the channels to find a station that was playing some old-school jams. Once he found Patti LaBelle belting out an old favorite, "If Only You Knew," he stopped right there and sang along. Soon enough, he was feeling real good—a positive sign that he was definitely doing the right thing. Now all he had to do was decide how he wanted to pop the question.

The romantic in him wanted to do something big and over-the-top. But when he started thinking about how his and Victoria's relationship wasn't really about the big things. In fact, Victoria really responded to smaller, intimate settings. Maybe he should go with a classic ring-in-the-champagne sort of thing. Or since she loved bubble baths so much, he could set the ring on like a floating rubber ducky. Did she like ducks?

His mind continued to spin and whirl with possibilities. The more scenarios he thought up, the more excited he became. *Maybe you should go to New York and surprise her.*

The moment that idea raced through his mind, his foot eased off the accelerator and it seemed like his heart started bouncing around in his chest. Why not? It would give him the opportunity to talk to her father first. It was the proper thing to do.

Inspired, Eamon slammed his foot down on the accelerator and he zoomed out to his house. He was almost tempted to keep the car running while he raced into the house and packed an overnight bag. But he thought better of it. Still, he nearly hopped out of the car before shifting it into Park.

Once inside he whirled around the place like a Tasmanian devil. He grabbed a bag and proceeded to shove things in at random. But when he remembered that he was going to have to fly commercial, he went back through it to make sure that he could get through security.

Bag reasonably packed, Eamon flew back down the stairs and went into Victoria's study. There, he found a birthday card her parents had sent her and smiled at the return address written in the corner.

"Jackpot." He turned and rushed toward the door, but when he opened it, he nearly jumped out of his skin at the sight of Xavier standing on the other side.

"Damn," Xavier gasped, after springing back from the door. "You really know how to scare a brother."

"What are you doing here?" Eamon asked, grabbing the bag he'd dropped. "You damn near gave me a heart attack."

"Figured I'd come and crash with you for the night and make sure that you call your girl."

Eamon's face lit up. "I'm going to do one better than that. I'm headed out there to surprise her in New York right now."

Xavier folded his arms and bounced his head. "Well, all right. I must've really put a fire under your butt."

"I'm going to ask her to marry me." He shuffled the bag on his arm and then dug out the jewelry box and handed it over to his brother. "Tell me what you think about that."

Xavier opened the box and then emitted a low whistle. "Now, that's a ring!"

"Think she'll like it?"

His brother closed the box and handed it over. "If she's the kind of girl you described then I think that she'll like it because it's coming from you."

"Good answer." Eamon smacked his brother on the shoulder and headed out the door. "Make yourself at home. I'm going out to get you a sister-in-law."

* * *

Victoria was exhausted. After a twenty-four-hour turnaround, flying to New York, a full day with family and friends only to cap it off with a return trip to Las Vegas. But when the captain told everyone to prepare for landing, she was suddenly hit with a jolt of energy. Just to be back in Las Vegas closed that gulf she felt being so far away. After years of being so independent, it was strange for her to have these kinds of feelings. It wasn't that she needed to be with Eamon every minute of the day. She just wanted to be around.

Going through this, she couldn't help but have great sympathy for the women whose lovers went off to war for months or even years at a time—even women whose significant others had equally dangerous jobs like being a police officer or a fireman. It must take a certain amount of strength to endure that.

The truth was, for her right now, she didn't know where she stood in her relationship with Eamon. But she did intend to talk to him about it as soon as they finished making love when he came home in the morning. Not only that, she was going to make him breakfast. This time, hopefully, there will be no eggshells in his omelet or any coffee grinds in his cup.

*Hopefully.*

In less than thirty minutes after de-boarding the plane, she hopped into a cab and was on her way toward the suburbs of Las Vegas. It was nearly dawn and there was still a good chance Eamon might not be home from work just yet or he could already be in bed. Only time would tell. Restless, she kept glancing at the time and the meter in the cab. Her driver was clearly in no hurry to get anywhere— definitely not like the cab drivers in New York.

Victoria scooted up to the edge of her seat and tapped

the driver on the shoulder. "Excuse me. But is there any way you can go a little faster?" she asked with a smile.

The bored driver immediately started shaking his salt-and-pepper head. "Sorry, ma'am. I have to go the speed limit."

Still holding her attitude in check, she tried again. "What if I said that there's an extra twenty dollars in it for you?"

"I'd say that it would hardly make a dent in the speeding ticket I'll get."

"A hundred dollars?"

"Pfft." He shook his head.

"Fine. Two hundred."

He started to hedge.

"Three hundred, and that's my final offer."

Finally a smile ballooned across the man's face. "Buckle up." He slammed his foot down on the accelerator, and they had liftoff. It was more like one of those rides in Disneyland. He darted in and out of cars as if he drove in the Indy 500 part-time. In the end, she got what she wanted. They arrived at Eamon's place in a little more than fifteen minutes.

Climbing out of the cab, she was confused by Eamon's missing Porsche and the rental car in the driveway. Was his car in the shop or something? She paid the driver and then carried her purse and bag into the house.

Eamon was cooking or rather had cooked. The scent of banana-nut pancakes and link sausages wafted in the air. Victoria inhaled deeply as she crept toward the kitchen. But she was disappointed that it was empty.

Turning around, she grabbed her bags and elected to take the stairs up since, honestly, it was much faster. Halfway, up she could hear singing and the shower running.

*This was going to be even better,* she snickered to herself.

She pushed open the bedroom door and saw the bathroom door was closed.

She quickly put down her bags and started stripping out of her clothes. This would be a nice little payback for him interrupting her bubble baths. She grabbed one of her extra robes and then headed into the bedroom.

"'Ooh, baby, hot just like an oven I need some lovin'...'"

Was he singing "Sexual Healing"? Victoria chuckled as she tiptoed past the large tub and headed to the stand-alone shower. She smiled though she could barely make out his entire frame in the frosty glass door.

"'Whenever blue teardrops are fallin'...'" he wailed.

Victoria was slightly surprised that he was off-key, but she reached for the door and pulled it open. "Missed me?"

The man in the shower jumped and spun around. Their eyes connected a half a second before Victoria peeled open her robe and exposed herself to a complete stranger.

However, he wasn't so lucky!

Their screams tore from their throats about the same time. Just then she quickly slammed the door back and ran out of the bathroom slamming that door behind her, as well. Suddenly it seemed like she couldn't run fast enough. She gathered her clothes from the floor and tried to hurry and put them back on. She got the pants back on, but then the bathroom door flew open. Victoria clenched the robe tight across her bosom.

"Who are you?" she shouted.

The man stepped out with a towel, wrapped snuggly around his hips. "Whoa. Calm down," he said, holding his hands up. "There seems to be some type of mis-understanding. I'm Xavier King. Eamon's brother."

That answer managed to take a little of the edge off her panic.

"Xavier?"

He smiled. "Hello. It's, uh, nice to meet you." He cocked his head and looked at her. "You must be, uh...uh—"

"Victoria," she answered, a little annoyed that he didn't know that she lived here.

"Yes. I'm sorry. My brother told me about you." He cocked his head again like something was wrong. "He also said that you were in New York."

"I came back early," she answered, feeling her relief slowly trickle over her. "I thought that I would come back and surprise him."

"Well, I guess it's a good sign that you both think alike." At her obvious confusion, he added. "He flew out to see you."

"What?"

"Surprise." He shrugged his shoulders.

"Oh. Well." Victoria smiled and tugged a deep breath. "I guess then that it's nice to finally meet you," she said awkwardly. She didn't feel entirely comfortable walking back over to shake his hand, especially since she'd just seen him in his birthday suit. "I guess that's what I get for not answering your brother's calls."

"Yeah." He looked around. "Sorry about using your shower. There's seems to be something wrong with the one in the bedroom that I'm in."

"It's not a problem. I completely understand."

They started moving in a strange circle where he was slowly working his way to the door while she was working her way around from the door.

"You know, in a lot of ways you could almost pass for your brother's twin."

"We get that a lot," Xavier chuckled, but he still kind of looked at her odd.

"Is there something wrong?" Victoria finally asked.

"Not really, it's just… You look like someone I used to know. That's all." He studied her face again. "In fact, you could pass for her twin, too."

Victoria suddenly had a strange feeling come over her. "Really? Who?"

"Just this girl."

He tried to wave it off suddenly, but something told Victoria to press for an answer. "What was her name?"

"Karen."

## Chapter 23

Eamon arrived at the Gregory estate feeling like a teenager picking up his prom date. Only this wasn't an ordinary house. It was a huge estate that showcased the extreme wealth Mondell Gregory had amassed over his lifetime. He didn't know a whole lot about Victoria's father—just the basics. He knew that Victoria was very fond of him, which was why she chose the same career. He knew from experience that men of Gregory's status tend to be very proud and bullish, which meant this meeting was likely to be very painful.

Fortunately for Eamon, he wasn't intimidated by men like Gregory. In his mind, they both put on their pants one leg at a time. He only hoped that he would be able to win his approval to marry his daughter. If not, he was sure that they would miss him at the wedding.

He rang the doorbell and stepped back. While he waited,

he practiced his speech in his head. About a minute later, a stoic older gentleman opened the door.

"May I help you?"

"Yes. Is this the Gregory residence?"

"Yes. It is."

"Then I would like to see Mondell Gregory. That is if he's in."

"May I tell him who is calling?"

"Eamon King."

Finally the butler's expression changed. His brows stretched up a half an inch while his gaze raked Eamon from head to toe. "Please. Come in." The butler stepped back and opened the door.

"Thank you." Eamon flashed him a smile as he stepped into the house. His eyes roamed around the grand foyer and he immediately thought about his Uncle Roger's home in the Carolinas. His only hope right now was that Mondell Gregory was nothing like his uncle.

A chair scraped somewhere in the house and then there was a series of footsteps tapping and pounding the marble floor. A couple of seconds later, a large, trim older man who matched Eamon's height but had caramel-colored skin and piercing green eyes strolled into the foyer. Behind him stood an elegant woman with soft eyes and a kind smile.

"Eamon King!" The man thrust out his hand.

"Yes, sir. That's me." He threw his hand into the outstretched one and shook it mightily. There was instantly a subtle contest between them as the two extended their handshake a little too long.

"Mondell Gregory," he said. "Perhaps you may have heard of me? I have a daughter that you seem quite fond of."

"Yes, sir. I am quite fond of her—extremely so."

With those words, his wife clutched his hand while her smile stretched even wider.

Eamon turned his gaze toward her and offered her his hand, as well. "And you must be Ceyla." He waited until she placed her small hand into his before he lowered his head to press a kiss on the back of it. "It's a pleasure to meet you both finally. Your daughter has told me a lot about you."

"Well, I'll be honest, son, it's easier squeezing water out of rock than to get her to tell us anything about you. I don't mind telling you that I didn't too much like it."

*Oh, boy. This is going to be harder than I thought.* Eamon cleared his throat. "Yes, sir. I'm sorry about that. We should have come together a lot sooner than before now."

"You mean before you got my daughter to move in with you in that place they call *Sin* City?"

*Okay. Much harder.*

"Mondell!" Ceyla snatched herself from his side and quickly stepped in front of her husband so that she could loop her arm through Eamon's arm. "Please forgive him. He's a little cranky when he hasn't had his breakfast yet," she explained smoothly. "In fact, we were just getting ready to eat. Would you care to join us?"

Eamon expelled a long breath. "Actually, I'd love to."

"Good. Come with me." She started to lead Eamon away, but managed to flash her husband an annoyed look.

"What? We were just having a civil conversation," he said.

Ceyla didn't bother to answer but marched Eamon to the breakfast table. "Victoria had sent me a few pictures of you, but I have to say that they hardly do you justice, my dear."

"That's awfully nice of you to say," Eamon said, trying his best to mind his p's and q's. But after meeting Mondell, he knew that beyond a shadow of a doubt before this was all over with, he was going to be baptized by fire by the time Mondell got through with him.

When he was led into the dining table, there was an array of food spread across a grand mahogany buffet table. To his right, he saw a crowd of people already sitting and eating their breakfast. He flashed them all a big smile.

"Good morning."

The four women at the table all stretched their brows high while their eyes lit up with interest.

"Well, who do we have here?" one of the older women said, straightening in her chair and taking her time surveying every inch of Eamon—to the point that he almost felt violated.

"Oh." Ceyla patted Eamon's arm. "Let me introduce you to everyone," she said. "Right here, we have my *older* sister, Fiona."

"Hello, sexy," she said with what Eamon thought was a cougar growl.

"Uh, nice to meet you."

The woman held on to his hand. "No. The pleasure is *all* mine. Trust me."

There was another rake of her eyes and then Eamon had to forcefully pull his hand out of hers.

"Fiona, behave," Ceyla chastised in a low whisper. "And over here is my younger sister Brenda."

"How do you do?" she said simply.

Ceyla continued around the room and when they reached Lolita, she sprung out of her chair like she'd just been poked with a pin needle and stood so close that her breasts jabbed his chest.

"How do you do?"

"Uh, just fine." Eamon didn't need Ceyla to tell him that she was Fiona's daughter. Their kinship was more obvious in mannerisms than in looks.

Ceyla clasped her hands together. "I'm sure that all of you are curious to know just who this young man is."

"I'm hoping it's the new pool boy," Fiona said, slathering on some lipstick.

"Good lord," Mondell mumbled, looking like he was disgusted by everyone's performance.

"Actually, no," Ceyla said. "This is Eamon King."

"Hello." Eamon stood there smiling while one by one their mouths dropped open so wide, he was able to make out that a couple of them had their tonsils removed. There was one exception—Lolita. She looked so angry that with his head turned at a certain angle it looked like there was steam rising out of her ears.

"So this is how they grow them in Las Vegas?" Fiona finally said after picking up her jaw. "I now see why your daughter ran away from home."

Eamon laughed. "Actually, I was born and raised in Atlanta."

"I swear that girl gets everything," Lolita complained.

Eamon didn't know what that meant, but suddenly he thought he preferred to be grilled by Mondell than to continue to stand there like some prize Thoroughbred.

"Come." Ceyla tugged his sleeve. "Get something to eat. As you see we have plenty."

"Thank you." He drew another deep breath and grabbed one of the plates and started picking out what he wanted for breakfast. It was quite a spread but he kept it simple with eggs and bacon.

"Would you like some orange juice?" Ceyla asked.

"By God, Ceyla," Mondell barked. "There's no need to

mother hen him to death. I think that he knows how to fix himself breakfast."

There was a quick pop and Eamon turned around in time to see Mondell rubbing the back of his head while Ceyla hissed another warning, "Behave."

The small interplay reminded Eamon of his own parents and he relaxed a little bit more. When he returned to the table, he smartly elected to sit next to Mondell rather than what looked like his instant fan club.

"So," Mondell said, turning to him. "Victoria said that we would meet you soon. I didn't think it would be this soon. What was it? Were you hiding out at her apartment to see if the coast was clear for you to come and see me?"

Eamon didn't understand the question. "No. I decided to fly out here on my own." He cleared his throat when he met the man's gaze. Maybe he was a lot more nervous than he thought. "I really wanted to talk to you one on one."

Mondell's left brow lifted as Ceyla perked up.

"Do you, now?"

Eamon nodded confidently and then glanced around. "Is Victoria here?"

Her parents looked at each other and then turned their confused looks on him.

"What do you mean, dear?" Ceyla asked. "Victoria flew back to Vegas last night."

Eamon nearly dropped his fork. "Oh. I didn't know."

"I believe that she went back early because she was missing someone."

She gave him a telling look and it cheered him considerably. "Well, I guess we must've gotten our wires crossed. I came out here to surprise her and she came back home to surprise me. Classic."

Mondell's smile slid wider. "That means I'll have you all to myself."

Fiona spoke up. "You can always share him." The inappropriate joke fell flat while everyone gave her a shake of their heads.

"So what do you say that we finish our breakfast and then we can go to my study so that we can have a talk?" Mondell suggested.

"Sounds good." *Let's just hope that I survive it.*

He felt a vibration at his hip. He glanced down at his phone and read his brother's name on the screen. "Excuse me. I need to take this call."

The minute the name left Xavier's mouth he knew that he messed up. "You know what? Now that I'm really getting a good look at you, I see that I'm mistaken. Please, don't pay any attention to me and my ramblings. I'm sure if my brother told you anything about me, I tend not to know what I'm talking about pretty much most of the time."

Victoria just stared at him.

"In fact," he continued. "I even have very, *very* poor eyesight from time to time. I've been meaning to get my eyes checked. I've just been busy and—"

"Please. Stop," she said, shaking her head. Then she closed her eyes and drew in a deep breath. "You mean to tell me that I look exactly like Eamon dead ex-girlfriend? The one that died the day he was going to propose to her?"

Never in his life had Xavier wished like hell that there was such a thing as a time machine. If only he could just rewind the clock a few minutes and not have given her Karen's name. What on earth was he thinking? Eamon was going to kill him, but damned if she didn't look just like her. Same face, same height. How did Eamon not see the similarities? And now what was he supposed to say?

"Look. I think that maybe I should just get my things

and go." He started toward the door. "I'm really going to be late for my flight back to Atlanta."

Victoria pressed her mouth closed and Xavier could see a tide of anger rising. Yeah. He definitely put his foot in his mouth big time. "Hey, it was…really nice to have met you. I really hope to see you again soon," he offered weakly and then hurried up and got the hell out of there.

Once he made it to the safety of his car, he quickly grabbed his cell phone and called Eamon. "C'mon, bro. Pick up," he prayed. Just when he was convinced that he was about to be transferred to voice mail, Eamon came onto the line.

"Hello."

"E, man. Thank God you picked up."

His brother's voice suddenly dipped in concern. "What? What is it? Did something happen at the club, or has Quentin been arrested again?"

Xavier sucked in a deep breath. "I wish it was something like that."

"This sounds really serious. What is it?"

"First, you got to promise me that you're going to forgive me for what I'm about to tell you."

"Are you serious?" Eamon huffed out a deep breath. "I'm in the middle of something here. I don't have time to play—"

"I'm not playing," Xavier stressed. "Promise me."

There was a brief pause over the line. "All right."

"That's a promise?"

"Yeah. Yeah. It's a promise."

"Good." Xavier felt like a weight was lifted from his shoulders, but not much. "Your girl came back home today."

"Yeah. I just found that out. I'm up here at her parents' place."

"Look, man. I wasn't prepared when I saw her. I mean… had I known then I wouldn't have just—"

"What did you do? You didn't sleep with her, did you?"

"What? No." Xavier pulled the phone away and made a face at it for a second before putting it back up against his ear. "Give me a little more credit than that?"

"Sorry. It's just that you're really acting weird and I'm feeling a little pressure with Victoria's dad. He's not too happy that we've been living in sin apparently."

"I told her," Xavier spat. It was just best to put it all out there. Let it lie like roadkill.

"You told her what?"

*Is he serious?* "I blurted out that she looks like Karen. I mean, bro, the girl could pass for her twin. One minute I'm taking a shower, and the next I think I'm staring at a ghost."

The line went silent.

"Hello? Can't you hear me?" He pulled the phone away again, but this time to see that the call had been dropped. He pressed speed dial, but this time Eamon didn't pick up.

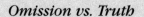

*Omission vs. Truth*

## Chapter 24

Dr. Turner's pen finally stopped scribbling. "So Eamon didn't tell Victoria that she looked like his dead ex-girlfriend?"

"Shocking, huh?" Quentin stretched and then shook his head. "It seemed like a move I would've pulled."

"Really? You don't believe in being honest in a relationship?" Turner asked.

"There's being honest and there's being honest," he said, though he knew that word-barf wasn't going to get past his therapist.

"Explain." Turner shifted in her chair and crossed her legs.

From the corner of Quentin's eyes he caught the slow movement and wished he had a pair a scissors to cut that ridiculously long skirt in half. Surely Dr. Turner was committing some kind of crime hiding those long beauties under all that material.

Alyssa laughed.

"What's so funny?" Q asked.

"You," Alyssa said, shaking her head. "You'll never change. Here you are, going to therapy because you supposedly can't get over me, but you're sitting there ogling the doctor's legs."

"What do you care? You're married, remember?"

"Mr. Hinton? Who are you talking to?" Dr. Turner asked.

"Huh?" Quentin jerked his head back toward the doctor.

The doctor frowned. "I asked who were you talking to."

Turning toward the window, he wasn't surprised to see his mirage had vanished. "No one. Just talking to myself."

The scribbling returned and Quentin rolled his eyes. *Great. Now she thinks I'm crazy.*

Alyssa reappeared. "You think talking to someone that's not really here *isn't* crazy?"

"Good point."

Dr. Turner looked up. "What was that?"

"Uh, nothing," Q covered and then narrowed his eyes at Alyssa.

She just shrugged her shoulders and mouthed *"Sorry."*

Dr. Turner cleared her throat. "Since you're not going to explain to me the difference between being honest and being honest—how did Eamon handle that latest development with Ms. Gregory?"

Quentin sucked in a deep breath and made himself comfortable again. "Well...the first thing he realized was that he needed to hurry and get his butt back to Las Vegas..."

## Chapter 25

Eamon disconnected the call and then rushed back into the dining room to announce to the crowd, "I'm sorry, folks, but I have to go."

Everyone turned toward him with shocked faces. "What?"

"I'm so sorry, but something major has come up that I have to go and take care of it. I hope that you all understand." He glanced over at Mondell. He wanted to promise the man that they would definitely have that talk when and if he came back. But something told him that it was one promise he didn't know whether he would be able to keep. Instead, he just nodded to the older gentleman and prayed that they would indeed have that talk.

However, Mondell wasn't a man who liked to be put off. He hopped up from the table and followed Eamon out. "Is there something wrong? Does it involve my daughter?"

"Ah. No. I—I just need to get back," he said, meeting

the man's eyes. He needed to be alone so that he could think. This whole mess probably could have been avoided, if he had just mentioned—

"You seem stressed," Mondell noted. "Tell you what. We can have that talk while my driver takes us to the airport."

It was on the tip of Eamon's tongue to refuse the offer, but unfortunately, he did need a ride to the airport. "Sure. Sounds good."

Mondell smiled. "Aaron, tell the driver that we need to go to the airport pronto."

"Yes, sir." Aaron turned and quickly strode off.

Then it was just the two men in the foyer.

"So. What's the emergency?" Mondell asked.

*Think. Think. Think.* But Eamon was drawing a blank and Mondell's eyes were following him like a hawk. This seemed like the perfect time for the truth. Turning, he looked Mondell straight in the eye. "There was something that I should've told your daughter that I didn't. Now she's found out and I have to go talk to her before she decides to leave me."

Mondell didn't blink. "Is this something…illegal?"

Offended, Eamon barked. "No. Of course not."

"Hey, I have to ask," he said, shrugging. "We are just getting to know each other, right?"

The man was right. He didn't know Eamon from the man in the moon. "Yeah. You're right."

Mondell nodded, but continued with his direct interrogation. "Is it another woman?"

Eamon paused not because of guilt but because of the absurdity of the situation. "Yes and no."

"I see," Mondell said, with enough sarcasm to make it clear that Eamon had just confirmed his long-held suspicions.

Eamon faced him. "No, sir. I don't think that you can possibly see. The woman in question was an old high-school sweetheart. My first love—"

"I don't give a rat's ass if—"

"And she's dead."

Mondell's mouth remained open in midsentence. His eyes rounded Eamon like he was confessing to be a murderer.

"She was killed by a drunk driver on her graduation day in Chicago. I was in Atlanta because my graduation was on the same day. I was hoping to propose to her the next day, but unfortunately I never got that chance."

Mondell's face finally softened.

"The problem right now between me and your daughter is that I did tell her about her. It's just that I never told her that she looked a lot like her. Really a lot like her. My brother just called to tell me that he let that little bit of information slip. I'm hoping to be able to repair the damage so that when I give her this ring that's in my pocket that she will know *and* believe that I'm giving it to *her*. Not Karen."

"How can you be sure, son? I mean, within your own heart?"

"Because she's *not* Karen and because I'm smart enough to know the difference. I'm not with your daughter for who she looks like. I'm with her for who she is. How she makes me feel."

"Still. There's a part of you that has to be compar-ing—"

Eamon shook his head. "When I first met your daughter, I was physically attracted to her, yes."

Mondell shifted uncomfortably.

"But it had more to do with her presence. She's a hurricane when she's angry. I was blown away more by that than anything. And it's true still. I want nothing more than your daughter's happiness and I'm praying to God that she gives me that chance."

Their gazes remained locked for a long time and then Mondell slowly started nodding his head. "I sure hope that you're telling me the truth because I sure in the hell don't like being lied to."

"I am. Now I just have to get your daughter to believe me." Mondell's expression didn't give him any hope.

"All I can do is wish you luck, son." He patted Eamon on the shoulder. "You're going to need it."

Victoria cried the entire time she was packing her things. It got so bad at times that she couldn't see and would have to sit down. Then it would keep happening. After Xavier left, she was just numb all over. She didn't know how to process news like that. At the same time, she couldn't understand how Eamon never told her that she was a dead-ringer for a woman he once thought that he would spend the rest of his life with. Did that mean that every time they were together, he was making love to Karen and not her? Was the initial spark in his office the day they met more about another woman?

Did it matter?

She wanted to pick up the phone and call him, but she wasn't sure what to say, either. *Hello, I'm leaving you because you might be two-timing me with a dead woman?*

"I should've known that all of this was just too good to be true. *He* was too good to be true." She collapsed on the edge of the bed and waited for the stabbing pain to pass. This is what she got for leaping off cliffs and flying with her eyes closed. Didn't she know that she was going to crash at some point?

She heard the front door of the house slam closed and she hopped back up and tried to dry her eyes before she headed back downstairs. She had listened to enough of the voice messages that Eamon had left her on her cell phone to know that he was due any minute. One thing that Victoria didn't want to do was to just run out of here without telling Eamon to his face why.

"Victoria!"

Another tear fell just because she was going to miss the sound of his voice.

"Victoria, are you here?"

"I'm coming," she said and then cleared her throat before leaving their bedroom for the last time. By the time she walked down the staircase, she had pulled herself together…well, as much as she could anyway. The moment that she saw his face, she paused. She had to fight everything that was in her not to just go running down the stairs and leap into his arms like one of those black-and-white movies that duped generations of women into believing that's how true love worked.

"Victoria, we need to talk," Eamon said. His eyes pleaded with hers.

"I think the time for talking has passed," she said, sounding stronger than she felt.

"It's never too late." He took a step up the staircase. "I love you."

A sad laugh fell from her lips as a whole new wave of tears washed over her. "Now? You want to tell me that you love me *now?* The truth was too inconvenient before?"

"It wasn't like that."

"No?" She shook her head and settled her hands on her hips. "Are you going to tell me that you never noticed that I looked like Karen?"

"Of course I noticed. It just wasn't a big deal."

"Not a big deal? You were in love with her!"

"Yes! And now I'm in love with you! Doesn't that count for anything?"

"I don't believe you." She shook her head and then continued her way down the stairs.

"Why not? I've never lied to you!" He reached for her hand as she tried to pass him on the staircase, but she pulled away.

"It's a lie of omission," she reasoned. "You kept something *that* important from me."

"Please," Eamon said, following her. "What good would it have done to tell you? Answer me that. If I'd told you the day we met that you looked just like my old girlfriend, how many times do you think you would've been obsessing over whether I was in love with you or a woman that's been dead for over a decade? Besides, when we initially got together it was just a casual relationship. *Just sex* I believe were your words. As it grew into something more, you would have done exactly what you're doing now. Leaving."

"You don't know that."

"Don't I? If not, why are we talking about it now?"

"Because it's too late!"

Eamon tossed up his hands. "Then I don't know what to tell you. All I can do is apologize and tell you that I love you."

Victoria fought a valiant war with herself. His face and voice were so sincere but she couldn't help but feel like she'd been betrayed somehow. And she didn't expect it from him. He'd always been so direct and honest—at least she thought so. "Goodbye." She picked up the last bag that was by the door and turned to head out.

"Just know this," he called after her. "I waited. I waited until I was sure before I said those words to you. I was prepared to say them before all your family and friends, too. That's why I flew out there. That has to count for something, doesn't it?"

*Maybe.* She took another step.

Eamon had one thing to say. "I also want you to know that…I'll be here. When you realize the mistake you're making…the happiness that you're about to throw away… I'll be here."

Victoria stood there, for nearly a full minute. His answers seemed so rational, but at the same time so wrong. His words of love now seemed so convenient instead of sincere. For once, she didn't want to just fly off the handle and say and do things that she didn't mean.

When she hadn't moved toward the door, hope bloomed in Eamon's heart. He quickly rushed down the stairs and put his arms around her waist. "Stay," he whispered from behind and then placed a kiss on the back of her head. For a moment, he closed his eyes and inhaled her signature sent of jasmine and white roses. What would he do if he couldn't smell that scent on her skin again? How would he pick up the pieces after losing out on love for a second time?

Just as he was willing her not to leave him, she pulled away and walked out of the door, taking his heart with her.

# Chapter 26

*Two weeks later...*

"Are you sure that you want to sell your share in the club?" Quentin asked Eamon for like the tenth time in the last twenty minutes.

"I'm absolutely sure," Eamon insisted with a smile. "Not that it hasn't been fun—it has been. I just think that it's time for me to move on and concentrate on the restaurant business. Benito is a great manager, but I'm ready to be more hands-on over there. Plus, it comes at a time when a man gets a little too tired of the nightlife, if you know what I mean."

Xavier, Jeremy and Quentin gave him a blank stare like they couldn't image *ever* getting tired of the club life.

"Maybe it's just me," Eamon said.

They started nodding at that because it made more sense that he was an anomaly.

"Well, all right. We're all more than happy to buy you out if you're sure that's what you want?" Q asked again.

"I'm sure. I'm sure. Please stop asking."

"All right. I guess that's it," Q said, turning to the lawyers at the table. "Let's do this."

The lawyers started passing documents around the room and the men all leaned forward and started putting their signatures on the dotted line.

It was a little harder than Eamon was letting on. But deep in his heart, he felt like he was doing the right thing. It was time to move on, work a regular job and regular hours. This time after heartbreak, he vowed not to kill himself with work, but maintain enough of a workload not to become a bum. Maybe he would start working on his music again. Most artists swear that the best songs come from heartbreak. If that was true, then he would probably be walking the red carpet at the Grammys next year.

When all the documents were signed, everyone exchanged handshakes. But his brothers and Quentin were looking like they were sitting at a funeral.

"C'mon, guys. Don't do this. We're still family. You're not getting rid of me that easily."

The boys shrugged their shoulders and gave him half-hearted smiles.

Eamon tried to play around by delivering a soft jab to Xavier's shoulder and then swinging his arm around Jeremy's neck. "The Dollhouse will go on and you guys are going to continue being successful, but I'm here if you ever need me. You know that, right?"

"Yeah, yeah." Jeremy shook his head. "It's just not going to be the same without you around."

"You'll be all right." He headed back to his office to get the box with the last of his things off his desk. But standing outside was Hayley with her lips turned down.

"I can't believe that you're actually leaving," she said. "I can't imagine this place without you here."

"Are you kidding me? I was hardly coming in to work as it was." He entered the office.

Hayley followed. "True, but still. You're, like, the best boss that I've ever had."

Eamon cocked his head and looked at her. "You do know that you don't have to kiss up to me anymore. I don't decide your raise anymore."

"Oh, yeah. Right." She snapped her fingers and then smiled again. "Old habits are hard to break."

"Well…" Eamon grabbed his box. "You better get yourself a new set of habits, because from what I heard you're going to be managing this location."

"What? Shut up!" Out of excitement, she swung and delivered a stinging slap against his biceps.

He smiled. "You deserve it."

"What about Quentin?"

"He's headed to Atlanta for a while. He's a good bartender, but managing may be pushing it a bit."

"You know, he really hasn't been that bad around here. The employees love him and though he's a master bartender, I haven't seen him drinking that much lately. Maybe he's finally gotten over that girl his brother married."

"Maybe."

"They say that time heals all wounds," Hayley reminded him.

Eamon nodded. "That's what I'm banking on." He started to head for the door when Xavier popped up.

"Mind if I talk to you for a minute?"

Eamon glanced at Hayley.

"I was just leaving," she said with a smile and then left the two brothers alone.

"So what's up?"

Xavier closed the door behind Hayley and turned to face his older brother. "I just wanted to check and see whether we're still cool. I mean, I realize that I really screwed up and everything. I just didn't think and—"

"Hey." Eamon set the box back down. "It's cool. It was not your fault. It had to come up sooner or later, whether it was you or Mom and Dad. Eventually someone was going to say something. I should've told her from the jump. That was on me, man. Forget about it."

"Forget about it? But—"

"I mean it. I don't blame you, so please don't think that Victoria and I breaking up is your fault. Please." He walked up to him and threw his arms around Xavier for a quick brotherly hug. "I love you, man. We're cool."

Xavier drew in a deep breath and finally nodded. "I just didn't want to see something like what happened between Sterling and Quentin happen to us."

"Never," Eamon assured him and then turned around again to grab his box off the desk. "There is one thing that you can do for me," he said.

"Name it," Xavier said.

"Walk me out."

"Sure."

Together the brothers exited the office and headed out through the main floor of the club where the staff was busy getting ready to open. At the bar a familiar face stood out.

"Charelle, what are you doing here?"

She beamed a smile at him while plopping a hand against her hips. "Looking for a job, and since I heard that you were leaving, I thought it would be the perfect time."

He was prepared to let that roll off his shoulders. "Well, I wish you the best with that."

She shook her head. "I also came because I heard that you got your heart broken so I wanted to see for myself how you were handling it. But I see you're doing just fine. Damn."

*Only if you're judging by the outside.* "I guess I'll leave you to your job interview." He and Xavier started for the door, but Charelle called after him.

"Well, are you at least going to go after this one?"

He turned, frowning.

Charelle just rolled her eyes. "I swear. I don't know why the good Lord made fine men as dumb as stumps. I told you before, a woman wants you to chase after her."

Eamon smirked. "And I told you that I don't play games."

"Then you ain't met the right woman," she volleyed. "Love *is* a game and only your pride won't let you play."


Victoria only cried for the first week. That was all that she was going to allow herself. It was a good thing, too, because her bed was littered with at least a dozen boxes of Kleenex. On the second week, she started her days back in boot-camp fitness training…and her striptease workout classes. She didn't know why. She didn't take any when she was in Las Vegas. But now that she was back home, she felt compelled to do it. That was as far as she wanted to examine the matter. Anything deeper than that and it might land her back in bed with another dozen Kleenex boxes—and her nose wasn't going to be able to handle that.

Returning to her father's office after such a long absence was just strange, too. But it wasn't like she'd been out of the loop or hadn't been working with some of the staff out in Las Vegas so that was going all right. It was seeing the twins after all that bragging that made her feel like such

an idiot. Now it was like they were tiptoeing on eggshells
around her. Then again, they weren't the only ones. Her
parents took turns calling her almost every hour, claiming
they were just checking on her.

All of them had their hearts in the right place, but she
didn't know how to tell them that they didn't need to treat
her with kid gloves. She was going to be fine…eventually.
She just needed a plan to work her way through this and
that's just what she had worked out.

On the first day of the third week she could barely get
out of bed. She didn't bother turning on the television
because all she did was just cry at the silliest commercials.
Tonight her father was being honored as The Mortin
Foundation's Man of the Year and she was determined to
go and show her support, *if* she could get up.

"You know you don't have to go," her mother called to
tell her. "Your father will understand completely if you
don't."

"No. No. I'm coming. What kind of daughter would I
be if I didn't show up to support him for an honor as big
as this?"

There was that pause again that would occasionally
hang over the line.

"I'm not worried about what people will say, Mother.
Lord knows that I'm not the only woman in New York
who has had their heart broken."

"Well…have you at least heard from him since you've
been back?"

Victoria sighed while another wave of tears crested her
eyes. "No," she lied. "I'm sure that he has moved on."

"Tsk. I don't know. I just got the sense that…oh, well.
I guess we'll see you tonight."

"Okay, Mom." She hung up the phone and immediately
felt guilty for not confessing to a dozen or so phone calls

that she'd received from Eamon that she allowed to go straight to voice mail. When the phone line beeped, Eamon always hung up. He never once left a message. At least that was a sign that he was still thinking about her. But what did that mean? Eventually, he would stop and she had a strange feeling that was just going to make things even worse.

Not until she had about an hour to get dressed did Victoria finally climb out of bed. She had to rush to at least look halfway decent for tonight's gala. To show just how far she had fallen, she had agreed to allow Kent Bryce to escort her.

At exactly seven o'clock he knocked on her front door. She took one more look at her black-and-white Roberto Cavalli dress and went to answer the door. The moment she saw Kent on the other side with that cocky smile, she realized what a mistake she had made. She couldn't stand this man, so why had she said yes when he asked at the office?

*I just wasn't thinking.*

She could say that about everything from now on.

"Are you ready to go?" Kent asked.

Victoria swallowed the bile that was rising in her throat. "Sure." She plastered a smile on her face and accepted his arm. During the limousine ride to the gala, Kent droned on and on about himself and how he saw his star rising in her father's company. There was something about them making a great couple, but she couldn't be sure. She was blocking it all out and staring out the limousine window.

Not surprisingly, her mind drifted back to Eamon and she wondered what he was doing now. *Why didn't he just tell me?*

*"What good would it have done to tell you? Answer me that. If I'd told you the day we met that you looked*

*just like my old girlfriend, how many times a day do you think you would've been obsessing over whether I was in love with you or a woman that's been dead for over a decade? Besides, when we initially got together it was just a casual relationship. Just sex I believe were your words. As it grew into to something more, you would have done exactly what you're doing now. Leaving."*

Was he right? Would she had just left earlier?

*Probably.*

She shifted in her chair. Who knows what she would've done? *Was it possible that he loved me?*

"I'm starting to have second thoughts about this," Eamon said, riding in the back of his limo.

Xavier, Jeremy and Quentin turned and gaped at him.

"Now you say something? After trekking up here to New York and spending two hours to get ready for this fancy shindig?" Quentin asked incredulously. "You have to be kidding me."

Eamon shook his head. "What if we can't get in? What if she turns me away?"

"What if she's with another dude?" Jeremy tossed in. When every eye shifted in his direction, he shrugged. "What?"

Q reached over and popped his cousin hard on the arm. "You're really lousy at this, you know that?"

Defensive, Jeremy frowned and rubbed his arm. "Sorry, but my middle name isn't *Oprah*."

"No, it's *Clueless*," Xavier said, shaking his head. "Look, Eamon. This is going to work. We're going to get you in, she's going to see you and the tears will flow—it'll be a classic tearjerker moment. Trust me."

Eamon nodded his head, clearly trying to convince himself that his brother was right. Then just before he turned to look out of the limo's dark-tinted windows his eyes crashed with Quentin's. "And what do you think?"

"Me?" Quentin pressed a hand against his chest and then looked around. "You're asking me?"

"Why not?" Eamon said. "You have an opinion on this, I'm sure."

"Oh, God," Xavier groaned, closing his eyes and pinching the bridge of his nose.

"Glad to see that you have so much confidence in me," Q said to Xavier and then turned his gaze back toward Eamon. "You *really* want to know what I think?"

Eamon sucked in a breath. "Hit me."

The cousins' eyes locked for a long moment.

Jeremy and Xavier held their breaths.

Finally Quentin spoke. "I think that what you're doing is incredibly brave. Clearly Victoria means a lot to you."

Eamon nodded, but even he seemed to be holding his breath.

"A part of me wants to tell you to run like hell—don't look back," Q said honestly. "But I'm not going to tell you that because I know if you did take that lousy advice, you'd regret it for the rest of your life. I'm starting to suspect that finding true love is rare and if you don't grab it when you can, you might never get another opportunity."

All the King brothers' brows lifted in surprise.

Quentin smiled. "What? I can be deep."

Nodding, a smile hooked Eamon's lips. "That you can, cuz. That you can."

"God, it's hot," Victoria complained and rolled the windows down. She was tired of the same question circling in her mind and she was tired of this growing dread that was spreading up her body.

"Looks like we're here," Kent said just as their vehicle rolled to a stop.

"Thank goodness." She couldn't wait to get out. It was hot as an oven.

The valet opened the door and she calmly stepped out. But when she had to accept Kent's arm again, she thought that she was going to be sick all over again.

Within minutes they were smiling and mixing with the other guests. Iris and Grace came with their latest dates, but immediately flocked to her side to check in with her.

"How are you holding up?" they asked in unison.

"Fine. I can handle being around people for one night."

They flashed a sympathetic smile and encouraged her to be strong. And she was. When it came to putting on a brave face, no one did it better than she did. But while she was mixing and mingling, she felt a charge of energy in the room. She ignored it at first, but then she felt as if there was something or someone closing in on her.

Then Victoria recognized his scent and then slowly started to turn around. When she did, her heart fell down to her feet. "Eamon."

Sexy as hell in a black tuxedo, Eamon King had captured more than just her attention. From the corner of her eye she could see more and more women slowly turn their heads.

"What are you doing here?"

One side of his face quirked up. "I came to take you back home, where you belong."

Victoria's heart started to flutter wildly in her chest. "I am where I belong."

Eamon glanced up at Kent, a man who looked like a pebble standing next to Eamon. "You can go now."

Kent's mouth dropped open. But for some reason, he didn't say a word.

"What in the hell?"

Eamon gently but firmly took her by the elbow and started escorting her away from the thick of things.

"Eamon, unhand me," she hissed.

"In a minute." He turned and looked at her. "And if you're thinking about causing a scene, I can get crunk with the best of them."

She didn't doubt it. But it was only because this was an event for her father that she didn't test him on this.

Finally they arrived at a secluded corner and Eamon turned toward her.

"Now that you've got me over here, what do you want?"

"The truth," he answered. "Do you love me?"

The question was so direct and unexpected that she actually started sputtering. "W-what?"

"You heard me, so answer the question."

"I don't see what the hell that has to do with anything."

"It has everything to do with it. Because I love you and I think that sixteen days is long enough punishment for me not having told you that you look like an old girlfriend of mine. You were right. I was wrong. But if that's the only thing that's keeping us apart, then I have to say it's insane. With all the real problems in the world, this is nothing. I *know* that you love me. So what are we doing? Playing games? Is that it? Fine. I'll play them with you if that's what it takes to win you back.

"You don't believe that I love you? How about I shout it to the whole world right now?" Eamon turned and with a booming voice announced, "Excuse me, everyone. Can I have your attention?"

Victoria's eyes bugged out. "Eamon, what are you doing?"

"I just wanted to announce to everyone that I love Victoria Gregory. I'm totally, insanely in love with this woman!"

The entire ballroom fell silent.

"And I came here tonight to ask her if she will marry me!"

Red with embarrassment, Victoria belatedly caught that last line. "What?"

Eamon turned back toward her and slowly lowered himself onto one knee. "I said, Victoria Gregory, will you marry me?" He lifted up a jewelry box and nestled inside sat an emerald-cut diamond ring.

Victoria's mouth sagged open. "You can't mean… I mean…are you sure?"

Eamon chuckled. "Of course I'm sure. The question is will you have me?"

*Don't think.* "Yes," she said simply, her face exploding with a smile. "Yes! Yes!"

Eamon quickly removed the ring from the box and slid the diamond onto her finger. When he stood up, he opened his arms just in time to catch her in his embrace. The entire ballroom erupted in cheers.

"I always liked that one," Mondell said, nodding.

Ceyla rolled her eyes at him, but smiled proudly at her daughter who had never looked happier in all her life.

From the other side of the room, Xavier, Jeremy and Quentin watched Eamon and Victoria's reunion with unusually large smiles on their faces.

"I told you that there would be tears," Xavier said, nodding.

Jeremy shrugged. "I said that there would be another dude here with her, too."

Q and Xavier glanced over at him.

"What?" Jeremy's eyes widened like a deer caught in headlights. "I'm just saying."

Xavier shook his head. "I swear. We can't take you nowhere."

While the brothers gave each other the evil eye, a slow smile crept across Quentin's face. "You do know what this means, boys?"

"What?" Jeremy asked.

At seeing the twinkle in Quentin's eyes the brothers were suddenly able to read his mind and they all said in unison, *"Bachelor Party."*

*Then There Were Three*

## Chapter 27

"So all's well that ends well?" Dr. Turner said, smiling.

Quentin shrugged. "I guess that all depends on how you look at things."

"Let me guess. You just view it as another fallen soldier?" the doctor surmised.

"Look at that," he said, peeking at his watch. "After two hours, you know me so well."

She shook her head. "I doubt that. You strike me as a very complex man who deflects tough questions, laments about the absence of true love while doing all he can to avoid even being in its presence. You're proud of your business success though you're surprised by it. You miss your family, though you choose to remain in a self-imposed exile."

He sat up from the chaise and looked at her stunned. "You mean all I have to do is click my heels three times and everything will be fine?"

Dr. Turner waved her pen at him. "Oh, yeah, one more thing. You think you're funny."

Alyssa sat down next to him. "Oooh. She's good. I think I like her."

Q frowned and cut his eyes toward his imaginary Alyssa, only to have her shrug her shoulders.

"What are you looking at?" Dr. Turner asked.

"No one," he answered too quickly and watched as his therapist's brows hiked in the center of her forehead.

"*No one?* It's a person?"

His smile stretched from ear to ear while he casually glanced at his watch again. "I've definitely gone over my time for the day."

There was a long silence before Dr. Turner nodded her head. "Very well." She closed her tablet and stood up from her chair. Their awkward silence continued as she walked him to the door. "Same time next week?"

Quentin hesitated. After two hours of talking, he didn't feel any different—or any better.

"Who knows," the doctor said, crossing her arms. "We might even get around to talking about you."

He shrugged. "Or I can tell you another love story."

Interest lit her eyes. "Another fallen soldier?"

"Those damn love wars."

"I'll be waiting here with bated breath."

Quentin winked and strolled off, catching the receptionist's eye again as he made his way to the office door.

"One question," Dr. Turner asked, holding up a finger. "Are Eamon and Victoria happy?"

"Disgustingly so. But I think that it has a lot to do with the incredible stripper we got him on the last night of his bachelorhood…."

# *Epilogue*

"Welcome to The Dollhouse, Las Vegas!" Quentin shouted, raising his glass to the raucous bachelor party as nearly two hundred men poured into the doors of the club. Because the number was so great, Quentin, Xavier and Jeremy elected to close the club for one night only to regular patrons so that their guests could enjoy the entire club. They were going to take a small hit, but in their minds it was more than worth it in order to throw one of their own a hell of a party.

The only problem was that they had to literally drag Eamon to his own bachelor party. Given what had happened during Victoria's last fiancé's bachelor party, Eamon had a hell of a time allaying her fears that the same thing could happen again. Sensing her unease, Eamon tried to get his brothers to call off the party.

They laughed in his face. And then kept him in the dark about his own party until tonight when they kidnapped him from the back office of his restaurant, threw him into a trunk and brought him there. As he glanced around, he saw that his brothers…and Q…had spared no expense for the elaborate seventies' disco theme that had waiters and waitresses sporting everything from platforms shoes to large hoop earrings and enormous Afro wigs.

Even Quentin looked ridiculous with thick, glued-on sideburns and vintage aviator sunglasses. But clearly the guys were into it, so he put on his best face and tried to go with the flow.

"Now, I don't have to ask which one of you poor bastards is getting married in the morning," Q said. "Because we all know and we're all grieving in our private way. We're losing a formidable player. A man's whose black book will be going on the auction block after we get him so drunk that he passes out."

The men laughed.

"But while we look on as this noble Casanova jumps off a cliff, undoubtedly each and every one of you are calculating in your minds right now just how much higher your booty ratio is going to go up after tomorrow. Let me put your minds to rest, for I have the answer for you." Quentin lifted his glass even higher. "The number for each of you is exactly—*two*."

All the men grumbled and then exchanged confused looks among themselves.

Quentin wasn't finished. "Two for each of you while I, humbly, sacrifice myself at the altar for promiscuous women everywhere."

The grumbling grew louder.

With his free hand he tried to gesture for them to lower their voices. "No. No. Please don't try to talk me out of it. I *want* to do it."

Xavier finally stepped up and grabbed Q by his oversize

collar and pulled him off the stage. "Don't pay him any mind." He dismissed Q with a wave. "Where's Jeremy?" He scanned the crowd. "C'mon up, bro."

Jeremy made his way through the crowd.

Once on stage, Xavier wrapped an arm around his neck and then together they turned toward Eamon. "As you know, tonight is our big brother Eamon's night. And we really wanted to take a moment to tell him just how proud we are of him. Clearly, he's marrying one hell of a woman. She has to be if she wants to spend the rest of her life with you."

Jeremy bobbed his head and grabbed the microphone from Xavier. "Yeah, it's one thing to have to put up with you because of blood. It's a whole 'nother story for it to be a choice."

Eamon refrained from flipping both of them the bird.

"Ladies," Jeremy yelled. "It's time to make it rain up here!"

On cue the music jumped up another five decibels while DeShawn, Brittani, Cassie, Delicious and Cotton Candy all made their grand entrances on their assigned poles and the men all flocked to their favorite girl's station.

But before Eamon could take a step, a black sack was slipped over his head and once again, he was being kidnapped, this time seemingly from his own bachelor party.

"Wait. Where are you taking me?"

"That's for us to know and you to find out," Q said.

A second later his two brothers appeared at his sides to help lead him upstairs. Before long, he realized they were taking him to the V.I.P. room.

"Guys, I don't know what you got planned, but I'm not going to cheat on Victoria. So if y'all have a hooker up here—"

"Will you pipe down?" Xavier mumbled. "Nobody said anything about you cheating on anyone. Geez. Is that invisible collar already on?"

"Yep," Jeremy answered for Eamon. "It has a two-inch leash on it, too."

Eamon rolled his eyes under the black bag. "Ha. Ha." He was shoved in a chair and his bag was snatched off his head.

"Enjoy," his brothers said. They patted him on the back and then turned and marched off the stage and out of V.I.P.

"Wait!"

The DJ hit the turntables and T-Pain's auto-tuned song "I'm In Love With a Stripper" blasted over the speakers.

Eamon jerked back around.

A second later, Victoria stepped onto the stage, dressed in skimpy, purple belted hot-pants that looked more like a pair of panties, with a matching banded tri-top. But what really put a smile on Eamon's face was the huge Donna Summer hair. He remained stunned for a few seconds until Victoria made her first swing around the pole. Then he realized that his baby had been practicing.

He eased back in his chair as Victoria met his steady gaze while simultaneously rolling her hips. From that moment on, he was caught up in a trance, and when she climbed the pole and did her first introverted V-pole slide all the way down to the floor, he was as hard as a rock. Hips swinging, ass clapping, Eamon had transformed into Gollum himself. Once again, he broke the club rules and reached out and squeezed her luscious, golden butt when she waved it one too many times in his face.

Victoria laughed and pulled away, but only so that she could strip out of her top and toss it onto his face.

Eamon quickly snatched it off so that he didn't miss a

move and good thing, too. Because the next thing he knew, his baby was sitting on his lap and grinding back on him like the rent was due in the morning. Breaking another house rule, he reached around and cupped her full breasts, loving how her hard nipples rubbed against his palms.

"Hmm. You're going to mess around and get pregnant tonight instead of tomorrow," Eamon said against her ear.

Victoria shook her head and pulled his hands away. "Sorry, sir. But I'm really going to have to ask you to keep your hands to yourself. Club rules." She stood back up and this time, her itty-bitty hot-pants came off and those, too, hit him in the face.

By the time he'd removed them, Victoria was back on the pole and hanging upside down by her calves. But as she took her time sliding her hands all over her body, Eamon started finding it more difficult to remain in his chair.

Slowly, she reached for the bar, opened her legs into V formation and glided back down, her pink flower visible for Eamon's eyes only. Trying to keep his butt planted in the chair was bordering on torture. The next song, "My Chick is Bad," started playing and Victoria was back to grinding on his lap and lifting her breasts high enough so that she could give her nipples a lick.

Eamon's hands came up and Victoria bounced out of his lap so fast, it nearly made his head spin. "Sorry," he apologized, feeling like a strip-club virgin. The next thing he knew Victoria grabbed her discarded bra from off the floor and then tied his hands behind his back.

"There. That should help you behave." She smiled and then walked back around the chair and resumed her routine.

He tried the knot and was surprised by how secure it was.

Victoria's smile widened. "Are you trying to be a bad boy?" she whispered against his ear before pulling his lower lobe in between her teeth and sucking it.

Eamon hissed while his cock pressed painfully against his zipper.

"Yeah. You're trying to be a bad boy while I'm trying to give you a nice show. Don't you like the show I'm doing for you, baby?" She pushed her butt down harder for a slower grind.

"Y-yes." Eamon's eyes damn near rolled to the back of his head.

"Don't you know that there's no touching or I can't dance for you?" Victoria released his earlobe and then ran her tongue down the column of his neck.

He quivered.

"I hear that you're getting married in the morning," she panted.

Eamon no longer trusted himself to speak so he just nodded his head.

"Do you love your fiancée?" she asked.

"Y-yes."

"Are you going to love and cherish her?" She reached for his zipper.

"Y-yes."

"Through sickness and health?" She slid the zipper down.

"Oh, God, yes."

She reached into his pants and pulled out his cock. "For as long as you both shall live?"

Eamon swallowed and tried to slow his heartbeat down, but her silky fingers made that nearly impossible.

"Hmm? I didn't hear you, mister." Victoria reclaimed his earlobe.

"Yes. Yes. Yes."

"That's a good boy."

Before he could draw another breath, Victoria eased down onto his steel-like erection until she was seated completely into his lap. For a few seconds they remained still, sharing each other's breath until Victoria started working her hips again. "From now on, I'm the only one that dances for you."

Eamon's chest heaved up and down while his head kept spinning.

"You got that, baby?" She stopped circling and started bouncing.

He opened his mouth, but no words came out of his mouth.

Victoria bounced and grinded. "Look at me, Eamon."

Their eyes locked while she continued screwing his brains out. "No one. All of this belongs to me. You got it."

The chair started creaking.

"I—I got it."

She reached up and grabbed the back of his head. "Let me hear you say it all belongs to me."

A smile crept across his face. "Every inch of me belongs to you—forever and ever." With one great yank, he freed his hands and then grabbed her hips so that he could slam her body down onto his cock. Before either of them knew it, they were flying as high as their tangled emotions, while their bodies met each other thrust for thrust. By the end of the fifth song, they were on the stage floor, Victoria with one leg wrapped around Eamon and the other one wrapped around the golden pole. When her third orgasm detonated, Eamon was right behind her, growling her name.

For several songs afterward they just laid there, holding each other and smiling contentedly.

"You know," Victoria said. "I think I'm going to have one of these installed in our bedroom."

"Then I'm going to make sure that I keep plenty of dollar bills tucked away in the nightstand drawer."

They laughed and then sealed the deal with a kiss.

\* \* \* \* \*

# REQUEST YOUR FREE BOOKS!

## 2 FREE NOVELS
## PLUS 2 FREE GIFTS!

**KIMANI**
ROMANCE
™

### Love's ultimate destination!